A Beautiful Game

Emma Mooney

Discover us online:
www.crookedcatpublishing.com

Join us on facebook:
www.facebook.com/crookedcatpublishing

Tweet a photo of yourself holding
this book to **@crookedcatbooks**
and something nice will happen.

To my Mum and Dad
For everything

About the Author

Emma Mooney is not a football fan and, to her, it doesn't matter which teams win or lose, but she does care about young people and it's this passion that inspired her to write A Beautiful Game.

Emma has completed courses in creative writing at both Glasgow and Edinburgh University and for six years was an editor for Ironstone New Writing.

This is her debut novel and she hopes you enjoy getting to know the main character, Robbie, as much as she did.

Find Emma at **www.emmamooney.co.uk**

Acknowledgements

My thanks go to Steph and Laurence Patterson of Crooked Cat Publishing for believing in this story, and to Simon Marshall-Jones for his superb editing skills. Thanks to the Cats too for such a warm welcome.

I have been lucky enough along the way to learn from some brilliant and talented writers and I'd especially like to thank Magi Gibson, Ian MacPherson, Helen Lamb and Kate Harrison for their encouragement and support. Thanks also to my fellow writers in these groups because you all helped me bring Robbie to life.

A special thank you goes to my wonderful friend, Ellie, for always asking questions and pushing me to delve deeper into the world of my characters. You never let me take the easy way out! Thanks also to Liz and Lesley for taking the time and the courage to read the first draft, and to the rest of the 1912 Book Club I raise a glass and ask you to be gentle with your reviews. To Dawn, Jenni, Jackie and Catriona, I thank you for always being there and for believing in me.

Thanks to my amazing husband, Tony, for never once doubting that I could do it, and for insisting that the dreaded rejection letter that all writers face should be called a 'not yet' letter. For that, and a million other reasons, I love you.

And finally to David, Andrew and Laura - all the time I thought I was teaching you about the world and it turns out you were teaching me!

Emma Mooney
August 2014

A Beautiful Game

One

I wrap the scarf around my neck and it feels good. Heavy. I picture Dad telling the story of how he gave it to me on the day I was born. He loves that story. Tells everyone. As soon as he heard it was a boy, he left the match and went straight to the hospital. Draped his scarf over the cot for everyone to see. Hearts won 3-1 that day. He said I was their lucky mascot.

I go through to his room and watch him get ready.

'A hundred and sixteen years.' He struts in front of the mirrored wardrobe, admiring the maroon shirt stretched tight over his belly. 'A hundred and sixteen years since we last played them in the cup final.' He grins. 'And I'm going. Can you believe it?'

He doesn't notice the scarf around my neck.

'Right, son,' he turns to me, 'I'd better get going; the bus leaves at twelve and I need to grab a few beers first.'

'Can I see your ticket, Dad?' I want to hold onto him for a wee while longer. The ticket cost him a fortune but I'm still hoping he'll produce an extra one for me, like a magician revealing a bouquet of plastic flowers from his sleeve. Dad pats his pockets, checking he's got everything, and I hold my breath. But there's no Willy Wonka moment. No golden ticket. Dad never takes me to the games anymore.

He stands in front of me and I lean forward onto my tiptoes until I'm nearly the same height. I'll be thirteen next month. He holds on to my scarf. 'You look out for your old man in the crowd,' he says. 'West stand.'

I nod. I'll be watching the game in my bedroom 'cause

3

there's no way Mum will let me watch it on the big screen in the living room. She hates football.

The doorbell rings and Dad's face lights up. 'That'll be Big Steve,' he says, 'now be good for your mum.' He races downstairs. It's eleven o'clock. Four hours 'til kick off. The front door slams shut and I listen to their singing as they disappear down the path.

The plastic stars on my ceiling faintly glow and I try to imagine I'm somewhere else, somewhere far away from the orange glow of the city. I remember a book Mum used to read to me when I was little. The boy in the story was called Max and he sailed away in a boat. I close my eyes and pretend I'm Max on his deserted island. But then I remember the ending. Max came home.

I open my eyes but I can barely see the stars anymore. Mum bought them for me the first time she left. Since then the presents have got better. Last time she brought me back the latest racing game.

The street outside my bedroom window is busy. I listen to the singing and chanting, and I strain my ears to hear Dad's voice. But I can't. All of Edinburgh is either out celebrating or drowning their sorrows, depending on the colour of their shirt.

A thin slice of light cuts across my pillow and I know Mum is standing in the doorway. I close my eyes again.

'Still awake?' she asks.

I squeeze them shut even tighter.

'Can I come in?'

I lie there, pretending to be asleep, and listen to her footsteps as she carefully avoids the scattered piles of books, comics and dirty clothes. She sits down on the edge of my bed and I'm trapped beneath the covers.

'I wondered if you'd heard from him.'

I pick up my mobile from the bedside table. No new messages. No missed calls. I shake my head. 'He'll be out celebrating,' I tell her. 'It was a great result.'

I look up at the signed shirt on my bedroom wall. Dad bought me it for my first Christmas but I only know one name. John Robertson. Robbo. My dad says he's the greatest. Scored twenty-seven goals against Hibs. That was before I was born. Mum refused to let him call me Robbo, so instead I'm Robbie. Close enough.

She leans over and kisses me on the forehead and I can smell her perfume. 'You go back to sleep,' she whispers. 'I'll wait up for him.'

I lie still and watch the minutes slowly change on my alarm clock. It's half past eleven. The Station Tavern shuts at midnight so he won't be home for at least an hour yet. I picture him falling out of the pub, searching his pockets for enough loose change for a kebab. If I'm lucky he'll come straight home and share it with me.

I open the book Miss Green gave me and start from the beginning again.

Tom!

No answer.

Tom!

No answer.

What's gone with that boy, I wonder? You Tom!

The book grows heavy in my hands and I'm nearly drifting off when I hear his key turn in the lock.

'Championees, championees.'

I jump out of bed and grab my scarf, throwing it round my neck and nearly tripping as I race to the top of the stairs. He's holding on to the banister, grinning up at me. 'Olé, Olé, Olé.'

I leap down the stairs, two at a time. 'What was it like, Dad, when the ref blew the final whistle?'

'Magic,' he says. 'Absolute fucking magic.'

'Don't swear in front of Robbie,' Mum cuts in.

'Don't fucking interrupt,' says Dad.

'Yeah, Mum,' I say. 'Let Dad tell me what it was like.' I turn

5

back to him. 'Tell me everything.' He hands me a white paper wrapper. A kebab. 'Thanks Dad.' I open the wrapper and my heart sinks. Wilted lettuce and some chilli sauce are all that's left. I dip my finger in the sauce and tell myself I don't care.

'Time for bed,' Mum says.

I ignore her. 'Tell me more,' I beg.

'Grab a can of beer out the fridge for me, son, and I'll tell you about the whole match. Minute by fucking minute.' His words are slurred but I don't care. I'm his only audience and I'm loving it. I go to fetch his beer.

Mum puts out a hand and stops me. 'It's late,' she says. 'Go back to bed.'

I start to argue but something in the way she looks at me makes me stop and so instead I turn and make my way upstairs. I stop at the landing and watch through the wooden spirals of the banister.

'Leave the fucking kid alone,' says Dad. 'He just wanted to hear about the game.'

Mum steps towards him. Her lips are painted red and she's wearing that denim skirt. The one she wore to parents' night and Mr Cameron couldn't take his eyes off her legs the whole time he was supposed to be talking about my science test. Her blouse is only fastened half way and I can see her bra. It matches the colour of her lipstick.

She reaches out to Dad. 'I thought maybe you and I could celebrate,' she pauses and moves closer, 'together.'

I blush. Shit! They don't know I'm here.

Dad pushes her hand away. He steps back and looks her up and down.

'I made myself pretty for you,' she says.

'Pretty?' He laughs out loud. 'You must be joking.' He grabs her wrist and twists it. Hard. 'You look like a fucking tart.' He pushes her against the wall and leans in close. 'The best day of my life,' he growls, 'and you're spoiling it.'

I run to my room and hide behind the door. Out of sight,

out of mind. A sudden memory returns. I'm little, maybe four or five, and we're at the kitchen table. It's dinner time. Dad's holding a fork and he's poking Mum's arm with it. Blood soaks into her sleeve and she's crying. I squeeze my eyes shut. I squeeze them until it hurts. If I can't see them, they can't see me and none of it is real. That's my plan. But Mum's saying something. She keeps saying sorry over and over again but I can't remember what she's sorry for.

And now I'm hiding again. Only this time it's behind my bedroom door. I hear the first blow and I know she'll leave again tonight. I crouch into a tight ball and cover my ears but I can still hear everything. She's begging him to stop but he won't.

'Best day of my life,' he says again.

Two

Tracey throws the bloodied towel into the laundry basket. What had she been thinking? Had she really believed he'd rather fuck her than punch her? The bastard does what he likes. She's his rag doll and this time he didn't care where he hit her. Didn't care about hiding the bruises. This time she knows she can't pretend that nothing happened. She looks in the bathroom mirror and sees her eye is already swollen.

Her bra presses tightly against her breasts and it hurts. She reaches round, unhooks it and lets it fall to the floor. Bruises are blossoming across her chest forming a hideous bouquet of red, purple and blue where he twisted and pinched the skin. *Dirty little slut.* She falls to her knees and vomit splatters inside the toilet bowl. She leans against her ceramic altar and silently prays. *Please God, let him be passed out on the sofa so he can't hear me.* He hates her making a fuss.

She doesn't dare flush in case the noise wakes him and so she covers up the mess with thin strips of toilet paper. Bile rises into her throat once more but she forces it back down and lays her head against the cold bathroom tiles. The red lace lies coiled on the floor in front of her as though waiting to attack. She sees it, reaches forward and hooks the bra at arm's length with one finger. She dangles it over the laundry basket, ready to add it to the pile of washing but stops. She pulls it back and drops it in to the bin instead.

Taking care not to make a sound, she slips through to the bedroom and looks in the wardrobe for something loose to wear. It strikes her that she owns a lot of long sleeved tops with high necks and she chooses a baby blue cotton jumper and carefully pulls it over her head. It doesn't hide the bruises on her face.

Her bank card is tucked into the front cover of her library book, somewhere she knows he'll never look. Mrs Carmichael insisted she put a little bit away every month. Just in case. She hasn't managed to save much yet but at least it's something. She puts the card in her pocket and grabs a few bits and pieces. Her mobile phone is lying on the bedside table and she hovers over it, undecided. She barely knows how to use it but if she takes it with her she can phone Robbie and check he's okay from time to time. She reaches out to take the phone but hesitates. What if Robbie tells him she's been in touch? Would he be able to find her from her signal like they do on TV? She opens the drawer and drops the phone inside. It's not worth the risk.

She sneaks through to Robbie's room and finds him sound asleep on top of his bedcovers and she smiles as she sees him lying on his back with both arms thrown out to the side. He's slept this way since he was a baby and she remembers how his arms used to stick out through the bars of his cot. She sits down on the edge of the bed and strokes his hair backwards, away from his eyes. If she wasn't here Robbie wouldn't have to hear the fights, wouldn't see the punches. She watches him sleep and wonders what he's dreaming of, scared that he hears the sound of his father's fists in his dreams.

She never worries that his dad might hurt him, he adores his wee boy. His lucky mascot, he calls him. They've always been close. As soon as Robbie could walk, he took him to the park to kick a ball about. On his fifth birthday, he took him to his first Hearts match. They never stopped talking about it for days after and she could see then the same glint in her boy's eye that his dad has when talking about a game.

And Robbie loves his dad. Worships him. But that's okay, little boys should worship their dads. Shouldn't they?

Three

Dad bursts into my room and drags open my curtains.

'What's wrong?' I ask.

He holds out his hand and pulls me up from the bed. 'What's wrong?' he laughs. 'The only thing that's wrong, lad, is that you're still in bed. Now get yourself dressed and come downstairs for breakfast. I've got some sausage and eggs on the go but you'd better eat them up quick. I don't want us to miss a thing.' He leaves the room and I listen to him whistle as he goes downstairs.

I've no idea what he's talking about. What doesn't he want us to miss? I'm still in yesterday's clothes but that's okay, a quick spray of deodorant and I'm ready. Dad won't care about whether I've changed or not and Mum's not here to notice. I watched her leave in a taxi last night from my bedroom window. She didn't look up as she left. She never does. But it's okay, she'll be back again tonight. She always is.

Dad is draping a fried egg over a heaped pile of sausages, bacon, tattie scones and beans. It smells amazing and I'm starving.

'Perfect timing,' he says and hands me the plate. 'Now eat up.' We sit down opposite each other at the small round table in the middle of the kitchen and he shoves a massive forkful of food into his own mouth. 'I reckon we should leave as soon as possible. They're saying the trains and buses are gonna be jam-packed.' He's waving the remote control towards the TV which is showing the highlights of yesterday's game. 'The open top bus is leaving the City Chambers at two and making its way through the city centre and then back to the stadium. The whole team are gonna be on it and they're expecting thousands to line the streets. Thousands. Can you imagine it? I reckon it'll be best to catch it somewhere on Gorgie Road near the entrance to the stadium and if we go now we should get there early enough to bags a good spot. Somewhere we can cheer them on as they bring the cup home. Show the lads our support. It's going to be magic. Absolute fucking magic.' He looks me up and down. 'But first you'll need to get changed.'

I look at my clothes. How did he know?

'Go and get your strip on, everyone's going to be in maroon today.'

'But I don't have a strip.'

'What are you talking about, of course you do. I bought it for your birthday. Now quick, go and get changed. I think we should start making our way. Grab the best spot.'

'Dad, you got me it for my eighth birthday.'

'And?'

'I'm twelve.'

He's still looking at me confused.

'It hasn't fitted me since Primary Six. Mum handed it into a charity shop on Dalry Road ages ago.'

'A charity shop?' He shouts the words at me and I back away. I know not to mention her when she's gone so why did I open my big mouth? 'She gave it to a fucking charity shop? That was brand new. Cost me a fortune. And now some wee ned is walking about in your strip.'

He's right. I should have stopped her. Dad bought that strip for me and it was mine to keep. But it really didn't fit me any longer. 'Maybe I could wear one of your old tops,' I say and his eyes light up.

'Great idea. You're growing up so fast, soon you'll be as tall as your old man.' He slaps me across my back and grins. 'Wait here. I'll go and grab one of my old shirts while you finish your

11

breakfast.' He runs upstairs and as he reaches the top he stops and shouts back down to me. 'It's going to be a great day, son. Wait 'n' see.'

The streets are already buzzing as we make our way along Gorgie Road towards the stadium. The road is still open and passing cars toot their horns, waving maroon flags and scarves out of windows. Dad throws his arm around me. 'Soak it all in, son. I want you to remember this for the rest of your life. Just think, you'll be able to tell your own boy about this one day.' He holds both hands out in front of him. 'I was there with my old man, you'll say. It was a glorious sunny Sunday and the streets were lined with Hearts supporters. Everyone was smiling. Everyone was happy.'

I look around me and he's right. Everyone looks like they've won the lottery. 'Everyone was celebrating,' I add.

He grins at me and I can't remember the last time I felt this happy. It's a glorious sunny Sunday right enough.

'Come on,' he says. 'Let's cop a squat down here.' We sit on the sunny side of the street on the edge of the pavement and soon others join us.

A family with a kid in a buggy stop at a gap next to us. The wee kid in the buggy is sleeping. They've come prepared with a cool box and a picnic rug and I watch as the mum unfolds the tartan rug and spreads it across the kerb. They plonk themselves down next to us and she adjusts the parasol on the buggy to keep the sun out of the kid's eyes.

'Look at that,' says Dad. He's pointing at the toddler's t-shirt.

50% dad
50% mum
100% Jambo!

'Love your wee boy's t-shirt,' he shouts to the man beside us and gives him a big thumbs up. The mum throws Dad a dirty look and checks to see her son's still sleeping.

'Were you there?' the man asks.

Nobody needs to ask where he means.

'It was magic,' Dad says and I'm glad he stops there 'cause I get the feeling the wee boy's mum won't like Dad's swearing.

They start their own minute by minute match commentary and I switch off and look around me. A gang of teenagers line up along the wall behind us and share out a six-pack they've brought with them. I turn away before they catch me looking and I switch my gaze to the road in front of me. The police have stopped the traffic from coming along this way and there's a guy walking towards us with a bundle of Hearts flags. 'Two pounds a flag,' he's shouting at the top of his voice and the mum next to us digs into her pocket and hands over a ten pound note. She takes the flag and tucks it into the buggy where it shudders gently in the breeze.

She catches me looking. 'Would you like one?' she asks me. I shake my head and stare at the pavement. It's getting hotter and the sun stabs like needles on the back of my neck. Dad's stopped talking to the man on the picnic rug and he's up on his feet. 'Keep my space,' he says. 'I'm going to grab something to drink.'

He disappears into a small newsagents and I grin at the headline emblazoned on the sandwich board outside the shop; *Scottish Cup Final - Hearts 5 Hibs 1.*

Behind me the teenagers have started singing, 'We only won 5-1, we only won 5-1.' I join in and soon the whole street is singing along too. The mum says something to her husband, probably about the noise, but he shrugs his shoulders and laughs. The toddler is still sleeping anyway so I guess everything's okay, but I hope they wake him when the bus comes so that one day he can tell his own son that he was there. He saw the cup coming home.

Dad sits down beside me and lays a few cans of lager at his feet. He takes one and it opens with a hiss. He hasn't got me anything.

The man on the picnic rug opens up his Sunday paper and

it's so enormous it takes up the whole rug. I wish I'd brought my book with me. The wee boy in the buggy stirs and the mum pops a dummy in his mouth. The dummy moves up and down as he sucks on it and it makes me even thirstier than I already was.

Dad finishes his can and crushes it under his heel, leaving it in the gutter alongside the fag ends. He pulls open another can and takes a long sip. This is killing me. It's scorching hot now and I'm dying for something to drink. 'Dad,' I start and he flashes me that look that says he knows I'm after something.

'What d'you want?'

'Nothing,' I say.

He leans back with his elbow on the kerb and takes another drink.

'Can I get some money for a drink of juice?'

He tosses me a fifty pence and I jump up from the kerb, already imagining the cold amber liquid pouring down my parched throat.

'And make sure you give me the change.'

The shop is cool and dark after the heat out on the street. It's packed with half-naked, sweaty men buying cans of beer and cigarettes but the banter is friendly and everyone's in a good mood.

I open the fridge door and lean forward to enjoy the cold vapour that comes out to meet me. I wish I could climb inside, only for a minute, but that'd be long enough to cool down. I grab a bottle of irn-bru and take it up to the counter.

'Seventy-nine pence.'

I open my palm and smile at the guy. 'It's all I've got.'

'Well, it's not enough.'

'Aw mister,' I try. 'It's roasting out there and I think I'm gonna pass out if I don't get a drink.'

'Well, fuck off outside and make sure you don't pass out in my shop.'

'Have you got anything for fifty pence?' I ask and he points to a shelf at the back of the shop where the bottles of fizzy juice have a picture of a koala bear on their label and don't even look big enough to wet my lips but hey, it's better than nothing so I hand my coin over.

I twist open my bottle of warm, cheap cola and the juice fizzes up and splutters over my hand. I try to catch the froth that's spraying over the sides but I'm not quick enough and a sticky puddle gathers at my feet. The bottle's half empty now and I cradle it in both hands, determined not to lose another drop.

Outside on the street everyone's still singing and I sit back down beside Dad and lift the bottle to my lips. Droplets of fizzy sweetness fizzle on my tongue and trickle down my throat. Heaven. I greedily glug more and more but it stops too soon. There's none left and I'm still thirsty.

Loud shouts erupt around us and people are saying that the bus is round the corner. I don't know how they know this because I'm looking down the street and I see nothing, but everyone's getting excited and they're shoving each other to try and get as far forward as possible. The toddler in the buggy wakens and starts screaming but no-one notices. The dad is too busy squinting through his mobile phone waiting to catch a video clip or picture and the mum is hanging over his shoulder, screeching in his ear to 'take a picture, take a picture.'

I smile at the wee boy. The 100% Jambo! I take the plastic flag from his buggy and wave it in front of him but he screams louder. I try shushing him but he can't hear me above the shouts and chants of 'We only won 5-1, we only won 5-1.' His mum still hasn't noticed he's awake so I search my pockets for something to quieten him down but all I find is a squashed packet of chewing gum. I take the yellow wrapper off and uncover the silver paper below. This catches his attention and the screams quieten to a sniffle. 'Look,' I say and hold it out for him to see, 'it's shiny.'

He stops crying and reaches out to the silver wrapper with chubby fingers. I unwrap the stick of chewing gum and hand him the silver foil. He studies it carefully, turning it over in his tiny hands. I pop the strip of gum in my mouth but it's tasteless and breaks into pieces as I bite down.

My dad's on his last can now and the boy's dad has given up waiting and put his mobile back in his pocket. The excitement around us starts to settle as rumours go round that someone in the crowd got a text from someone watching at the city chambers who said the bus has just left.

The singing stops and a strange hush falls over the crowd.

'Help!' The mum with the picnic rug breaks the silence. 'He's choking. Quick, do something.' She yanks her son out of the buggy and the poor wee boy starts crying all over again. 'He's choking,' she screams, but surely if he's crying like that he can't be. I look at his hands and see he's still got the ball of silver paper in his fist.

'He's fine,' I try to tell her but she's not listening.

'You gave him chewing gum.'

'What's going on?' Great, now my dad's getting involved.

She throws her arm out and points at me. 'He gave my baby some chewing gum.'

Dad wallops me over the head. He's so fast I didn't even see it coming. 'What the fuck d'ya do that for?' he yells at me. 'You could have killed him.'

And now she's screaming that her baby's gonna die and Dad looks at me like I'm something stuck to the bottom of his shoe and I'm trying to tell them that I've got the gum in my mouth but nobody's listening.

Dad sticks his wee finger in the boy's mouth. He must be looking for the gum that isn't there and suddenly he screams and yanks his finger out, waving it in the air and jumping up and down. 'The wee bastard bit me.'

'It's the bus,' someone shouts and chaos breaks out around

us. We've been so busy arguing we didn't notice the teenagers have pushed their way past us to the front of the kerbside. Dad forgets his sore finger and grabs one of them by the shoulder and spins him round. 'That's our spot,' he shouts.

'Well, you shouldnae have moved.'

Dad pulls himself tall and I swear he suddenly looks over six foot. 'I promised my boy we'd have the best spot,' he says, 'and we will. Now move aside.'

I hold my breath. Even the boy in the buggy has stopped crying.

A giant shadow falls over us. 'Dad,' I shout, 'it's the bus.' We turn just in time and the bus is right in front of us. It's right there. My dad throws his arm around me and squeezes tight. We stand there and cheer with the team as they hold the cup above their heads. I watch Dad's face light up as he waves to his heroes towering above him.

Four

The sun has been shining all day but they haven't left the house once. Haven't left the bed. He never said a word when she turned up on his doorstep, just held her until she stopped crying and then led her by the hand through to the bedroom. It hurt when he touched her but she managed to hide it from him. She's good at that. After all, everything heals with time.

'You okay?' he asks and she nods without looking at him.

He leaves the bed and Tracey can soon hear water running in the next room. She swings her legs round, sits on the edge of the double bed and looks around her. Red and silver striped curtains hang in the window, falling in perfect pleats from a chrome curtain pole. Light switches and plug sockets match the metal pole and she turns away before she can see her tainted reflection looking back at her. A framed Vettriano print is centred above the bed, and she stares with envy at the glamorous, young woman dancing barefoot along the beach.

John reappears with a towel tied loosely around his waist and his hair still wet from the shower. 'Here.' He throws something in her direction and she flinches as it lands on the covers beside her. It's a key. 'I want you to think of this as your home.' In the taxi on the way over here last night she'd imagined John would be furious when he saw the mess she was in, thought she'd have to stop him from racing straight over there and beating him up. But he didn't say a word about the bruises and he asked no questions. She picks up the key. She knows she should say thanks but she can't summon the words up to her mouth.

'And I'll make some space for your stuff.' He starts to empty the top drawer in the chest by his bedside.

'It's okay,' she says. 'I don't have much with me and I can keep it in this bag for now.'

He looks at her plastic carrier bag and laughs out loud. 'Don't be stupid. You can't use a poly bag as a wardrobe.' He shows her the empty drawer. 'You can keep your things in here and I'll clear some hangers for you to use.' He reaches for her bag but she pulls it close to her chest. He holds his hand out and she hands the bag over like a little girl. He smiles and tips the contents out across the bed. A handful of knickers, a bra, a couple of t-shirts and a blue toothbrush. That's all she thought to bring with her. She's embarrassed to see her knickers are washed out and look more grey than black, and she wishes he'd hurry up and put them away in the drawer.

'Looks like we're going shopping,' he says.

'I'm fine for a few days.'

'And then what? You can't go back to that,' he pauses to search for the right word. She waits. Monster? Bastard? But he chooses neither. 'You can't go back. Look at you.' He takes hold of her chin and turns it towards the only mirror in the room but she doesn't look. She doesn't need to. She knows the mess her face is in. It still hurts.

'I'll need to go back to collect some of my things.'

'You don't need any of your old things. I'll buy you everything you want. There's nothing in that house that you need anymore.' He holds out a pair of faded knickers for her to take. 'I've left you a towel in the bathroom. It's on the radiator, keeping warm.'

She covers the bruises on her breasts with one hand, lifts her clothes with the other and goes through to the bathroom.

John's flat is on the top floor and is only a stone's throw from the stadium. Chants of 'We only won 5-1' drift through the open bathroom window and she knows her boy is out there somewhere, singing along with the crowd. She stretches onto her tiptoes, presses her nose flat against the steamed up window and tries to look through the open crack at the top but all she can see are rows of rooftops disappearing into the distance.

The hot water from the shower stings and she turns the pressure down until it's nothing more than a trickle. She dips her head under the pathetic dribble of water and a roar erupts from outside. Her boy is so close it hurts. She's never stayed away for more than one night before and she knows he'll be expecting her to come home tonight. He's probably wondering what present she'll bring him this time. Another roar erupts from the crowd outside and she can't help it. A single tear escapes and rolls down her cheek. She wipes it away.

Her things are still lying on the bed when she comes out of the shower, and she picks them up and tosses them into the empty drawer. They look lost and she tries rearranging them so that they take up more space but no matter how she lays them out they barely cover the bottom of the drawer. She tries adding a few other bits and pieces from her handbag, including some tampons, a hairbrush and a lipstick, but it makes no difference. She dresses quickly, grabs a quick look in her purse just to double check the bank card is still there, and goes through to the kitchen.

John offers her a cup of tea, but the noise of the boiling kettle only drowns the singing out for a short time. Neither of them mention what's happening outside but when they switch the TV on, news of the open bus parade fills the screen and she scans the crowd for their faces. She knows they'll go home tonight and watch it played back on the telly, looking to see if they can spot themselves in the crowd.

It's Sunday night and that means a curry in front of a repeat of Match of the Day. She closes her eyes and pictures Robbie lying asleep on top of the covers when she left last night. She can hardly see the details of his face and panic bubbles in her chest. She slows her breathing and imagines his hands. They're surely as big as her own hands now, yet in her mind all she can see is a tiny fist curled around her finger. She watches the pictures on the screen and tries to spot her boy but it's like a cruel game of *Where's Wally*. Thousands of people have come out to see the bus travel through the city streets and they're all dressed in maroon. Everyone is cheering and clapping and having a great day and she knows her boy is okay. He and his dad are having a fun time together.

Maybe she'll phone him later, just to hear the sound of his voice. But what if *he* answers? He'll know it's her straight away and what if he traces the call to here. Maybe she should use a phone box. As long as she's careful, she knows he'll never come looking for her here. He's never even heard of John. She made sure of that.

Five

It's lunchtime and so far I've survived science, history and double maths with Mr Johnson. Double maths on a Monday morning, what a killer. Johnson hates first years, told us that on our very first day with him. Most teachers don't know you exist, you're just another annoying, little first year. They don't even bother asking your name. Except Miss Green. She's different from all the other teachers.

Mum didn't come home last night. I sat outside on the front step with my book until it got too dark to read, and then I went back inside and watched for her from my bedroom window. I waited and waited, sure she'd be home any minute, but I must have fallen asleep. When I woke up this morning she still wasn't home. It's okay, I'm not worried about her, but she's never been away for more than one night before.

Miss Green's already in class by the time we get along to English. She's leaning against her desk waiting on us all to settle down and pay attention, and then she says good afternoon and we repeat the words back to her in the mind-numbingly slow, tuneless chant that we all perfected way back in primary school. 'I know this is normally our library period,' she says, 'but I promised you something special and if we don't get started soon we'll never finish by the end of the year.' She ignores the groan that erupts and reaches under her desk and pulls out a pile of books. I watch her. Mesmerised. Quietly, she walks up and down the rows, putting a copy on everyone's desk. I try not to look, I don't want to spoil the surprise.

She stops at an empty desk. 'Does anyone know where Dean

Thomas is?' Dean Thomas is the class clown and a bully. I'd hoped to get rid of him when I came up to the academy but no luck, he's in almost all of my classes. So far this year, I've managed to keep my head down and stay out of his way.

'He's too embarrassed to come in to school today.'

I look round and see it's one of Dean's mates, a boy called Callum.

Miss Green looks confused.

'Lost 5-1 to a bunch of tarts.'

As usual Callum's trying to be a fucking smart ass.

'Don't worry Miss,' I say, 'it's only football.'

She shrugs her shoulders and smiles at me. I think I'm her favourite because she never gives me a row when I hand my homework in late, and she always picks a book out for me when it's library period. Last week she gave me her very own copy of *Tom Sawyer*. I read it all straight away.

Something hard hits me on the side of the head and a ball of paper lands at my feet. I bend down and pick it up before she sees it. I have a quick look around but everyone's pretending to study the book in their hand. I place the ball of paper in my lap where she won't see it and unravel it. The threat is scrawled across the back of a receipt in red pen.

Ur fucking getting it!!

I know Callum's waiting for me to react so I scrunch the receipt back into a tiny ball and shove it into my pocket. He's nothing without Dean and I'm not scared. But I still don't look his way. I'm not that stupid.

Miss Green stops at my desk, 'You're going to love this one,' she says and places it straight into my open hands. The book weighs practically nothing and I'm disappointed. There must be less than a couple hundred pages. She sees my face and mouths, 'Trust me.'

I turn the book over and study the front cover. *Animal Farm* by George Orwell. Never heard of him.

The room has gone quiet and everyone's feeling the same

disappointment. We were hoping for a bit of adventure, a bit of excitement. Let's face it, after everything she said about us being ready for something more grown up and mature, we were all hoping for something with a bit of sex in it. Not exactly *Fifty Shades*, but something a bit more exciting than a book about a farm.

'What's it about Miss?' I ask.

'Let's open at the first page,' she says, smiling, 'and find out.'

Six

It's been an extremely long day and Anna Green is shattered but the smell of cooking cheers her up as she walks through the front door.

'Just in time.' Matt comes rushing out of the kitchen to meet her, wiping his hands on a tea towel. 'Dinner's almost ready and I've even got you a mini apple crumble for pudding.'

Apple crumble is her favourite and since she fell pregnant she can't get enough of it. Matt takes the bag of school work from her and puts it down next to the front door. She looks at the overflowing pile of jotters and worksheets that need to be marked for tomorrow and feels that familiar knot in her stomach. 'Haven't you done enough work for today?' he asks, but it's not really a question and she doesn't answer him. She knows she's working too hard at the moment but she's going on maternity leave soon and needs to make sure everything's up to date.

She peels her swollen feet out of a pair of black high heels and as she tosses the shoes into the cupboard under the stairs she swears never to wear them to work again. Then she remembers that she said the same thing last week. She turns her back on the school work and goes through to the kitchen.

'How were the kids today?' Matt asks.

'Okay.' she says and melts into the leather dining chair, relieved to take the weight off her feet. 'I started reading *Animal Farm* with my first years today.'

'And how did that go down?'

She shrugs her shoulders.

'I remember hating that book. That and bloody Shakespeare.' Matt hands her a glass of blackcurrant juice and she wishes it was red wine. They've had the Shakespeare conversation a thousand times and she can't be bothered arguing her point again.

'How did the class bully like the new book?' he asks.

'He was off today.'

'Probably hung-over after yesterday's celebrations,' he says. She watches him serve a spoonful of pasta on each plate next to a slice of garlic bread. She'd really rather go straight to the apple crumble.

'Apparently, his side lost.'

'A Hibee! Wow, he's brave owning up to that in that school.'

'I don't think anyone would be brave enough or stupid enough to take Dean Thomas on.'

'Wait and see,' Matt says and opens a bottle of beer for himself. 'He'll meet his match one day. They all do.'

'Oh, for God's sake, he's only twelve; stop assuming that he's got no chance at a future.'

She hears her tone and quickly changes the subject before she loses her temper with him. 'So how was your day?'

'Great. And after I cleared my desk I decided to come home early to make my fiancée a special dinner.' He puts both plates down on the table and she feels bad for snapping at him.

'Looks lovely,' she says.

He puts down his drink and sits opposite her. 'I'm sorry,' he says, 'I just worry about you getting so caught up in their lives. I don't want you to be disappointed if things don't go the way you hope for them.' He takes her hand, 'And I wish I could see more of you.'

'It'll soon be the holidays,' she says.

He rubs her shoulders but the knots of tension are tight and refusing to let go. 'Have any of them noticed?' he asks.

'A couple of girls were whispering in class so I guess I'm maybe rumbled, either that or it's the usual gossip about who fancies who. And as for the boys, well, you know what boys are like. I could be nine months pregnant and they still wouldn't notice.' She takes a sip of blackcurrant juice. 'Did you really hate *Animal Farm*?' she asks and he laughs.

'The whole idea of farm animals taking over the world totally freaked me out and I've never trusted them since.'

'So you'll not be taking junior to a farm then,' she says.

'Of course I will.' He reaches across and gently strokes her stomach. 'I'll just make sure I keep an eye out for the pigs.'

Seven

Mum's been away for a week now and I don't know where she's gone. Since she left, Dad's forgotten I exist. He fell asleep on the sofa last night with a pile of empty cans lying on the floor beside him and he's still there this morning. Snoring. I tiptoe through to the kitchen and pour the last of the cornflakes into a bowl only to discover there's no milk in the fridge. Avoiding the creaking third stair, I carry my bowl back up to my room and switch on the Xbox. I eat my cereal dry.

I can't concentrate on my game and keep getting killed. Where can Mum be staying? She never tells us about any of her friends because it makes Dad angry. He says we should be enough for her. The screen in front of me fades to grey, I've been killed again. I give up and switch it off.

She's never stayed away this long before.

I try reading the next chapter of *Tom Sawyer* but I can't concentrate.

What if she's hurt?

I reach for my mobile and call her phone.

The crazy frog ringtone revs into life and I follow the sound through to their room and there, in the top drawer of the bedside table, is her phone. I slump onto the bed. Now there's no way I can get in touch with her.

I pick up her phone and go to the contacts folder. After me and Dad there's old Mrs Carmichael's number. I remember I used to play in her garden while Mum cleaned her house. Sometimes Mrs Carmichael would come out into the garden to chat and she'd bring me a glass of lemonade and a chocolate digestive. On rainy days I'd sit behind her sofa and stare at all the books in her bookshelf. Some of them were so old they smelled kind of musty, but that never bothered me. She didn't mind me reading them as long as I was careful with them. I was always careful. Most of the books were romance books but the ones I liked best were the ones with pictures of cowboys on the front that used to belong to her son. If I promised to be really careful she sometimes let me take a book home with me. The last time I saw Mrs Carmichael she was really ill and she couldn't talk without getting out of breath. Mum insisted that I give her a kiss when we were leaving but she smelled a bit like one of her old musty books and I couldn't make myself do it. Instead, I gave her a quick hug and ran out the door. Mum was mad with me and didn't speak the whole way home on the bus. I never saw Mrs Carmichael again because she died a couple of weeks later. Mum was really upset.

Downstairs, the toilet flushes and I freeze. *Please don't come upstairs.* I hold my breath and listen. The living room door slams shut and the TV is switched on. I relax and begin to rummage through the top drawer of her bedside table searching for anything that might tell me where she's gone.

The little purple address book is hiding at the very back of the drawer. I'd given it to Mum for her birthday last year. I found it in one of the charity shops along Gorgie Road, the one across from the pub Dad goes to. Barnardo's, I think. I'd traipsed up and down that street all morning trying to find her something pretty that cost less than the five pound coins I had in my pocket. She likes pretty things, especially butterflies. She used to take me down to the railway bridge to see them in the summer. She'd point out the buddleias growing wild beside the track, their big purple flowers always covered with all different kinds of butterflies. Mum could name every one but I only remember a few. My favourite is the painted lady. It's a beautiful red and black butterfly that shouldn't really live in Scotland. According to the scientists it should live further south in hot countries. Who cares? If I had wings I'd go wherever I want. I couldn't find anything with butterflies on it for five pounds but when I saw the address book I knew she'd love it. It's a deep shade of purple, the same colour as the buddleia bushes that grow along the railway lines. Wild, like Mum. The sticker in the shop said six pounds but when I showed the old woman behind the counter the coins in my pocket she smiled and told me that by luck it had been reduced that very morning to five pounds.

I open the book and flick through the pages and there under M is Margaret MacFarlane. Gran. I close the book and smile. It all makes sense now and I don't know why I didn't work it out earlier. Mum has gone to stay with Gran. Gran is my dad's mum and she's the only family we've got although we don't see her very often. Nobody told me what happened but I think there was some kind of big fallout at Mum and Dad's wedding.

Downstairs, the TV is blaring in the living room and I know he'll probably be in there for the rest of the day watching the cup final over and over again. Normally I'd sit beside him. Not today. I slip the address book into my pocket and head downstairs. He won't even notice I'm gone until he runs out of beer. I close the front door quietly behind me.

It's Sunday morning and the street's quiet. I head towards the railway bridge, and spot an old woman walking her dog on a lead. It's a black Labrador and I cross the road so that I can find out its name. I love dogs. I stop and bend down to stroke it but the woman yanks sharply on the lead, dragging the poor dog across the road to the side I just crossed from. 'Be like that,' I shout but the woman keeps walking, 'I only wanted to know your dog's fuckin' name.' She looks back over her shoulder and I see she's scared. I blush. Mum would kill me if she knew I was shouting at old women in the street. I kick an empty irn-bru can and walk on, shoving my hands deep into my pockets.

When I get to the bridge I stop and take out my phone. I take a deep breath and punch in the number but nothing happens. No signal. I shuffle round a bit and hold my phone up high. Nothing. I walk backwards until a couple of bars appear in the top left of the window. It rings. I hold my breath and wait to hear Gran's voice but there's no answer. Shit. What am I supposed to do now? I don't want to go back home and face him. I pick up some loose stones from the road and start throwing them onto the track below. Maybe if I wait long enough Dad will go out. Last time Mum left, he spent the whole time in the pub. I let the pile of stones in my hand fall to the ground and try the number again. Still nothing.

A train goes racing beneath the bridge, blowing its horn as it passes, and I watch it disappear. I wonder if Mum tells Gran about the fights. Probably not. Maybe she says Dad's working away for a few days. But that wouldn't work because then she would have to take me with her. I throw a few more stones. Maybe she tells Gran that Dad and I have gone away fishing together for the weekend. That'd work.

I put the phone back in my pocket and wander further down the street and on to the tow-path where it's quiet. My plan is simple and I go searching for the perfect weapon. This feels weird, looking for something to hit myself in the face with but when she sees that I'm hurt she'll feel bad for leaving. Then I'll tell her how much Dad's missing her and we can go home together, and everything will be back to normal again. I go over everything in my head. It's perfect. I pick up an empty bottle but I don't want to end up in A & E so I put it back down and keep searching. Then I see the buddleia bush. Its dead flowers from last year hang down, ashamed of their ugliness. I spot an old forgotten brick underneath the bush and I pick it up and wipe away the moss and rotting leaves. It feels heavy in my hands. Solid. I don't dare pause, so without thinking about what I'm about to do I lift it and smash it into my cheek. *Jesus Christ!* There had better be a fucking, massive bruise to show for this.

Now all I need to do is turn up on Gran's doorstep and by tonight everything will be fixed. I empty my pockets, desperately hoping there might be a couple of pound coins for my bus fare but all I find is a squashed packet of Hubba Bubba that's covered in fluff and an unused condom still in its wrapper. I *hadn't* forgotten that was there. It appeared in my jacket pocket a few days ago and my guess is that Dean Thomas slipped it into my pocket in class. I flip the red and silver foil packet over in my hands before putting it back with the other junk. I open a piece of bubblegum and start to chew. It tastes of nothing but I'll need the energy if I'm going to make it all the way to Gran's house.

I remember the time we took the bus to Gran's because Mum thought it'd be fun. An adventure, she said. But the bus took forever and by the time we got there Mum was in a bad mood and hardly said a word. It wasn't really an adventure 'cause nothing exciting happened. I love adventures. All of the best books have one. Right now, I'm like Tom Sawyer, setting out into the big world without anyone knowing where I am or when I'll be coming home. Except, I'm not going to live on an island in the middle of the Mississippi, I'm trying to get to my Granny's house. I wish I hadn't thought that 'cause now I feel more like Little Red Riding Hood than Tom Sawyer or Huckleberry Finn. I never liked the story of Red Riding Hood. How can anyone expect you to believe that Granny could still be alive after she'd been cut out of the wolf's stomach?

Well, I'm not carrying a basket of flowers, sandwiches or a cake, and my Granny's not ill in bed so I'm happy to say I'm nothing like Red. I try to think of which adventurer I'm most like. Robinson Crusoe? I don't have a boat and I'm not stranded. D'Artagnan? I don't have any musketeers to keep me company.

I keep walking until I come to a faded street sign that tells me I've made it. I slow down and say the numbers out loud as I search for the right house. Twelve, Fourteen, Sixteen. Not far now.

Number twenty-four looks neglected and sad. Rubbish litters

the pavement outside and the fence looks like it was kicked in a long time ago. I stand in front of the iron gate, staring at the broken house in front of me. Faded red paint is peeling off the front door, revealing a sickly green colour beneath while grubby net curtains hang in the windows. I bet Red Riding Hood's granny never lived in a dump like this. Weeds climb out of every crack in the broken walls but none of them are brightly coloured like the buddleia. These weeds are jagged with their thorns warning me to keep away. I almost do what they want but what would have happened if the prince in Sleeping Beauty had been put off by the wall of thorns. Sleeping Beauty was my mum's favourite book when she was little. I might not be a prince but I'm tired and hungry and I'm sure Mum is inside waiting on me. Waiting to be rescued. So I pluck up the courage and put my hand on the rusted gate, expecting it to creak or groan as I push it open but it does neither and opens silently. I take this as a good sign and step forward, over the threshold and into the garden. I'm not sure I can call it a garden because there doesn't seem to be any plants or flowers growing here, except for the weeds.

I reach my hand out to press the doorbell but I'm already guessing it won't work so instead I bang my fist on the door. I peer through the tiny pane of glass in the door hoping to see signs of someone coming but the inside door to the rest of the house is closed and all I can see is the small porch. Several pairs of shoes lie scattered over the mat and I look to see if any could belong to Mum. I bang on the door again but still there's no sign of movement. Maybe they've got the TV on. I jump off the front step and try to peer in the front window. Carefully, I push aside a bunch of nettles and place my foot on a large rust-coloured stone. I grab onto the window sill and pull myself forwards, trying to see into the living room.

'What are you doing?'

The voice comes from behind me. 'Gran?'

It takes her a moment to recognise me but when she does she

nearly squeezes me to death. 'Robbie,' she gushes. 'Why didn't you phone to let me know you were coming? Stand up tall and let me see how you've grown.'

I stand in front of her and she does the predictable comparing our heights thing that all grown-ups feel obliged to do when they've not seen you for a while.

'I don't believe it,' she squeals. 'You're taller than me.'

I've been taller than Gran for a long time now but I don't tell her this.

'And what's this?' She points to my eye and I wonder how bad it looks. She takes hold of me by both shoulders. 'Did someone hit you?' she asks and I wonder who she thinks did it to me.

'No,' I say, 'I got hit playing rugby at school.' Shit, this isn't going the way it was supposed to. Where's Mum?

'Rugby, eh? Think you should maybe stick to football. It's a lot less dangerous and keeps your Dad happy.' Gran slips her hand through the crook in my elbow as though I'm the one chaperoning her and leads me up to the front door where she takes out a key from beneath a broken plant pot on the bottom step.

'I'm not sure that's a good idea.'

She cuts me off before I can finish. 'Nonsense,' she says. 'I've lived here for nearly thirty years and not once have I worried about being burgled.' She gives me a look. 'Until today,' she says. She looks behind me. 'Where's your mum? Did she send you here on the bus by yourself? Wait 'til I have a word with her.'

'No, it's okay, Gran,' I say. I feel dizzy and sick. Mum's not here.

'Come on in,' she says, holding the door wide open for me to go through.

I do as I'm told and walk slowly through to the hallway. But my head is spinning. If Mum's not here, then where is she? I squint through into the living room and then the kitchen, but there's definitely no sign that anyone else is staying here. A single mug and plate sit by the kitchen sink, waiting to be washed.

'I suppose your mother sent you here so you'd get a decent meal 'cause she's too lazy to get off her backside and look after her own boy,' she mutters under her breath as she shuffles through to the kitchen. I'm not sure if I was supposed to hear or not but I suspect she knows there's nothing wrong with my hearing.

She rummages through the cupboards looking for something to feed me and I feel guilty for landing on her like this but I don't say anything because I'm really hungry.

'Has she got one of her migraines?' Gran asks.

I look at her and wonder how much she knows but she's not looking at me. She's gathering a pile of ingredients on the bench. I see the box of eggs and hope she's gonna make me a fry up.

'Omelette?'

My stomach growls at the thought of food and I nod enthusiastically.

'Grab a seat.'

My plate is soon empty and I've answered all of Gran's questions about school, teachers and girlfriends. She disappears upstairs to fetch something and I plan my escape. I think about asking to borrow some money but that will only make her suspicious. I listen at the door, making sure she's busy upstairs and then I grab a chair, climb up and carefully lift down the Toby jug that sits on top of the kitchen cupboards. First time lucky! I hear her footsteps on the stairs and quickly put the Toby jug back, promising myself that I'll put the five pounds back next time I'm here. Gran comes back into the room as I'm putting the chair back under the table. I look up above the kitchen cupboard. Shit, I've put the jug back the wrong way. Toby's facing the wall.

'Here,' says Gran, holding out a pound coin, 'Buy yourself a bar of chocolate or something nice on the way home.'

I stare at the money in her hand, my ears burning.

'What's wrong?' she says. 'Is it not enough?'

I take the coin and try hard not to look up at the Toby jug.

I can hardly breathe when I get off the bus. Please, please, please let her be home. I don't care if she gives me hell for getting a black eye just please let her be home. But as I push the front door open I see the hook where her jacket should be hanging is bare and the top shelf of the shoe cupboard is still empty.

I run upstairs to the bathroom and lock the door behind me. My face is a total mess and I open the bathroom cabinet and take out a small make-up bag decorated with pink and red roses. Inside are lots of tiny brushes, pencils and a mixture of miniature jars and containers. I find a red lipstick and picture her in that short denim skirt with the open blouse and red bra.

The tube I'm looking for is at the bottom of the bag. Foundation. This is the stuff Mum used on me the time I had a black eye. It was my last year in primary school and I was given the part of Fagan in the school show. Mum was more excited than me and helped me learn all my lines. She even made me a proper costume. The week before the show I stayed late to rehearse and when I came out it was already starting to get dark. A boy from my class called Callum Evans was waiting for me behind the bins and I never had a chance. He landed a punch before I knew what was happening and then his pals ran to fetch the teacher, making up some story about me calling Callum's mum a whore. One of his pals was Dean Thomas. The next day I was called into the headteacher's office and the part of Fagan was taken away from me. I was now an extra in the choir. Mum didn't say a word when I told her what happened and I still don't know if she believed me or not. On the night of the show she covered up the bruises with several layers of foundation but she didn't come to watch.

36

I open the tube of foundation and squeeze a little of the brown liquid onto my finger. Gently I try smoothing it over my cheek, trying hard not to flinch as I touch my swollen face. I study my reflection as I rub the cream in, desperately hoping it might magically make the bruise disappear, but it doesn't. It clumps and gathers at the edges where my skin is grazed and makes it look worse than before. I dampen some toilet paper and try rubbing it off but all I end up with is tiny bits of paper stuck to my face.

'Is that you?' Dad bangs on the bathroom door. 'Answer me,' he shouts. 'Who's in there?' He's been drinking.

'Only me,' I say and realise that he isn't looking for me, he's hoping it's Mum. He probably never even noticed I was gone.

'Open the fucking door.'

I do as he says.

'What the fuck have you been up to?' He's leaning against the doorway and he's spotted my face.

'Nothing,' I say.

'Don't lie to me.' He steps into the room and my eyes flick to the front door. Is it locked?

'Have you let someone beat you up again?'

What does he mean? 'Nobody beat me up,' I tell him.

'Don't lie to me.'

'I'm not lying.'

'I heard about the last time.'

'What did Mum tell you?'

'She was worried that you were getting bullied.'

'And?'

'And I told her it served you right for getting up on that stage singing and dancing like a girl. Probably knocked some sense into you,' says Dad. 'Got rid of all your fancy ideas of being a singer.'

'An actor,' I whisper.

'Whatever,' he says. 'They're all jobs for poofters.'

I know better than to argue.

37

'So who beat you up this time?' Dad asks.

'Nobody. I got into a fight with this gay kid in my class for looking at my arse,' I tell him.

Dad nods his head in approval and I breathe a sigh of relief. He believes my story.

Eight

Margaret MacFarlane puts two heaped spoonfuls of sugar in her coffee and pulls out a seat at the kitchen table. She turned seventy last month and prides herself on knowing when something is wrong and something was definitely wrong today. Robbie never comes to visit her by himself, in fact he never comes to visit her at all. His mother made sure of that a long time ago. And how on earth did the boy get that black eye? His story about getting hit by a rugby ball was obviously made up but why was he lying? Surely Tracey didn't hit him. And why did she send him here when she knows Margaret will see the bruises on the boy's face? She pretends she's busy all the time with her cleaning jobs, always looking for sympathy, but she forgets that Margaret had to bring her own son up all by herself after his father died. She's probably got herself into some kind of trouble. Usual story, she's been nothing but trouble since the day they married.

She sips her coffee but it's still too hot so she gets up to tidy away the dishes. She stops. The Toby Jug on top of the cupboards has moved and he's facing the wrong way. Robbie must have helped himself to some of her bingo fund. Carefully, she pulls out a kitchen chair and reaches up to the ceramic jug. It originally belonged to her own mother who used to keep it locked away behind the glass doors of the sideboard in the front room. Her mother used to keep her housekeeping money in it which was only ever enough money to buy food for the week. The meals were always pretty basic, lots of potatoes on their plate and whatever meat there was would be stacked on Father's plate, usually a slice of gammon or a pork chop if there was a special offer on down the butchers. Then her brothers would get the next biggest share because they were growing boys who'd be out making a living soon. That's what Mother always told her whenever she caught Margaret looking longingly at their full plates. She'd slap her hand, hard, if she ever caught her picking from their plates as she served them up.

She counts the money in the jug, stacking the different coins into neat piles in front of her on the kitchen table, and then counting the few notes that she's managed to save. She counts again one more time and is sure there's five pounds missing. Not a lot of money, she tells herself, but then she doesn't have a lot to take. Should she ask him about it next time she sees him? The answer would normally be yes, it's simple, the money belongs to her and what her grandson did is stealing. But she's got a feeling that right now he needs the money more than she does. Next week, she promises herself, she'll catch the bus into town and visit him, just to check everything's okay.

She looks at the money on the table and tries to think of a new hiding place.

Nine

The bus is late, as usual, and by the time I get to school the bell has already rung. If I don't hurry up I'll be late for registration but first I want to double check that she's not been trying to phone me. It's chucking it down with rain but I hang back and wait 'til everyone else goes into the building before I take my phone out. Mum hates me having it, says I'm too young and she's always going on about how it might melt my brain or something. It took me forever to wear her down and finally give in and get me one. She got me this one second-hand down the market and it's so embarrassing I never take it out on the bus or in class. Daren't. If any of Dean's gang got a hold of it my life would be a total misery. There's no messages or missed calls. What should I do? I thought about going to the police station to report her missing but then I'd have to tell them what happened the night she left, and then they'll arrest Dad and I'll have to go into care. Then I had a dream that I put up posters with Mum's photo on them all over Edinburgh and when I woke up it seemed like a great plan, but by the time I had breakfast I knew it was a dumbass idea.

I put the phone away and run towards registration. I have visions of Miss Green calling my dad to ask why I'm not in school and my stomach churns. As well as being my English teacher, she takes the register every morning which makes getting up for school a whole load easier. I've got English last period today. My favourite class. I wish Dean wasn't in it too but he's different with Miss Green though. Maybe he fancies her.

41

I push open the classroom door, ready to spin a story about missing the bus.

'You're late.'

Shit, it's Mr Johnson, my maths teacher. I slip in behind my desk, take out my homework diary and start copying the dates from the board.

'Robert MacFarlane.'

He always calls me Robert, says Robbie's not a real name. I look up. 'It's Robbie sir.' From the look on his face, I should have kept quiet.

'Robert MacFarlane,' he repeats. 'When the bell rings, please stay behind.' He peers over his glasses. 'You and I need to have a chat.'

I don't have long to wait before the bell sounds and soon I'm left alone in the classroom with my maths teacher. I stay seated, staring at my desk.

Mr Johnson stands up and strides across the classroom, stopping directly in front of me. My neck strains as I look up to him. 'School,' he shouts, in the same tone he uses if he catches you running in the corridor, skipping the dinner line or fighting in the corridor. It doesn't occur to him to lower his voice now he's right in front of me. Maybe he can't or maybe he doesn't want to. 'School,' he shouts again as if I didn't hear him first time, 'starts at eight thirty precisely.'

I look at him and wonder what he was like when he was my age. Was he the quiet kid who sits at the back of the class, or the geek whose hand is stuck in the air waiting to answer every question, or was Mr Johnson the Dean of the class, squashing everyone he meets? Suddenly I see it. Mr Johnson was the class bully in school. In fact, he's never stopped being the bully. And here he is now, picking on me. Why me?

'Why were you late?'

I wish Miss Green was here. 'I missed the bus, sir.'

'Liar.' He slams his hand down on the desk with a bang that makes me jump out of my skin. 'I already checked with one of your classmates and he tells me you were on the bus same as he was.'

There's no need for me to ask who the obliging and helpful classmate is.

'Smoking is forbidden on school property,' he shouts. This time I'm ready for the bang but instead he steps back and slowly circles my desk. His claws are in and he's playing with me like our next door neighbour's cat plays with a shrew.

I sit still in my seat and keep looking forwards. I say nothing. Mr Johnson looks disappointed and I know I'm winning.

'Detention,' he snaps. 'After school today.'

I stand and pick up my bag. I'm now late for science which means a row from Mr Cameron. Today is turning out to be a shit day.

I run all the way to the science lab and scramble on to my stool just as Mr Cameron enters the room. He stands in front of the board and surveys us all from above his glasses.

'Dean Thomas?'

I look at the back of the class to Dean's empty seat and allow myself a small smile. It seems Dean is late for class. I give a small shake of my head to show my disapproval of late comers and look at my watch.

Mr Cameron grunts and starts drawing a diagram of a plant cell on the board.In unison, we pick up our pencils and start to copy his drawing into our jotters. I sigh. It doesn't look like we're getting to do any experiments today.

Dean enters the classroom and skulks to the back row of benches. Collectively, we hold our breath and watch. He's almost in his seat. We wait. Mr Cameron spins round and takes aim. We sit back and get ready to watch the fireworks. Dean doesn't get a chance to speak. Our science teacher fires his assault rapidly, barely stopping to take air while Dean hangs his head and stares at the floor. I've never seen him give in so easily before.

'And make sure you stay behind at the end of the day for detention.'

Shit. I don't believe it. Dean's going to detention too. Just when I thought my day couldn't get any worse.

The rest of the day drags by until finally it's last period. English. Miss Green is patiently waiting for everyone to settle down and I watch her from my seat as she absent-mindedly loops a strand of hair round one finger and tucks it behind her ear.

When everyone's ready she stands up and begins. 'Imagine your best friend has been murdered and you know who did it.' She has our attention. 'In fact, everyone knows who did it and the person has been found guilty in a court of law.' The class falls silent. Today, she tells us, we're going to write a discursive essay, giving arguments both for and against capital punishment. The class are hooked and soon everyone's talking about the electric chair, lethal injection and hanging. I sit quietly, watching the smile on Miss Green's face as everyone throws a mix of ideas into the discussion. The argument soon begins to bounce back and forwards like a tennis match between Scott and Hannah, the two class swots. Scott is arguing that lethal injection is too soft and Hannah's nearly in tears at the thought of frazzled flesh from electrocution. Scott is winning his argument.

'But imagine that the guy in the chair killed your mum,' he says. 'Your mum.' His voice is soft, trying to convince Hannah he's right. 'How would you feel if she'd been brutally murdered?' He pauses for effect. 'Or raped.'

The hairs on the back of my neck rise and I remember that my mum is missing. What if something's happened to her?

Scott is still going. 'Suppose that guy sitting in front of you raped and then stabbed your mum.'

'Right,' Miss Green cuts in, 'I think that's enough discussion. It's time we all start writing.' She gives us the title and a few pointers on how to start our essay and then asks us to begin. I copy down the title but then I stop. A picture of my mum lying stabbed and mutilated like a body in a CSI episode fills my head and I can't get rid of it. I feel sick. She could be lying dead right now and I don't know. Miss Green stops in front of my desk. 'Can I have a word?' she says. She's not smiling and I know it's about this morning.

My chair weighs a ton as I push it back and stand to follow her to the front of the class.

She sits down at her desk and opens a folded sheet of A4 paper. 'I've got a note here from Mr Johnson. It says you were late for registration.'

'My bus was late,' I say without looking up.

'Mr Johnson says you were late because you were smoking.'

'He's lying.'

She puts her hand on my arm and I feel myself blush. 'Robbie, we've spoken about this. You can't say that about a teacher.'

'I wasn't smoking. I told you, the bus was late.'

Miss Green gives my arm a gentle squeeze. 'Robbie, I'm trying to help you.'

'He's lying.'

'You can't say that.' She lets go of me and turns to mark a pile jotters, clearly signalling that our conversation is finished. I'm not done.

'Why do you believe him?' I ask. 'The man's a liar.'

'Lower your voice, Robbie.'

'Why should I?' I shout. 'You're as bad as he is.'

'Go back to your seat.' Her voice is shaking but I don't care.

'You're all the same.' I sit down and stare at the title on the piece of paper in front of me. Capital Punishment: For and Against. I pick up my pen and write in big black letters across the page - *Who Fucking Cares?*

The bell rings but I don't wait to be dismissed. I walk out of class, tossing my literary masterpiece on to her desk and then fight my way against the one way system to the detention room only to find Mr Johnson himself perched on the edge of a desk. I take a seat by the window away from the fourth years who are doing their time until they can leave at Christmas. Another two and a half years for me. Miss Green keeps telling me I should stay on and do some higher exams. She reckons I could be the next Stephen Hawking, but I'm not sure if she believes I could be the next great astrophysicist or if she thinks I'll end up in a wheelchair by the time I'm twenty-one. I picture her face when she finds my paper. I groan and hide my head in my hands.

Someone sits down beside me and I turn my back on them and stare out the window only to see the school buses pull out of the playground. Great, I'll have to catch a service bus now, or walk. I'm going to be late anyway so I might as well use my bus money to buy a bag of chips. It's not like dinner will be waiting for me.

'I thought Johnson was a bit rough on you this morning,' the voice next to me says. I turn to find Dean Thomas sitting in the seat next to me.

'Cheers,' I say, not sure what else to say. 'Why were you late for science?'

'Got a message to go to the school office.'

'Why didn't you tell Cameron that?'

'None of his fuckin' business,' says Dean. 'Besides, you saw him, didn't give me a chance to say a thing.'

I nod. That's true. 'Everything okay?' I ask. Usually a visit to the school office means something's up.

He shrugs his shoulders and I think he's about to tell me something when Johnson appears beside our desk. 'Boys,' he shouts, even though he's standing right next to us. 'No talking.'

Dean and I sit side by side and stare out of the window waiting for our half hour of misery to be up.

When we're finally let go, we walk out of the school playground together. Dean lights a cigarette and offers me a drag. It makes my eyes sting but I manage to keep it to my lips

46

for several seconds before handing it back to him.

'Listen,' Deans says. 'A few of us are camping out on Friday night if you fancy coming along.'

'I'd love to,' I say too quickly. Not cool. I should have at least hesitated, told him I thought I was busy, that I would have to get back to him tomorrow. Too late, I'd jumped in like a wee kid being offered a sweetie. But Dean doesn't seem to notice. He's grinning at me.

'Great,' he says.

We're at the school gate and he's spotted a bus coming. I think about jumping on the bus with him but then I'd have no money for chips and I'm starving.

'See you Friday,' he shouts, 'and remember to bring your sleeping bag.'

Ten

The staffroom is empty and Anna makes herself a cup of coffee, a hit of caffeine to get her through the mountain of marking in front of her. Thank God the rest of the kids are on study leave, it means she's only got half the usual jotters to mark. She picks up her blue pen (she refuses to use red) and starts with the essays on capital punishment.

After marking the first couple, she feels like giving up. The handwriting is barely legible, the spelling is atrocious and they've totally missed the point about putting forward both sides of the argument. She tries not to feel too disheartened, after all it's the first time she's asked them to do anything like this and presenting both sides of an argument is something her fourth years still struggle with. She rummages through the pile of jotters hoping to find one that'll cheer her up and her heart sinks when she sees his name. Robbie MacFarlane. She could kick herself. Why did she give him such a hard time about smoking? She didn't even stop for a second to think that maybe he was telling the truth? Johnson said it was Dean Thomas that said he'd seen Robbie going round to the smokers but why would anyone believe a word that boy says? Robbie doesn't need another grown up giving him a hard time; he needs someone he can speak to. Already she can see he's starting to switch off.

She should have known better than to listen to a word Derek Johnson says. Unless a student is a maths genius, Johnson doesn't want to know them. The man hates kids and only went into teaching when he realised there was nothing else he could do with his postgrad in advanced calculus. Apparently when he first started he wanted the students to call him Professor. What a tosser! She can easily imagine him teaching in an all-boys private school with a black cape flowing behind him as he monitors the corridors. But at their school, he's a bully. A bully who happens to be the head of his faculty and that makes him a dangerous man, and until she has a permanent contract she has to do what he says.

The staffroom door is thrown open and Johnson strides in, imaginary cape sweeping out behind him in a theatrical gesture. 'Mark my words,' he announces to the room even though she's the only person in it. 'That boy is going to end up expelled before the year is out.'

She raises her head to acknowledge him and turns back to Robbie's jotter amused to discover the cover is decorated in tiny doodles of cartoon characters. She smiles as she recognises caricatures of some of the teachers. She turns the jotter over looking for Derek Johnson and there he is, depicted as a vampire complete with a stake through his chest. Droplets of blood are drawn dripping off the page and she barely manages to suppress a wee smile as Johnson continues twittering on.

'He deliberately ignored my words of advice and spent the whole half hour staring out of the window.'

She wonders if mathematically you can get a whole half hour but she says nothing.

'And then, guess who I see him chatting to as he leaves school, as if the pair of them have been best friends forever.'

If this man doesn't leave soon, she's going to scoop up her pile of jotters and take them back to her classroom to mark them there where she can get some peace.

'Dean Thomas! Can you believe the irony? He's chatting away to the Thomas boy as if the pair of them have been friends forever. The same boy who grassed him up for smoking in the first place.' He laughs through his nose.

'Who?' she asks. 'Who are you talking about, who is best friends with Dean Thomas?'

'That boy of yours,' he says pointing at her. 'The first year from your registration class. Can't remember his name.'

'Robbie,' she says. 'Robbie MacFarlane.'

'Robert,' he snaps. 'Robbie is not a proper name. The boy should be called Robert. After all, he's not a dog.' And with that ridiculous sentence, he sweeps back out of the room. She looks at the drawing on Robbie's book and promises herself that next time she'll stand up to Derek Johnson. If she doesn't stand up for these kids, who will?

She opens the jotter in anticipation. Robbie didn't say much during the discussion, but to be fair nobody else can ever get a word in over Scott and Hannah. They both think they're the best in the class, probably because that's what their parents have told them ever since they emerged from the womb. And yes, they're good, she's never had a problem reading their handwriting and their spelling is always correct, but there's no spark. They're good because their parents want them to be good, and she has no doubt they'll get top marks in their exams but that will be down to pressure from their folks and personal tutors, not any natural talent. Robbie's different. He might not have the neatest handwriting and his homework is never handed in on time and it's never signed but he's a bright kid. He totally gets it.

She turns the page and freezes. Scrawled beneath the title of the essay are three words: *Who Fucking Cares?*

She slams her hand down hard on the desk. There must be something she can do. She's not going to let Derek Johnson be right about this one.

Eleven

It's Friday and I still haven't heard from her. I keep playing the night of the cup final over and over again in my head like an action replay. Why didn't I stay in my room like Mum had told me to? If I hadn't gone downstairs to see Dad when he got home after the game, they wouldn't have argued. She's never been away this long before and it's all my fault. I feel sick. I want to ask Dad if he's heard from her but he's stomped around the house in a bad mood all week and I don't want to get him going.

Tonight's the night I'm supposed to go camping but Dean's hardly said a word to me all week and he's totally ignored me in class. I kept trying to catch his eye in French today and I'm sure he was avoiding me on purpose. I guess he's changed his mind about inviting me along. Who cares? I pick up my book and try to find my place. I've never been camping before unless sleeping in a tent in my back garden counts. It was the summer holidays and I'd been playing outside in my pop-up tent the whole afternoon. I kept pestering Mum to let me sleep in it until she finally gave in, but she only said yes once I agreed to let her sleep in it too. We waited 'til Dad had gone to the pub and then we filled some bowls with Smarties and Pringles and played a game of cards by torchlight. It was great fun. But when it was time to go to sleep, I got really scared and kept imagining someone coming and stealing me away during the night. I tried hiding deep inside my sleeping bag but that was worse. Then I remember Mum tapping me on the shoulder, asking if we could go back inside to sleep because she was scared. She made a big fuss in front of Dad saying over and over again how sorry she was for spoiling my night. But later on, when they thought I was asleep in bed, I overheard her telling Dad how she'd pretended to be scared herself to give me an excuse to come inside.

'That boy needs to get himself a pair of balls,' Dad said.

I thought he meant footballs.

The bus is already in the school car park when the bell rings for the end of the day and I grab a seat near the front. Only the cool kids get to sit up the back. It's the law. A few minutes later Dean gets on with his arm draped over the shoulder of some girl. I swear she's in third year, how does he do it? I can't even look at a girl without dissolving into a drooling wreck. He waves to someone and I turn round to see who, but there's no one there and I realise he's waving to me. I hold my breath as they walk towards me. I figure they're heading straight to the back of the bus but Dean slips into the seat behind me.

'You still up for tonight?' he asks.

I try to sound like I don't care. 'Whatever,' I mutter.

'See you behind the old church about seven,' he says, 'but tell your Dad you're staying at a friend's. Make someone up if you have to'

'Okay.'

'Think you can smuggle a bottle from the house?' he asks.

'Of course.'

He gets up to move to the back of the bus. 'And remember to bring a sleeping bag,' he says. 'It's still fuckin' freezing at this time of year.'

'You got a tent?' I ask.

'Leave all that to me,' he says. 'Your job is to bring the bottle.'

The two girls in the seat in front of me turn and stare. 'What are you fuckin' looking at?' I ask and they quickly turn to face the front of the bus again, but before they do I see their faces

52

and I know they're impressed. I sit back in my seat and smile. Maybe next week *I'll* be sitting up the back.

Twelve

It starts to rain as the school bell rings and Tracey looks to the sky and mouths thank you because it's easier to hide when you're holding an umbrella. Rows of buses are waiting on the road outside the school playground and she hopes she'll be able to see him from here. The front doors of the school burst open and a red and black swarm erupts from the building like locusts, flooding the playground. Damn. She doesn't even know which bus is his, so how on earth is she going to spot her boy amongst this bunch?

She grips the umbrella and scans the crowd, looking for him. He must be in there somewhere. Most of the kids aren't wearing jackets despite the rain that is now falling heavily from the sky. The older girls wear skirts that would serve better as belts and their ties hang below the top buttons of their blouses which are unbuttoned to reveal cleavage. Dark make-up painted around their eyes gives them a tribal, predatory look and she fears for the boys walking towards their bus, hands deep in pockets, heads bowed low. Robbie hasn't mentioned any girls yet, he's still too young to notice their existence.

She spots Dean Thomas come bouncing out of the school with two other lads, and they're laughing and shouting to a group of girls walking in front of them. These girls are younger than the others and have their mousey brown hair pulled back in a pleat and their ties are still done up to the top button. Dean breaks free from his friends and swaggers up behind the girls and Tracey can sense their fear from here. They keep their heads down and almost run on to their bus leaving Dean bent over with laughter. She watches as a girl with bright pink hair walks up to him and wraps her hands around his neck. They kiss open mouthed in front of the whole school and she looks away. Thank God Robbie doesn't hang about with boys like him.

On his first day at primary school it was obvious that all the boys already knew each other from football lessons. All the mums knew each other too but nobody bothered to notice Tracey standing alone at the gate. And then the party invites started. She'd dress him in a smart shirt and turn up with an expensive present wrapped in Spiderman or Batman paper and watch as the present was carelessly tossed on to the pile and her wee boy stood in a corner by himself watching all of the other boys run around together.

That was hard enough but then one day Robbie came out of school in floods of tears. All the boys in the class had been invited to a football party for Dean Thomas' birthday. All the boys except Robbie. She couldn't believe it. Dean's mother hadn't invited her wee boy to the party? The bitch always acted the part at the school gates, all made up and dead glam and she'd stand there and in her loudest and put on posh voice she'd announce to everyone where they were going on holiday. It was always somewhere tropical and hot but that never explained why she had an all year round tan. It was clearly out of a jar.

Tracey lost it when she saw Robbie come out of school crying and she didn't stop to think. She marched straight up to Dean's mother at the school gate, but she was never any good at confrontation and she crumbled when she stood in front of her. 'You forgot to give Robbie an invitation.' It was better than walking away.

But then Dean's mother laughed at her and something inside clicked. 'What kind of sick bitch doesn't ask a wee boy to a birthday party?' The school playground fell silent. Everyone stopped talking and turned to watch what was going on. 'My Robbie's breaking his heart 'cause he's the only one that didn't get an invitation. You should be ashamed of yourself.' She didn't hang around to hear the reply. She'd made enough of a fool of herself already. She dragged Robbie by the arm and marched him past the play park where already exaggerated stories of the encounter were spreading. Robbie was never invited to another party after that day.

Dean's dad walked out a year later. Left her for a younger model. The fake tan soon faded to a tint of Scottish blue and Dean didn't have any more football parties. From what she heard he started to get into trouble after his dad left.

She stands across the road and watches as the crowd in the school car park begins to dwindle. Where's Robbie? Damn, she was too busy watching Dean Thomas and she's missed her boy. Then she remembers Dean only lives a few streets away and she's sure he gets the same bus home as Robbie, probably gets off at the next stop, so she waits to see which bus he gets on. He and his girl finally come up for air and make their way towards the bus nearest to her. She scans the seats along this side looking for her boy but she can't see him. The bus is almost full and everyone looks the same in the red and black uniform.

Her stomach is tied in knots. The sensible bit in her head knows that she's probably missed him in the crowd but there's a nagging doubt forming in the back of her mind. What if he's not in school? Robbie's never ill, never takes a day off. The tiny bubbles of panic are growing and she feels sick. Why is he not in school? What could have happened? She watches Dean climb on board and wave to someone on the bus, probably another loser friend. She looks to see who he's waving to and almost drops her umbrella.

It's Robbie. She's sure it is. It's hard to see clearly through the steamed up window but she recognises her own boy's silhouette. Dean drops into the seat behind him and for a split second Robbie looks out the window and their eyes meet. She lifts the umbrella too late. Did he see her? She's not sure, it was only a brief glance and he's probably never thought of her once since

56

she left. The bus pulls away and she lowers the umbrella, letting raindrops mix with her tears. Her boy is so close and yet it feels like he's a million miles away. She watches the bus disappear round the corner. Thank God he's okay and still going to school, but why is he sitting beside the class bully?

She wishes Mrs Carmichael was still here. She'd know what to do. She had two children of her own, a son and a daughter, who were about the same age as Tracey. Her daughter seemed nice enough but her son never bothered to visit, not even when he knew his mum was dying. Tracey watched him at the funeral spilling his crocodile tears. She didn't go to the wake, couldn't stand to watch him pretend to care. He cleared the house out like a vulture, and within a week of the old woman's death he'd been in and packed up her ornaments, her jewellery and every piece of furniture that was worth something. He was only interested if it had a price tag attached and he'd have taken the light bulbs if he thought he could sell them.

About a week before she died, Mrs Carmichael told Tracey to choose something from the house to keep. *Take whatever you fancy.* She must have known she didn't have long left. Tracey didn't need to think about it. She'd fallen in love with the china butterfly the very first time she'd cleaned the house and she'd dusted very carefully around it every week for nearly twelve years. She doesn't think it's valuable, not in the way Mrs Carmichael's son thinks, but it's beautiful. Hand painted, Mrs Carmichael said. Cleaning for her was Tracey's first job after Robbie was born and, although she cleaned for lots of different people, from a young doctor in Morningside to a wee furniture shop on Slateford Road, nobody else was ever as kind to her as Mrs Carmichael was.

The china butterfly now sits on the kitchen windowsill at home where she was able to admire it several times a day while washing the dishes. She wishes she'd brought it with her when she'd left. Mrs Carmichael once told her that if you hold a butterfly too tightly, you'll knock the dust from its wings and it'll never be able to fly again. The trick, she said, is to let it land where it wants and admire from a distance.

Thirteen

Dad won't be home until after five which gives me a couple of hours to get organised. I'm not worried about telling him that I'm staying away for the night, I doubt he'll even ask where I'm going. I look in the fridge. Two cans of beer. No chance. He might not notice if *I'm* gone but he'll definitely notice if a can of beer is missing. I grab a bottle of irn-bru and empty it down the sink. The bottles of spirits are kept in a cupboard in the living room. I take a look. There's Bacardi at the back that looks like it's hardly been touched and next to it there's a bottle of advocaat left over from Hogmanay. Mum drinks it every New Year and this year she insisted that I should have a wee glass to celebrate with the bells but Dad went mental, said he didn't want me drinking a poofter's drink. They were so busy shouting at each other they didn't notice me leave the room. I flushed the sickly, yellow drink down the toilet and went to bed. I was still awake when the bells chimed midnight, and by then the arguing had stopped and they were singing Auld Lang Syne at the top of their voices. Neither of them bothered to come upstairs to wish me a Happy New Year.

The empty irn-bru bottle is sitting waiting on the sideboard. I take the lid off the Bacardi and pour some in and it immediately turns orange. I guess I should have washed the bottle out but it's too late now. I put the advocaat back and take out a bottle of vodka instead. Bacardi and vodka look pretty much the same so I figure it's okay to mix them but I don't want to take too much in case Dad notices it's missing. After I've added the vodka I lift the plastic bottle up to the light but it's not even a quarter full. I'm going to have to add something else so I take all of the bottles out of the sideboard and line them up on the floor in front of me. Tia Maria. That's Mum's favourite so I put that one back straight away. Gin. That'll do. Next there's a bottle of ouzo that they brought back from holiday. I add some ouzo and look for another clear liquid to mix with it but there's only whisky left. I open the bottle and take a sniff. It smells disgusting so I only add a little. Now my bottle looks like it's filled with pee. I decide it'll have to do and screw the lid back on tightly.

The doorbell rings and I jump and hit my head on the cabinet door. I shove the bottles back in as quickly as I can, not caring about what order they go in. The bell rings again and this time whoever's at the door starts knocking. They're clearly not going to leave.

'Robbie,' Gran is shouting through the letterbox.

I answer the door and Gran pushes past me into the hallway. 'Are you home all by yourself?' she asks.

'It's fine,' I say. 'I know not to answer the door to anyone.'

'You're too young.'

I'm holding the juice bottle in my hands and I quickly hide it behind my back. Wait. Now that looks more suspicious, so I bring it back round again. But what if she notices that the juice isn't orange and asks me what's in it. Even worse, what if she's thirsty and asks me to pour her a drink. It's suddenly got very hot in here and I don't feel so good. Gran's still speaking but I've no idea what she's saying. She's looking at me, clearly waiting for an answer. 'Sorry?' I ask.

'I was asking where she is.'

'Who?'

'Your mum.' Gran holds her bony hand against my forehead and shakes her head. 'You don't look so good,' she says. 'Maybe you're coming down with something.'

She's going to spot the bottle in my hand any second now.

'Why don't you climb into bed and I'll make you some

soup.'

Dad will be home soon and if they're in the same house together it's gonna end in a fight. It always does. 'I'm fine,' I say. I need to get her out of here before he comes home and before she starts asking more questions about Mum. 'I'm going for a shower.'

She stares at me. 'Well, I'll just pop the kettle on and wait for your mum coming in.'

'She won't be back,' I snap. 'She's meeting a friend after work.' I wait to see if she'll believe me.

She slams her umbrella down on the hall table and I look at the water puddling there. 'I've taken a night off my bingo, come all this way on the bus to see her and you tell me she's going out with a friend. Where's she going?'

Before I can think of an answer, she's off on another rant. 'She's going to the pub, isn't she? There's probably some karaoke night on. Typical. Never thinks of anyone but herself.'

Water from the umbrella is now dripping off the edge of the hall table and on to the floor.

'I've come all this way into town only to discover my selfish daughter-in-law is going out for a night on the town, leaving her young boy home alone.'

She's shouting now and it's scaring me.

'I can get her to call you in the morning,' I say. What the fuck am I saying, how am I going to get Mum to call anyone in the morning when I don't know where she is?

'Don't bother,' Gran says and it's not fair 'cause now it feels like I'm the one getting the row. 'We don't need her, do we? I'll pop the kettle on and we can sit down with a cup of tea and watch the telly together.'

She hangs her wet jacket over the banister and walks through to the kitchen, leaving her umbrella and the growing puddle behind.

'Wait,' I shout. Gran turns round and looks at me. 'We can't,' I'm not sure what to say and I stumble over my words.

'I'm going for a shower, remember?'

Gran looks at me as if I've lost my mind.

'And then I'm meeting some friends.' There, I've said it. That wasn't so bad. I wait on Gran to complain about how the youth of today are always busy, always on the go, no time for anyone but themselves. But she doesn't say a word. Without a sound she walks back into the hall, slips silently into her raincoat, picks up her bag and walks towards the door. I stand and watch her walk out the door leaving nothing behind but a puddle of water on the laminate floor and the sour taste of guilt in my mouth.

I think about shouting her back for a cup of tea but I haven't got time. I gather all my things and stuff them in an old rucksack I found in the garden shed. It's getting late and Dad's not back yet. I'm supposed to meet Dean up at the churchyard in ten minutes and I can't be late or he'll think I've bottled it. I scribble a note and stick it to the fridge door, the first place Dad always heads to when he gets home. My note doesn't go into any specifics, just says that I've gone camping with some friends and I'll be back tomorrow sometime. He might be mad at me but I doubt it, he's more likely to be glad to see the back of me. I pick up the rucksack and the sleeping bag. I got my sleeping bag for my birthday a few years ago but I've never used it so I hope I can still squeeze into it. It won't matter, at least I managed to get some drink. The bottle is wedged firmly in between my torch and Miss Green's battered copy of *The Adventures of Tom Sawyer*. I sling my rucksack over my shoulder and imagine I'm setting out on an adventure like Tom. I love that story so much I'm reading it again. I close the front door behind me. Maybe next time I open the door, Mum will be home, waiting to meet me.

Turns out I'm the last one to arrive in the churchyard.

'You're late.' It's one of Dean's mates, a skinny weasely looking boy whose name I can't remember.

Dean gives him a look, warning the boy to be nice to me.

'Alright, Dean,' I say casually, hands deep in my pockets.

'Did you bring a bottle?' The boy who asks me this is Callum Evans, the same boy that lost me the part of Fagan in the school show.

I reach into my bag and show him the half filled irn-bru bottle.

'What the fuck's that?' he asks.

I decide it's probably best if I don't list the mixture of drinks.

Dean grabs the bottle out of my hand. 'Not bad,' he laughs, 'not fuckin' bad.'

I relax. Things seem to be going pretty well.

'Fancy a can?' Callum is holding a can of lager out to me. I take it from him and open it as if it's the most natural thing to do. I've never had my own can before, just a wee sip of Dad's when he's not looking. It feels good in my hand. Callum and the boy whose name I can't remember are watching me. I take a sip and force myself to keep my face straight. The boys look disappointed and go back to playing on their phones.

'Drink up,' Dean says. 'I need your help putting up this tent.'

I throw back a mouthful of warm lager and grab the ground sheet and pegs. 'You sure we're allowed to camp here?' I ask.

Dean laughs. 'What d'ya expect, permission fae the big guy upstairs?'

I shrug my shoulders. 'Don't want to get thrown out in the middle of the night.'

'Stop worrying,' he says. 'My Mum knows the minister and he said it was fine for us to camp here. Even offered to bring us hot chocolate.' He laughs to himself as he starts unravelling the tent.

I take hold of the other end and we begin building it in silence. It's a small four man tent and doesn't require much more effort than the pop up tent I had as a kid. I remember how sometimes I'd put my tent up in my bedroom and fall asleep inside, dreaming I was somewhere else.

At last, the tent is up and we knock a couple of pegs into the ground with our heels. Dean goes to shout on the others and I take the ground sheet inside and wrestle with it until it sort of covers the wet grass. The tent's barely big enough for me to stand up in so I sit cross legged in the middle waiting for them to bring all the gear round. The orange gore tex shell ripples in the wind and rain begins to batter against the sides.

I hear them coming, racing against the driving rain to get everything under shelter. Their shadows loom over me for a brief second before they burst into the tent, falling inside in a heap of laughter. Nobody shares the joke.

I wrap my hand around the can and drink some more, surprised to discover it's nearly empty. I drain the last mouthful and make a big show of crushing it loudly in one hand before tossing it into the corner.

'Oi,' Callum shouts at me. 'Throw your fuckin' litter elsewhere.'

I don't say a word but quietly retrieve the crushed can. I go to put it in my rucksack but it's not there. 'Has anybody seen my bag?' Shit, my words are slurred. No one answers. 'I said has anybody seen my bag?'

Dean puts down his can and looks at me. 'Where'd you leave it?' he asks and the others burst out laughing. The bastards. They've left my stuff outside. I duck through the tiny zipped doorway and out into the pouring rain. Where is it?

The freezing cold wind is driving into my face and I can hardly see a fucking thing. I'm sure I left it on the steps leading up to the church's main entrance. Shit, where is it? It's got Miss Green's book inside. Have they hidden it? Maybe this whole night is planned to take the piss out of me. No point in denying it, a part of me's been wondering that since I got here. Rain is running down the back of my neck and I'm beginning to wish I'd stayed in with Gran. Right now we'd be sitting in front of the telly watching re-runs of the Antiques Roadshow on UK

Gold.

I stand in the shelter of the front door to the church and watch the cars go by. Should I jump on the nearest bus home or go back to the tent and confront them? Who am I kidding? There's no way I'm brave enough to face up to Dean and his mates but maybe they've done it for a bit of banter. My bag might be in the tent already while they wait for me to come back laughing. Shit, I feel sick.

I hear a group of women approaching and I duck back into the shadows out of sight. They're dressed in feather boas and cowboy hats and the one in front is wearing a pink sash with some writing on it but I can't read it from here. There was a bunch of women dressed up like this when we were at Pizza Hut once and Mum made some comment about a prison sentence. I waited 'til she went to the loo and asked Dad why the women were dressed up and he told me that it's what they do on their last night of freedom before getting married. I asked him what men do on their last night of freedom but he turned bright red and looked at the menu. I think I can guess.

And then I see it. My rucksack is lying on the path, in a muddy puddle. I grab it, and dive back into the tent. Their laughter stops.

'Here,' says Dean and he passes me another can of lager. 'Last one 'til we hit the hard stuff.'

I force a smile. 'Great.'

Callum winks at me. 'I see you found your bag.'

I shuffle into a corner of the tent and start emptying my things out. It's not as bad as I feared. The rain hasn't reached Miss Green's book and my sleeping bag is snug and dry inside its own wee sack. I'm grinning as I drag it from its cocoon and start unrolling it across the far end of the tent.

'Fuckin' hell,' Callum squeals. He fastens his coat around his neck like a cape, punches one fist high into the air and starts humming the theme tune from Superman. 'We've got a superhero in our tent.'

Dean is pissing himself laughing. 'Wrong song, Dickhead,' he says.

I look down at my sleeping bag and a life size image of Spiderman stares straight back at me, hidden behind his mask. Aw, fuck, how am I gonna get out of this one? 'Thought you'd appreciate it,' I say and laugh along. Nice recovery. I don't know if you've ever tried laughing along when someone's ripping the piss out of you but it's fucking hard. I seem to have got away with it though and soon we're sharing a cigarette and the subject has changed to Mr Cameron.

'Wanker,' Dean says and we all agree. He takes another drag on the cigarette then passes it to Jamie. He catches me watching. 'What you looking at?'

'Nothing,' I say and reach for my can. It's empty but I can't remember finishing it. 'When are we opening the hard stuff?' I ask.

'When I fuckin' say,' snaps Dean.

Jamie and Callum are arguing over who scored the best goal in the cup final.

'Who fuckin' cares,' Dean shouts, 'just shut up the pair of you before I smash your fuckin' skulls together.'

I'm guessing the rumours about him being a Hibs fan are maybe true. Callum rolls his eyes but he shuts up like he's told.

'I'm bored,' Dean announces and I try to think of something cool to do.

'We could take the torch and read some of the tombstones,' I offer.

'Fuck that,' laughs Jamie. 'I've got some better reading material.' He snorts through his nostrils as he laughs and a bubble of snot inflates like a tiny balloon and hangs there. He wipes it on his sleeve then rummages around the inside of his bag and pulls out a tattered copy of a girly magazine. That's what my dad calls them. I found his secret stash last summer at the back of the garden shed in a box filled with nails, rawl plugs and old light switches that he'll never get round to using. I was looking for some elastic for a catapult because I had some mad idea about killing a pigeon and cooking it over an open fire for our dinner. I think it was round about the time I was reading Swiss Family Robinson. I'd borrowed some books on surviving in the wild from the library and I'd just finished a chapter on hunting wild game birds. Well, in Dalry a pigeon is probably the wildest game bird we have and I intended eating one for my dinner.

But I never finished making my catapult, not after I discovered the bundle of glossy magazines hidden in the bottom of the box. Let's just say that my interests expanded that summer. For the first time ever I'd found some literature where I was more interested in the pictures than the words.

Gradually though, I got bored and returned to my library books.

'Look at the tits on her,' says Jamie, and Callum and Dean are hanging over his shoulder, mouths wide open. They remind me of the old *Tom and Jerry* cartoons I used to love watching when I was wee.

Dean snatches the magazine out of Jamie's hand for a closer look. 'Fuckin' Hell, do you think they're hers?'

'Of course they're hers, who the fuck else's could they be?' Jamie asks.

'He means are they implants,' says Callum.

'Or they could be Photoshopped,' I add.

They all turn and stare at me. 'Photoshopped?'

'You know, like you can make someone look slimmer or get rid of their spots in a photo.'

They're still staring at me.

'You can just about do anything to a photo if you've got the right program.'

'And have you?' Deans asks. 'You know, got the right program?'

'I've got an old edition,' I say, 'but you can still do most things on it.'

'Like give Jamie here an enormous cock,' laughs Callum.

Jamie scowls and grabs back his magazine. 'Who cares if they're real or not,' he says, lost in the photo again. 'They're amazing.'

'Got a hard-on?' Callum teases.

'Fuckin' right I have. I'm not a fuckin' queer, you know.'

I can't see the photo from where I'm sitting but even I can feel my dick stirring to attention. It's all this talk of tits without having to whisper. I'm feeling brave. 'Give us a look,' I say and Jamie throws the magazine in my direction. 'Fuckin' hell!' These are way bigger than anything I've ever seen in my dad's girly mags and my cock is throbbing so hard it hurts.

'Think Robbie's got a hard-on too,' laughs Callum.

Dean shuffles into the centre and when he speaks his voice is so quiet that I have to really strain to hear him. 'Anyone up for a game?'

The two cans of lager and my enormous hard-on are encouraging me to be reckless. 'Go on,' I say, 'I'm up for anything.' The words are out my mouth before I can stop myself.

'How about...' He leans closer and I can smell pickled onion crisps on his breath. 'How about...'

'Go on.' I'm hanging on his every word.

'A wanking competition.'

I stare at him, not knowing what to say. A wanking competition? What the fuck's a wanking competition?

Jamie's eyes are twinkling. 'Definitely going to win this time,' he says and he's starting to undo his buttons.

'Slow down, Jamie boy,' Dean laughs. 'You've already got a head start.'

Jamie laughs. 'My head's definitely started doing something,' he says looking down and I see the purple tip of his cock straining to escape through the zipper.

'You know the rules,' says Dean. 'One minute with our

hands behind our backs looking at the picture,' he hesitates, 'and then we start.'

'Get your zip pulled up, you big cheat,' shouts Callum pointing at Jamie's peeking dick.

What the fuck? They've done this before.

Dean sets the timer on his phone and puts it down next to the girl with the gigantic tits. 'Our minute starts...' he presses start on the screen, 'now.'

The others tuck their hands behind their backs and stare at the photo. Looking at their faces, it's very clear what they're imagining but as I watch the contorted expressions on their faces my own cock begins to deflate. Fucking hell, no, this can't be happening. I look at the countdown.

40 seconds...

Oh fuck. There's no way I can face them in forty seconds time with a limp dick. Stare at the picture, stare at the picture. It's not working. Look at her tits, imagine you're touching them, holding them.

30 seconds...

Thank God, I can feel a slight stirring in my pants. I look down to check that my cock's standing to attention only to see I've got a pair of white y-fronts on. They'll definitely take the piss out of me if they see them. Why didn't I wear my boxers? Shit. I don't believe this, it's going floppy again. Concentrate, concentrate.

20 seconds...

Kissing them, licking them, squeezing them. It's working, it's working.

10 seconds...

I'm hard, I'm hard!

Dean starts the countdown from 5... and they start pulling at their trousers, undoing buttons, zips. I join in. Keep looking at the tits, keep imagining.

And then they start touching themselves and they're pulling, yanking, groaning. I try rubbing my hand up and down but nothing is happening.

Jamie comes first and he spurts his spunk all over his own hand. There's not much but he's definitely the winner. Thank fuck it's over.

But no. Dean and Callum are still racing to the finish line and I see now that failure to come is not an option here.

I look at the magazine again but nothing happens. The dick within my tight grip falls limp.

Fourteen

No matter how fast Margaret MacFarlane runs, she can't catch up with him. She's tired but she knows she can't stop. She can't leave him on the streets by himself; he's just a young boy. He turns the corner and disappears, and she pushes herself to run faster until she catches sight of him again. He's still ten paces in front, and she knows that if he chooses to run up one of the side streets she'll lose him forever. Why is her son running from her? She shouts his name but he doesn't look back. 'Wait for me.' Her legs are hurting but she can't give up. She can't let him get away from her. There's no one else who will look after him, only her. He has no-one else. If she keeps running she can reach him. Every step hurts but she's gaining on him. He's moving again but this time he's slower.

She doesn't understand. The boy running away from her looks like her son but why is he wearing that red hooded jacket? Her boy doesn't have a jacket like that. But the jacket looks familiar and she remembers seeing it on a different boy. She remembers the boy's name is Robbie. But where is her son? She stops running and so does the boy ahead of her. And then she remembers her boy is now a father and the boy in the red jacket is her grandson, and he's alone. Where is the boy's mother? Has she left him alone? Is her son alone too? Is it Robbie that's running from her? Not her son, her grandson.

'Robbie,' she shouts. He turns and looks back, and she sees the bruise on the side of his face is bleeding. 'Who hurt you?' she shouts but he just grins. He's clutching something in his hand but she can't make out what it is. She steps towards him and tries to see more clearly. At first, it appears to be a bottle of irn-bru, but as he lifts it to his mouth to drink it changes into the Toby Jug from her kitchen. 'Wait for me,' she shouts out to him but he raises the jug in the air as if making a toast.

'Cheers,' he shouts and smashes the jug to the ground. Coins scatter in front of her as he turns and runs away from her again. She tries to keep up but the road suddenly changes direction and now they're running uphill. She doesn't think she can keep going but if she stops now he'll get further and further away and she'll never be able to help him.

She's shouting his name as she wakes but already the tendrils of the dream are beginning to vanish, leaving behind only their dark shadows. She closes her eyes, desperate to continue, sure that this time she can catch up with him and make everything alright but the dream eludes her and she can't find her way back to where they were.

She pulls back the covers and slips out of bed. The other side of the bed has been empty for over twenty years now but she still sleeps on the side nearest to the window. She doesn't miss having him beside her, doesn't miss his physical touch. They only ever made love with the lights off. She laughs at the words made love. That man never made love to her once. He fucked her like an animal.

The house is cold and she grabs the dressing gown from the back of the door and wraps it tightly around her frail body. As her mother used to say, 'old age doesn't come easy'. She stumbles downstairs to the kitchen in the dark and pours herself a glass of water, not wanting to put the kettle on in case she wakes the neighbours. The sound of the running water drives her back upstairs to the bathroom where she switches the light on, hoping that the fear will disappear with the darkness. It doesn't.

She leaves the bathroom light on and crawls back under the covers hoping to fall back asleep but she can't shake off the feeling left by her dream.

Fifteen

'Get up, you lazy bastard.'

I open my eyes and Callum is standing over me, his tall figure silhouetted against the painfully bright sunlight that's streaming through the thin orange material. I squeeze my eyes shut against the light and try to push myself up to a sitting position but a shooting pain drives through the middle of my head and I bite down on my lip to stop me crying out. I feel like I've been hit by a whacking, big bus. It's bloody freezing and I'm aching all over. I must be coming down with something.

'Got a hangover?' His voice slices right through me and I want to tell him to shut the fuck up but I don't say a thing.

'A hangover,' Jamie laughs, 'after two cans of beer.'

I wish they'd both fucking disappear. I'm dying here.

'Get up,' Callum shouts in my face. 'The game starts in half an hour and I've still to grab my stuff.'

I open my eyes again to find everyone's up and they've got their bags packed. My head hurts like fuck, but if I squint against the sunlight it's not so bad. I shift in my sleeping bag and look up at Dean. 'Why don't you guys head off to your game and I'll pack the tent away?'

'No way,' says Dean. 'The tent belongs to my brother and he doesn't know I've got it.'

'No probs,' I say, trying to sound like nothing's wrong. 'I can drop it off later.'

'Are you fuckin' deaf? I need to get that tent home in one piece.'

Christ knows what Dean thinks I'm going to do with his tent but it's clear he's not leaving without it. My head is pounding and I'm scared that if I move I'm going to throw up.

'Get up, Floppy.' Callum says and Jamie bursts out laughing. 'Did you not hear the man, he says he wants his tent back.'

And there it is. My new nickname. Floppy. By break time on Monday the whole school will be calling me it and there's nothing I can do to stop it happening. I unzip my sleeping bag slowly, trying not to make any sudden movements in case I puke everywhere.

'I'm gonna be late for my game and it's your fuckin' fault,' Callum says and gives me a sharp kick in the ribs. 'We're playing St Mary's at eleven and I'm the star striker so you'll get the blame if we lose. I need a proper warm up, you know.'

'Leave him alone,' Dean laughs. 'He's probably still dreaming about her wi' the massive tits. Managed to get a stiffie yet?'

I can't hold it in any longer, and I crawl out of my sleeping bag and rush from the tent. Watery puke splatters outside the entrance and I look down at the ground only to see a blue rucksack covered in it. Oh fuck, please don't let it be Dean's.

'That's my bag,' screams Callum and I feel a small smile tug at the corner of my lips. 'You fuckin' retard,' he shouts, 'you've puked all over my stuff.'

'Calm down,' says Dean, 'at least he missed the tent.' He winks at me and mouths, 'Good aim.'

The guys pack up the tent, grab their stuff and disappear, leaving me to make my own way home. Every thundering step back to the house shudders right through me but I eventually make it. My stomach's going round and round and I hope I can make it inside before I'm sick again. And my head! Aw, man, my head feels like there's a million wee men in there jumping up and down on my brain like it's a giant bouncy castle. I make it to the front door but my stomach cramps and I know I can't hold it in. I throw myself to the left and lean over the flower bed beneath the living room window. Mum's pride and joy, I think a split second before I throw up all over her gladioli.

I slump down onto my knees and dig deep into my pocket searching for my key but it's not there. Shit. I must have dropped it somewhere. Christ, I wish I could magic myself into my warm, cosy bed and wake up when the pain's gone, but if I cannae find my key I'm gonna have to sleep it off right here on the front doorstep. I know it's a stupid plan but my head hurts too much to think any harder. I drop my bag on to the path and I see something glint in amongst the gladioli. My key. It must have fallen out of my pocket when I was throwing up. I try to ignore the smell of my own sick as I reach into the flowerbed. My fingers fumble around in the dirt until they find the cold metal of the front door key. I grasp it tightly, and ease myself back up to standing slowly, unsure if I'm going to be able to get inside to the bathroom in time. I steady my hand as best as I can and carefully line the key up with the lock but it refuses to go in. No matter how hard I push it and twist it, the key won't go in, and the wee men upstairs are really having a party in my head now. Why won't the key turn in the lock?

Suddenly, the door in front of me swings open.

'Where the fuck have you been?' Dad's standing in the doorway and he's already been drinking.

'I left you a note,' I say. 'I was camping with some boys from school.' I dump my soggy, stinking pile of belongings on the hall floor. It's not like Mum's going to give me a row for leaving them there.

'Don't fucking lie to me.'

He staggers towards me and I take a step back. 'I'm not lying.'

'You're a fucking liar.'

I try to take another step away from him but my back's pressed up against the front door and the handle digs into my ribs.

'Liar,' he shouts at me. 'You were with her, I know you were.'

'With who?'

75

'You were with her. Your mum.'

'I haven't seen her since she left. I was camping with some friends from school. Look, there's my sleeping bag.' I point to my things on the floor.

'Think you can fool me like that?' he asks but I see him looking.

'Check it out. My stuff's probably still wet 'cause we got caught in the rain camping up by the old church.'

'If I find out you were with her,' he says, 'I'll fucking kill you.' He turns and walks away.

I cuddle up under the covers and turn the page. Tom, Huck and Joe are sleeping round a campfire beneath the stars on Jackson's Island, a small island in the middle of the Mississippi. No-one knows they're there because they've left behind no notes and I wish I could do the same. But it's raining in Edinburgh and there are no islands in the middle of the Union Canal. If I was braver I wouldn't care about the rain. I'd run away to wherever I could. I dream of packing a bag and slipping out through the back door, disappearing into the night. Maybe I'll catch a train to London. I'd be invisible down there, just another stranger on the street.

I picture myself walking along a busy London street and suddenly I'm surrounded by Dad. His face fills all of the television screens in the window of Harrods and I stop to watch. I can't hear what he's saying but I know he's pleading to me to come home. Sitting beside him is a police officer, his hands clasped together and resting on the table in front of a row of microphones. My face is displayed on a giant poster behind them and I cringe when I see they've used my primary seven photograph. I'm mortified, surely they could have found a better picture of me.

And then I see her. I freeze. She's sitting on the other side of the police officer. Her face is puffy and she's clearly been crying forever.

Suddenly I'm back in my bedroom and somewhere out there she's hiding from me.

'Bitch.' It hits me that it's her that's playing the part of Tom Sawyer, not me. And that's not right, is it? I'm the child in this story. I'm the one that's supposed to be sorting out my feelings. Me. She's the grown up and it's her that's supposed to be waiting and worrying. She should be here in my place, staring out into the darkness wondering where I could be. That would serve her right. Serve both of them right. Maybe then they'd know I exist. Maybe then they'd care.

I tip out my rucksack, ignoring the damp, earthy smell, and I cram it full with a pair of jeans, a couple of t-shirts and my fleece. I take the lid off the empty irn-bru bottle, hoping there might be a couple of dregs worth draining in the bottom but the smell turns my stomach and I tighten the lid again and toss the plastic bottle into the bin by my desk. I throw an extra pair of socks into the bag for emergencies. When I was at primary school Mum always made me keep a spare pair of socks in my school bag in case I ever got wet feet. By the end of the year, they'd still be unworn and by then they'd be covered with pencil sharpenings and the little balls of fluff that always seem to gather in dark, forgotten corners. She also insisted that I keep a pound coin taped to the inside of my bag. *Just in case.* Every Friday I had to take a new coin from her purse to replace it after I bought a big bag of Haribo from the corner shop on the way home. Once I started the academy she never seemed to fuss anymore, said I was old enough to look out for myself.

That's when she started disappearing. The first time she left I didn't even see her go. She and Dad were arguing as usual and I stayed in my room. I'm quite good at shutting out the noise, I've had enough practice, and so I went to sleep tucked up under my covers with a library book and my torch. When I woke in the morning the torch batteries were dead and Mum was gone. At first I thought she'd nipped out to the shops but she still wasn't home by lunchtime and I remember feeling angry 'cause I was getting really hungry.

'Where's Mum?'

'Don't know.'

'When's she coming home?'

Same answer. Dad was in front of the TV watching the football highlights on Sky Plus. Nothing new there.

'Well, when's she making lunch?' I asked.

He didn't answer and by this time my stomach was starting to growl. 'I'm starving.'

Dad switched off the TV. 'You'll have to make your own fucking lunch.' Then he pushed himself out of the sofa, patted his pockets to check for his wallet and left the room. I stood alone, in the middle of the living room as I heard the front door slam shut behind him.

That night she walked through the front door as though she'd never been away, kissed me on the cheek and handed me a brown paper bag. Inside was the packet of plastic, glow in the dark stars which are now stuck to the ceiling above my bed. But what I remember most of all was the smell of the sausage and bacon frying in the pan as she made supper. She left again three weeks later.

The mobile phone by my bed beeps and I jump. It must be her. She knows I'm thinking about her.

what u up to?

It's from Dean. I tap on the message to reply.

Nothing much, do you want to meet up?

I stare at my message, my finger hovering over the send button. I take out the comma and change the word you to a single letter u. That looks better. But what if he doesn't want to see me, maybe the text was meant for Jamie or Callum and he picked me from his contact list by mistake. My palm is sweating and I delete the message and start again.

nothing much

No capital letters and no punctuation. Perfect. I press send and wait nervously with the phone in my hand. It beeps almost immediately.

meet me in 10mins
@ school gates

I grab my jacket and shove my phone in the top pocket. Dad's sitting in front of the TV and I tiptoe past the living room door and through to the kitchen without daring to even take a breath until I'm out the back door. It's finally stopped raining but the cars make loud sloshing sounds as they speed up through the oily puddles, soaking me as they pass by.

I'm at the school gates within minutes but Dean's not here yet so I lean back against the wall and hope he turns up. An elderly couple sharing a bag of chips walk past and the woman looks me up and down before keeping her eyes on the pavement in front of her. Her husband is feeling braver and he faces me, eye to eye. Wanker. What does he think I'm planning to do, mug them for their chips? I pull my hood up and laugh as I watch him put his arm around her shoulder. Her knight in shining armour.

I shuffle over towards the gates, away from the orange street light and watch them walk away with their bag of chips.

'Alright?'

I jump with fright and Dean bursts into a belly laugh. 'Ya big girl.' He punches me on the shoulder.

'Didn't hear you coming.'

'I saw you,' he laughs, 'eyeing up the old bird.'

'Eyeing up her chips more like.' I'm glad it's just me and Dean; it's easier to talk to him when Jamie and Callum aren't around.

'You hungry?' he asks.

I haven't had any dinner and the thought of food makes my stomach rumble.

Dean laughs out loud. 'Does your mother not feed you?'

I don't know what to say.

'You okay?'

'Just dreaming about that bag of chips.'

Dean laughs again and I'm hoping he believes me, he doesn't ask anymore. 'Come on.'

'Where?'

He turns back and gives me a wink. 'To get you that bag of chips of course.'

We head off in the direction of The Golden Fry and as we get closer the smell of fresh chips and vinegar makes my mouth water and my stomach growl. I'm practically wiping the drool from my chin by the time we see the yellow sign above the door.

'I've not got any money on me.'

'Me neither,' says Dean and I'm so disappointed I think I might actually cry. To make it all a hundred times worse, a man in a suit walks by, cuddling his warm bag of chips close to his chest. The smell drives me wild and my stomach is sounding like the great warrior Aslan as he prepares to go into battle.

I shrink into my jacket, trying to stay dry against the driving rain that's started falling again. Inside the shop, there's a queue of people waiting patiently as the women behind the counter build a small tower of paper trays. They're waiting on a fresh batch of chips. The best kind. So hot they scald the roof of your mouth but it still doesn't stop you from taking another. The young woman is in charge of creasing and folding the white card into the final tray, which the older woman then takes and adds to the toppling pile. They chatter away while the customers stand, the agony of waiting shown in pained expressions across their face but they know it'll soon be worth the wait. I watch as the round, Italian owner raises the cage out of the boiling fat for inspection. I can almost hear the silence inside the small shop as the customers hold their breath. He shakes his head and lowers the cage back into the fryer and the people in line start to dance from foot to foot, desperate now. 'Come on,' I say, 'let's go.'

'Don't you want your chips?' Dean asks and he's grinning in a way that both scares and excites me at the same time.

'I don't have any money,' I tell him again, although I know he hasn't forgotten. I know he has a plan but I'm not sure I want to hear it.

'You won't need money,' he says and I can see he's excited. 'Just go inside, ask for your chips and when she hands you the bag, ask for a can of coke and when she turns to get it that's your time to make a run for it.'

'Are you serious?'

'You'll be great. Nobody knows you.'

'They will after I do a runner. What if they put my picture on Crimewatch?'

Dean laughs in my face. 'Crimewatch,' he's actually bent over with laughter, 'for a bag of chips. Oh man, you kill me, you're so funny.'

I wasn't being funny, but it's kind of nice to hear him say that. 'Imagine Mr Johnson's face as he's sitting on his sofa eating his dinner and suddenly I pop up on his TV screen being chased by a police helicopter on Britain's Most Wanted.' Dean's laughing so hard he's crying, and I love it. I love that I can make him laugh like that. I pretend to speak through a megaphone, 'Put your hands up and step away from the chips.' Dean's nearly on the ground with laughter.

I start to walk away but he grabs hold of my arm. 'You'll be fine,' he says. 'Everyone's a bit jittery the first time.'

First time? Shit, how can you get away with it more than once?

'You should have seen Callum's face the first time he tried it. He was absolutely shitting himself.'

'Did he get caught?'

'Caught? He didn't even go through with it, bottled out at the last minute and handed his money over.' Dean shakes his head. 'Pussy.'

I smile at the image of Callum paying the woman behind the counter while Dean watched on. Not quite the hard man that he pretends to be, eh? I look through the chip shop window and see my chance to prove myself. I can do this, I know I can. Besides, I can't mess up once I've put in my order 'cause I've not got any money to pay with.

'Back in a minute,' I say to Dean and march into the shop before I can change my mind. The queue inside snakes around the wall and there must be half a dozen people in front of me waiting to get served. I should have waited until it was quiet, so I could go in and out in the one go. Too late, I've committed myself now and I'm not going back out to Dean without a bag of chips in my hand. There's no way he's going to tell Jamie or Callum that I'm a pussy. I grin as I think of Callum losing his nerve at the counter. There's banging on the glass behind me and I jump. It's Dean and he's pointing at my jacket. Now he's putting his hood up and down and I'm getting nervous because the man in front of me is looking too. I turn my back on Dean, still trying to work out what he's telling me. Shit, I've not got my hood up. Quickly I pull it up and have a look round for any cameras. There's one pointing at the till, well, that's okay, I'm not planning to rob the till. There's something on the ceiling above the counter but I can't make out if it's a camera or a smoke detector. It's probably just a smoke detector and besides, if it is a camera, it won't be working anyway, they never are. Still, I decide to keep my hood up, no point inviting trouble.

I imagine I'm a character from one of my favourite books but the closest one I can think of is Oliver Twist, which would make Dean like The Artful Dodger and that's not right. When my class did Oliver as the school show I remember waiting for weeks before the library could get me a copy of the book. They argued at first because I wasn't supposed to order adult books on my junior card but I persuaded them it was for a school essay and they eventually gave in. I shouldn't have bothered. It was full of long, boring descriptions and it took ages before anything actually happened. I was so disappointed because I loved the characters in the show, loved the setting, the story, loved the whole lot. Apart from the choir, I hated the choir, it was just an excuse to get every kid on the stage, and in the end that was where I got put after Callum Evans lost me the part of Fagan. Gran was the only one who bothered to come and see me. She said I was the best singer in the whole choir. Said she could hear me above everyone else, which I know wasn't true 'cause most of the time I mimed. It was nice of her to come though, and to say all those nice things. She even bought a copy of the DVD so that Mum and Dad didn't miss out. The box sits on a shelf by the TV. It's still in its wrapper.

A wee boy wearing a judo suit comes into the shop with his dad and they join the line behind me. The boy looks about five or six and the blue suit is drowning him. An orange belt is tied twice around his waist and I bet he dreams of getting a black belt one day. He's barely pausing to take breath as he tells his dad all about the new move he's learned but his dad is too busy texting on his phone to notice. I smile at the boy and almost ask him to show *me* the move when I realise that in a couple of minutes I'm going to be the baddy. Next week, this boy is going to tell everyone at his judo class all about the teenager who robbed the chip shop. He might even get his instructor to teach him a new move that stops a thief. I turn my back on the boy and hope he won't remember what I look like when the police ask him later on. Will they bring in a police artist for someone stealing a bag of chips? I almost laugh out loud at myself for being so daft. Nobody's going to call the police over a bag of chips. I stand up straight and check the line in front of me. Shit, there's only one more customer before it's my turn and I haven't thought about what I'm going to say.

I look at the black pegboard with the little white plastic letters spelling out everything there is to eat. Battered cod, smoked sausage, white pudding, the list goes on. I look for the price of chips and I'm given more choice; large portion, small portion, chip roll. The boy in the judo suit is trying out his moves on his dad, desperately trying to get his attention, and instead he keeps banging into me. *Get off your fuckin' phone and*

83

listen to your wee boy. My head's spinning and the smell of hot, smoking fat is making my stomach turn. Will Dean believe me if I tell him I'm not hungry anymore?

'What can I get you, love?'

I look at the older woman, the one who was building the tower of cardboard trays. 'Two fish suppers,' I blurt out. What the fuck did I say that for? I search the board for the price of a fish supper. Six pounds, what was I thinking? I'm supposed to walk out with a bag of chips, nothing more than a couple of pounds.

'What a miserable night,' she says as she scoops a portion of chips out the fryer. She's trying to make polite conversation as she gets me my two fish suppers. You don't have time to chat when you're getting a bag of chips. A bag of chips takes less than a minute, everybody knows this and so there's never time to chat. 'I bet you're looking forward to the summer holidays, eh?' Jeez, this is taking forever. 'Salt and vinegar?' At last we're nearly done. I shake my head and she starts to wrap the fish and chips in brown paper. Good, now hurry up and hand them over. 'You look soaked right through, love,' she says. Oh why does she have to keep being nice to me, just hurry up so I can get out to Dean. I bet he'll be impressed with the fish supper. And one each, he's going to love that.

She puts the parcel on the counter. 'Anything else, love?' she asks.

'No thanks.'

'That's twelve pounds exactly,' she says and holds her hand out for the money.

Shit, I was supposed to ask for a can of coke but I completely forgot. Now she's looking at me funny and she knows I'm up to something. 'And a can of coke,' I say.

'Twelve ninety,' she says without moving to get the can.

I rummage around in my jacket pocket. Why isn't she getting me the can of coke like Dean said she would? Because she's on to me, that's why. What if she's pressed an alarm beneath the counter? The police will be here any minute. Fuck it. I grab the fish suppers from the counter and run for the door. But the door doesn't budge, and I can hear the wee boy shouting, telling his dad to stop me. I clutch the two fish suppers and shove the door with my shoulder but it still won't open and I'm guessing they've locked me in. And then I see the sign on the handle. *Pull*. I pull the handle and the door opens first time.

I tuck the brown paper wrapping under my arm like a rugby ball and charge down the street as if the whole New Zealand squad is after me.

Dean's nowhere to be seen but I'm not about to stop so I keep running. I run all the way back to the school gates, hoping this is far enough away.

'Quick, get in here.' Dean is inside the school playground, under what used to be the bike shed.

I hold out the two squashed bags of fish and chips. 'Ta-da.'

Dean's grinning and takes the parcel from me.

'You should have seen her face when I grabbed the bags and ran.'

He unfolds the brown paper wrapping and then stops. 'What the fuck?'

I puff my scrawny chest out with pride. 'Pretty good for my first time, eh?'

Dean throws the parcel to the ground. 'You were supposed to get a bag of chips, how fucking hard can it be?'

I don't understand. 'But we're hungry, what good is one bag between both of us?'

'Nobody cares about one wee bag of chips.' Dean's furious. 'They don't give a shit about a few slices of fried fucking potato, costs them nothing.' He walks towards me, standing on the battered cod with his dirty trainers. 'But, oh no. Robbie here likes to think he's smarter than anyone else.' He's standing in front of me now but I hold my ground. 'Robbie doesn't care what everyone else does, eh? Naw, he just goes ahead and orders two fish suppers.' He leans in close until his face is just inches from mine but I don't back down. He raises his hand and places a finger on the centre of my forehead. 'What–the–fuck–were–you–think–ing?' Every syllable is emphasised with a sharp tap to my head.

'What was I thinking?' I say. 'Good fuckin' question. I'll tell you what I was thinking. I was thinking about how I was so hungry 'cause since Mum left I've not had a decent thing to eat. Since Mum left, I go to bed hungry, wake up hungry and nobody fuckin' cares.' I stand there, in the playground in front of the school hard man with tears rolling down my cheeks and the school hard man puts his arm around me and tells me he's sorry for shouting at me, and then he tells me not to worry 'cause he'll help me find my mum. After all, he knows people. Except of course none of this happens. It might have happened on the banks of the Mississippi, but this is Scotland and the year is two thousand and twelve and in Scotland men don't hug other men, and boys don't ever tell other boys that they're missing their mum.

The reality is I say none of these things. What was I thinking? Maybe I wanted to prove to Dean that I'm better than Jamie or Callum. Maybe I was hoping to get caught by the police who'd have to track Mum down to tell her that her boy is falling to bits without her. Or maybe I just got scared and couldn't remember what I was supposed to ask for.

'Fuck this,' Dean says. 'I'm out of here.'

'See you at school on Monday,' I say, but he's already gone.

I stand inside the old bike shed and stare at the graffiti on the walls. Generations have passed through this school and those who were brave enough have left their mark behind for me to find. The oldest markings have faded and been written over but if you look really carefully you can still make out some of the names. I trace the lines with my fingertips, imagining the ghosts of these tags walking beside me. None of the scribbles are probably that old but I like the idea. I find a faded love heart in the corner, Rab + Stacey 4ever scrawled inside. Rab. That could almost be me. I feel inside my jacket pocket for a pen. The blue biro barely leaves a mark on the wall and I give up by the time I get to the first letter b. Next time, I'll come prepared.

I turn to go home but see that one of the brown paper bags is still folded over. I pick it up and lean against the wall, accompanied by the names of hundreds like me. I slowly unfold the paper and the smell makes my stomach growl. I'm starving. Absolutely ravenous. The fish is cold and greasy but fuck it, it's better than nothing.

Sixteen

It's Saturday night and Tracey's sitting in front of the TV watching clips of home movies with grown men falling off rope swings, cats running round in circles and toddlers behaving badly at weddings. This used to be one of Robbie's favourite programmes but now it's just another thing he's grown out of and she can't remember the last time they sat down to watch it together. Come to think of it, she can't remember the last time they watched anything together. John is hooting and laughing through every clip and she's worried he's going to have a heart attack.

Because it's Saturday night he insisted they eat their dinner in front of the TV. *For a special treat.* He pushed twenty pounds into her hand and told her to get them a fish supper each from the chip shop round the corner while he stayed home to warm the plates. She couldn't believe it, she had a twenty pound note in her hand which was enough for a new wardrobe and she had to hand it over for two greasy fish suppers. She placed a card in the local newsagents window a couple of days ago, advertising herself as a cleaner, but no one's phoned yet and she's going to have to come up with another plan to get some money soon.

She looks at the battered cod on the white porcelain plate and dissects it with her fork, pushing it to the edge. She's not hungry anyway. What if she's wrong, what if he does hit Robbie? Is it possible that her leaving has made things more dangerous for her son?

'Put those thoughts out of your mind right now.' She looks up from her fish and chips and John is pointing his fork at her.

'There's no point in blaming yourself, that husband of yours is the only one to blame.' He winks at her. 'I keep telling you, you're much better off with me.'

She gets up and carries her plate through to the kitchen, scraping the leftovers in to the bin and running the tap to fill the washing up bowl. Maybe he's left Robbie alone at home while he's gone out drinking. What if he comes home drunk and she's not there for him to take his anger out on?

An advert for a furniture sale blares from the telly in the living room and John appears with his empty plate. 'Leave this to me,' he says and she knows she should be pleased that she's staying with a man who washes the dishes without being asked but she can't help but feel it's because she doesn't do it properly. John doesn't leave anything lying around. Everything is washed and put away as soon as it's used. The place is spotless. Last night she found him giving the plates another wipe after she'd washed them.

'Do you fancy a bottle of wine?' she asks.

He's in the middle of pulling on a pair of Marigolds and he stops and grins at her. 'Great idea.'

The change from the fish and chips is still in her pocket and she knows it's a waste of the money but it's an excuse to get out of the house and she should have enough loose change leftover for what she has planned.

For once it's not raining and so she leaves her umbrella behind in the shoe cupboard by the front door. John has a place for everything. The off-licence is around the corner but she walks past it, crossing her fingers that the phone box on Dalry Road is still there. When she gets there her heart sinks. The windows are shattered and the effect looks like some mad crazy paving from the seventies. What are the chances that the phone is still inside, let alone that it works? She pulls open the heavy door and the stench of urine hits the back of her throat but at least she can see a handset and it appears to be attached to the cable. She scoops the coins out of her pocket and childhood memories come rushing back. When she was a wee girl she'd stay with her granny in the summer holidays and she'd phone her mum every night before bed. She remembers building a tower of two pence coins on the shelf next to the phone book, excited about the thought of hearing her mum's voice.

Just like when she was a wee girl, Tracey stacks her coins on the shelf beside her, but this time the coins are silver and it's not her mum's voice that she's waiting to hear. Her mum died when Tracey was still young and she has no family left, except for her boy. The sticker beside the handset tells her it's sixty pence to make a phone call. Sixty pence. She almost laughs out loud, that would take a lot of two pence coins. She doesn't want to have a lengthy conversation with him, she just wants to check he's okay. Just wants to hear his voice.

She feeds three twenty pence coins into the slot and waits for the dial tone. Her fingers shake as she enters the number. The receiver smells of sweat mixed with God knows what else but she holds it to her ear and listens as the phone on the other end starts to ring. She pictures him racing downstairs, he always runs to answer it before anyone else. She's just about to hang up, scared she'll lose her money if the answer machine kicks in, when the phone is answered.

'Hello.'

It's *him*.

'Hello?'

She freezes and holds the phone tight in her grip. She knows she should hang up but she can't. She hears him breathe and it's as if he's right there beside her. She feels the rough skin on his calloused fingertips as he pinched her breasts. *Best day of my fucking life and you're spoiling it.* The smell of sweat and urine within the small phone box is replaced with the smell of his breath; beer, whisky and cigarettes mixed together making an angry cocktail. *You're nothing but a fucking slut.* She can almost taste him.

'Is that you, whore?'

He knows it's her. Hang up, she screams from somewhere deep inside but she can't. She's frozen. Paralysed.

'You filthy little slut, run off to your bit on the side, have you?'

How does he know about John? Does he know where she's staying?

'You'll come home,' he whispers down the phone line. 'You always do.'

She drops the receiver and runs out of the phone box leaving behind the pile of neatly stacked coins.

John is still sitting in front of the TV when she walks back in. She tucks a loose strand of hair behind her ears and takes a few deep breaths. Act as though nothing has happened. Her heart is hammering against her ribcage but she knows she can pull this off.

'Everything okay?' He's wondering if something's wrong.

'Fine,' she says and hopes her voice sounds okay.

'Where is it?'

What does he mean?

'The bottle of wine, did you get red or white?'

Shit. 'The shop was shut,' she says and walks through to the kitchen before he can ask any more questions. 'I'll make us a cup of tea instead.'

Seventeen

Nobody came to get me this morning and by the time I wake up I've already missed the school bus. I roll over and face my bedroom wall. I hate Monday mornings. What a way to start the week, science first thing with Mr Cameron and then double maths with Mr Johnson. But this Monday there's no Mum telling me to get up so I can stay in bed as long as I like. Except, I've got nothing to read. I finished *Tom Sawyer*, again, and I rummage through the pile of books beside my bed for something new but I've read them all. Maybe Miss Green will give me a new book this afternoon.

Our library period is first thing after lunch and I know I should give her the book back but I want to keep a hold of it a little while longer. I want to take one more adventure with Huck and Tom before returning it to her. There's some writing inside the front cover and I've tried to decipher what it says over and over again but the handwriting is smudged and slopes diagonally with fancy loops and curls. I can make out the name Anna and a date, and I'm guessing Anna is Miss Green's first name. Maybe she was given it on her birthday. If Mum was here I'd ask her to give me a copy for my birthday too, without telling Dad of course. Dad says reading is for girls.

I go downstairs to the kitchen and help myself to a handful of chocolate digestives for breakfast. I pour myself a glass of milk and figure that about makes it cereal. My stomach was killing me all day yesterday and I think it must have been that fish supper. Last time I'm getting anything out of there I tell myself, laughing at my own joke. The wooden floor is cold beneath my bare feet and even though the curtains are open the room is dark. It feels more like December than June. It's still raining outside and I picture Mum waiting for me under her umbrella and my stomach flips. I go to the window to look for her but all I can make out are the blurred shapes of the overgrown bushes and trees in the front garden. They remind me of the shapes I used to see at night time in my bedroom after the light was switched off when I used to think the dressing gown hanging on the back of my door was the bogey man.

I'm still hungry so I open a tin of peaches, grab a spoon and go back up to bed and turn on the TV. I've got a choice between cookery programmes, an antiques show or one of those shows where everyone's yelling and someone's taking a DNA test. Mum loves those programmes and she usually ends up joining in with the argument and shouting at the telly. I've even seen her standing in front of the screen yelling at some guy who's either run away with another woman or beats his girlfriend up. It's always the same old shit. I change channels and sit back to watch two teams race around a field buying old junk which nobody wants that they then try to sell at auction for a profit. It might be crap but at least nobody's shouting at anyone. In the end, both couples lose all their money, but still they smile and tell the fake-tanned host that they've had a lovely time. I switch the television off and go for a shower.

Dad's still sleeping off his hangover when I leave the house. If Mum was at home she'd wake him with a cup of coffee or if he was really out of it she'd phone his work and make up some story. Well, fuck him. I'm not going to lie for him. Mum's not here anymore to phone in sick for him and I'm not doing it. He can rot in his bed for all I care.

I get off at the bus stop nearest to the school and I can hear the noise straight away. It's lunchtime and the playground's full. I walk through the gates, but no-one notices me arrive. First years aren't supposed to go off the premises at lunchtime but most of us go to the chippy or the supermarket for crisps and sweets and nobody really cares.

I've timed it perfectly 'cause as soon as I arrive the bell rings and it's time to go in. I keep my head down and make my way straight to the library. Miss Green's already there and she smiles when she sees me.

'You weren't at registration,' she says and I blush. I hate lying to her 'cause she's the only teacher who's nice to me.

'Sorry Miss,' I say. 'Had a dentist's appointment.'

'All morning?' she asks.

'Thought I better wait until the jag wore off,' I say.

She smiles at me. 'That was probably a good idea.'

She believes me. I've got away with it. Brilliant. If I'm clever I can probably come up with a long list of good reasons for missing double maths from now on. 'I was wondering if you had another book for me.'

'Finished already?' she asks.

'I've read it three times.'

'Enjoy it?'

'Loved it,' I say, 'and I wondered if there are any other books that are like it.'

'Have you heard of Harper Lee?' she asks me.

I shake my head. 'Is it set in America?'

'Harper Lee is the name of the writer.' She laughs. 'She wrote a very famous book called *To Kill a Mocking Bird*. It's told through the eyes of a child. I think you'd like it.'

I follow her to the librarian's desk and sitting beside the computer is a thin book with a black and white image of a girl on a tyre swing on the front cover. I smile when I see the book has a yellow sticky on the front with my name on it. Miss Green has been planning to give me it all along. I pick up my new book and make my way to a quiet corner to read for the rest of the period.

'Wait,' Miss Green calls after me.

I turn round. Her copy of *Tom Sawyer* is lying next to my bed and I was hoping she wouldn't ask for it back yet. I'd like to read it again.

'Remember to bring a note from your mum,' she says.

I look at her, confused. 'A note?'

'For this morning's dentist appointment,' she says and walks away.

I sit in the corner and open my book at the first page but I no longer care what the book is about. I thought Miss Green trusted me, but now she's asking for a note. Why doesn't she believe me? I glance over the top of my book and watch her talking to a girl in my class. She hands the girl a book and I strain to see what it is. It too has a yellow sticky on the front cover. I thought I was the only one she picked books for.

'Alright, Floppy?'

Dean sits down beside me but I'm not in the mood to chat. 'I'm reading,' I tell him.

'Yeah, yeah, whatever,' he says and digs me in the ribs. 'I saw you looking at Rachel.'

I stare at the words on the page and hope he'll take the hint.

'Heard she broke up with her boyfriend,' Dean says. 'Why don't you ask her out?'

I close my book over. 'What are you going on about?' I ask.

He nudges me and points in the direction of the girl with Miss Green. 'She was seeing some boy in second year,' Dean says, 'can't remember his name, but apparently she was crying in biology last week.' He leans closer. 'Maybe you could give her a shoulder to cry on.'

I look at the girl with Miss Green. She is kind of pretty, and not many girls spend their time reading. Most of them spend the library period texting on their phones.

'Go on,' Dean whispers, 'ask her out.'

I've never really spoken to a girl before, never mind asked one out. 'I can't just go up and ask her out,' I say.

'Not when she's with Miss Green.' Dean laughs. 'Wait until

she's sitting down.'

'I can't.'

'That's what you said on Saturday night outside the chip shop and you totally nailed that one. Callum couldn't even get a bag of chips and you fuckin' came away with two fish suppers.'

I look at him to see if he's taking the piss but his face is dead straight.

'You're a genius,' he says and slaps me on the back. 'A legend.'

I look over at Rachel and watch as she plays with her hair, turning it slowly around her finger. I hold my new book in my lap in case Dean looks down and sees my dick standing to attention inside my polyester trousers from Asda.

Suddenly, Miss Green is pointing over at me and they're both laughing. Holy Fuck, have they spotted my erection? I tell myself not to be so stupid. But then, why the hell are they talking about me? I'm sweating and in polyester that means it's going to itch.

Fucking hell. Rachel's walking towards me. Where am I supposed to look? If I open my book and start reading now she'll think I'm not interested.

'Now's your chance,' hisses Dean and I wish he would disappear.

She's definitely coming this way. Should I look up and smile? The sweat's pouring off me and I'm dying to scratch. I can't quite bring myself to look her in the face but I let my eyes find her feet striding towards me. She's wearing purple boots. Cool. I raise my gaze. Purple boots. Black leggings hugging long, skinny legs. Hips. Waist. I dare to look a little higher. I stop breathing. Shit. I don't want her to see me staring at her tits, so I raise my eyes to her neck and I imagine kissing her soft skin. I bet it smells like Palmolive soap.

My heart pounds against my ribcage and I'm aware that Dean is sitting right next to me. Can he hear it? I take a deep breath and dare myself to look her in the eye.

Everything around me vanishes and all I know is that she's looking at me.

I smile and I'm sure she's about to smile back but suddenly she's pushed aside and Jamie and Callum barge through, knocking her book to the floor. I look down at the book and feel a stabbing pain in my chest. I can't believe it. Miss Green has given her *The Adventures of Tom Sawyer*.

'Hey there, Floppy.' Callum throws himself down on the seat beside me.

'Had a good wank lately?' asks Jamie and they both burst out laughing.

I look at Rachel and imagine myself picking up the book and handing it to her. She smiles at me and asks my name but of course none of this actually happens. Rachel picks up the book and marches straight past us towards the non-fiction section.

'Where have you been all morning?' Callum asks.

'He's been at home, practising with his Dad's porno mags,' says Jamie. 'Managed to get it up yet?' He punches me in the arm to let me know he's joking. Just a bit of banter. Just a laugh. But I'm not laughing.

'Seriously, mate. Where have you been?' Callum asks again. 'Johnson wanted to know why you weren't in maths. I reckon he's gunning for you.'

'Better get your mum to write you a note,' says Dean and I look at him. Even if Mum was at home, why on earth would she write me a note if I'd been skiving? Dean must see what I'm thinking. 'Tell her you were sick on the way to school and went home for a wee while until you felt better. She'll be dead impressed you went to school in the afternoon, think you're mature or whatever.'

'She can't write me a note,' I say quietly.

'Why not?'

'She's not at home just now.' I stare at my fingernails, waiting on Dean to ask where she is. I'm not sure what I'm going to say but I'm fed up of lying.

97

He doesn't ask. 'No problem,' he says. 'I'll write it for you.'

'What?'

'I've done it loads of times,' he says. 'Have you got a copy of her signature?'

I search through my school bag, looking for an old letter or note that I've forgotten to hand in. 'Here you go,' I hand him a form we were given in the first week asking for permission to get our photograph taken. It's a bit scrunched up and faded but you can still make out my mum's signature at the bottom of the page.

'Perfect.' Dean gets up and walks away without saying where he's going. Beside me, Jamie and Callum are squashed together on one chair, pouring through a tattered copy of *FHM*. I ignore them and glance over towards the non-fiction section. Rachel's sitting at a small table by herself with her back to me, her purple boots resting on the chair opposite her. I'm envious that she's entering the world of Tom Sawyer for the first time and I wish I could see her face to try and work out what she thinks of it. Maybe I could go over, pretend I'm looking for a book on micro-organisms or World War two or something, then I could notice the book in her hand and make some mature, witty comment. I try to think what my mature, witty comment could be but come up with nothing so instead I sit on my hands and look at her gorgeous, shiny hair hanging over the back of the plastic school chair. I can almost smell the Palmolive soap from here.

Dean comes back holding a sheet of A4 paper. 'Had to sneak a bit out of the photocopier,' he whispers. He reveals a pen from his shirt pocket and waves it in the air as though he's preparing to conduct an orchestra. 'What do you want me to write?' he asks. He loves the drama.

I shrug my shoulders. 'Sickness and diarrhoea?'

'Can't spell it.'

I doubt my mum could spell it either but I keep quiet.

'I told Miss Green I was at the dentist.'

'Not good enough,' says Dean. 'They can easily double check appointments like that. It has to be something smart, something they won't check.'

I stare out the window and wish I'd gone to double maths after all.

'Got it,' says Dean. 'A death in the family.'

'That's sick.'

'It's genius. Nobody's going to ask you any questions in case they upset you. Even Johnson won't dare to phone your house to check that your old Aunt Mary is dead.'

'Why would Mr Johnson phone my house?'

'Because that's the kind of bastard he is,' says Dean. 'If he thinks you're lying to him, he's like a dog with a fuckin' bone.'

I think of Dad getting a phone call from school and I remember the night of my primary six parents' night.

Mum had insisted that Dad come along, which meant that he missed going to watch the game in the pub and they'd had a raging argument before we left the house. She was in one of her brave moods.

They were still arguing in the car on the way to school.

'I don't see why we both need to come.'

'I told you, last parents' night the teacher said we should both be there, said something about a boy looking up to his dad as a role model. Besides don't you want to hear how Robbie's doing?'

'Robbie's doing fine, aren't you, lad?' Dad winked at me in the mirror and I felt sick. I'd been in trouble in the playground a few times and had got into a fight the week before with Callum Evans in the gym hall. I tried telling the teacher that he'd called my dad a loser but she made me sit out without bothering to hear my side of the story. I didn't mind. I hate PE lessons anyway.

'Well, I think it's a bit much expecting me to wear a shirt and tie.'

'It's important we make the right impression. She's not going to try and teach Robbie all the clever stuff if she thinks you work in a factory.'

'But I *do* work in a factory.'

'Yes, but you're not just any old worker, are you?'

'Don't know what you mean,' Dad said.

'Well, you're the union rep, aren't you,' said Mum, 'and that's an important job.' He hates when she goes on about it. She made me change the title of his job when I had a presentation to do on my family to my class and he was furious when he found out.

'There's nothing wrong with my job,' said Dad. 'I don't hear you complain when you're spending the money I bring home.'

Mum didn't say another word. Thank God.

Mrs Simpson wasn't smiling when she called Mum and Dad in to the classroom. My plan was to go in too. I was sure she wouldn't say anything bad about me if I was in the room but when I stood up to go in she pointed to the chair and told me to wait outside. I tried shuffling towards the door but I still couldn't hear what was being said.

Then Billy Walker and his mum and dad turned up and sat in the line outside the room and I had to listen while he showed his parents every single jotter that was in the neat pile in his tray. Billy was the class genius. My tray still sat, unlooked at, in the row outside the classroom. Maybe I could show Mum and Dad my work after they'd spoken to Mrs Simpson. I got up from my seat, collected my tray and sat back down with it on my knee. Billy's mum whispered something and I knew she was asking about me. I ignored them and picked up my maths jotter. The pages were curled at the edges and the squared paper inside was grubby and ripped in places where I'd tried rubbing out my mistakes. I glanced over at Billy's jotter. Even from far away I could see his pages were filled with neat rows of perfect sums.

Dad burst out of the classroom. 'Who the fuck does she think she is telling me how to raise my boy?'

'Let's just go home,' Mum said. I started sorting through the pile of jotters in my tray in the hope that Mum would notice them and want to stay and see my work. But she was already half way down the corridor.

'Hurry up,' Dad growled at me. 'I need a drink. I've wasted enough of my time in this place. Fucking teachers,' he shouted back over his shoulder, obviously hoping Mrs Simpson could hear him, 'they don't have a fucking clue about the real world.'

Billy's parents sat upright in the too small plastic chairs, their mouths hanging open like they were waiting to catch flies.

Mum and Dad argued the whole way home in the car. 'Fucking waste of my time,' Dad kept saying over and over again. 'Who the hell does that woman think she is telling me how to bring my boy up?' He turned round in his seat and stared at me. 'And who the fuck is this boy Callum Evans?'

I shrugged. 'Just a boy from school.'

'Does he bully you?'

I shrugged again. 'Kind of.'

'Kind of? What kind of fucking answer is that? Either he does or he doesn't.'

'He shoves me in the playground sometimes,' I said, 'and calls me names.'

'Mrs Simpson says we should talk it through with you, try and find out if there's something at the bottom of it all but I told her that it's just boys. Boys fight and that's that. Bloody woman started telling me that maybe I should spend some quality time with you. Quality time, what a joke! She should try working a full day in that factory, see how she feels at the end of a shift. Stupid cow. Doesn't have a clue. But I'm telling you to stand up for yourself. Bollocks to all this talking about your feelings crap. If someone hits you, you hit them back. Hard. Right? Only way to deal with bullies is to hit them harder than they hit you.'

I sat quietly in the back of the car, hoping that he'd get dropped off at the pub on the way home. He didn't.

Mum sent me to my room when we got home. 'Upstairs,' she said, 'Close your door and switch your television on.' Part of me wanted to argue. 'Let me take it,' I wanted to say. But I didn't. 'Quickly,' she said and pushed me firmly towards the bottom step.

I did as she told me, but the TV couldn't hide her screams and I crept out of my room to the top of the stairs. Through the wooden bars on the stairwell I could see Dad raising the belt above his head.

'It's your fault,' he said. 'If you weren't so soft on the boy he'd know how to stand up for himself.'

The leather belt sliced through the air, only stopping when it met my mother's back.

'He's a good boy,' she cried.

'He's an embarrassment.'

The belt sliced through the air again.

'Please,' she cried. 'He won't get in trouble again.'

I covered my eyes but the sound of the belt kept coming.

Eighteen

A man walks his Staffordshire Terrier past the house and stops to let the dog pee up against the wall. Tracey doesn't recognise him but she suspects it could be one of his mates, a pal from the supporters' bus, so she stares at the ground and waits until he disappears around the corner. The house looms over her and the key feels heavy and dangerous in her pocket as she runs a finger along its jagged edge. She only needs a few minutes to grab some things. A couple of t-shirts and another pair of trousers will do. At the moment it's a struggle to dry her jeans fast enough after they've been washed and she's got nothing else to wear. John doesn't have a tumble dryer and it's rained almost every day since she left so she's had to dry her knickers over his radiators.

She can be in and out in five minutes. Job done. But what if he comes back? Her hand is shaking as she reaches up to the fading bruise on her cheek. She looks up and sees that their bedroom curtains are still closed. What if he's in there now, watching her? He knows she'll have to come back sometime to get some of her things. She takes a deep breath and tells herself to stop being paranoid. It's the middle of the afternoon and he'll not be back from the factory 'til after five. She takes the key from her pocket and steps forward towards the front door. A shadow cuts across the pane of frosted glass. It's him. He's waiting on her.

She stumbles backwards keeping an eye on the door. Is he watching her right now? She turns and runs. She runs and runs until it hurts. Lamp posts and parked cars mesh together in a smudged blur as she races past them, her sides burning with a sharp pain until she gives in and slows down. But she doesn't stop until she finally reaches a street she doesn't recognise. She collapses against the brick wall and waits to get her breath back. No-one is watching through their net curtains but she doesn't care anyway. No-one in this street will recognise her. The stitch in her side is easing and she starts walking. She needs to get as far away from the house as possible.

The bank card in her purse is behind an old photo of Robbie taken at the beach. She's been saving what she can for months now like Mrs Carmichael said she should. Most of her cleaning jobs are paid for in cash and, although it's not much, she's been stretching everything and putting away the little that she could. Just a tenner here or there but it's been adding up. She never thought she'd need it so soon.

The Cashline machine is set back in a wall next to a pub. Very handy. Thirty pounds should be enough. She'll walk into town and get everything she needs from Primark. She slips the card into the machine and presses the cash button. She hasn't checked the account for a while, scared she might be tempted to spend it and maybe buy Robbie something nice. She always gets him a wee something when she's away but this time it's different.

She squints at the grubby screen.

What the hell?

Denied.

There must be a mistake. She can't remember the last time she used the card but there should be well over a couple of hundred pounds in the account. She presses the button for an account balance and waits.

Ninety-one pounds overdrawn. That can't be right. She wipes the screen with her sleeve, hoping the numbers in front of her will magically change but the truth is clear. The machine asks if she wants to carry out another transaction.

'Are you finished, hen?'

She spins on her heels. The man standing behind her is clearly waiting to get some more drinking money. She looks at the pub next door.

'I asked if you're finished. I dinnae have all fuckin' day to wait.'

She can't believe it. The bastard must have found her card. All of her savings have gone and everything she owns is back in the house. What is she going to do now?

Nineteen

I grab a can of beer from the fridge and stuff it in my school bag. Serves him right, he's so pissed these days he'll never notice. I'm surprised he's actually made it out of bed and into work this morning.

Dean looks for me as soon as he gets on the bus. This morning I dared to sit a few seats down from the back and I wave to him as he swaggers up the middle of the bus before slipping in beside me.

'You're in a fuckin' good mood,' he says. 'Bet you cannae wait tae watch Miss Green's face when she shows us the video.' I wonder what he's talking about but I let it drop.

A couple of quiet girls from our year get on the bus and the only seats left are the ones in front of us. They don't look at us as they sit down.

Dean nudges me in the ribs and gives me a wink. He leans forward between the two girls. 'Hi sexy.' Both girls freeze but neither is brave enough to look round. 'Fancy sucking my cock?' He laughs out loud and crimson flushes from under their collars, creeping upwards, but they say nothing.

The bus pulls up outside the school and Dean's out of his seat before it's stopped. 'Come on,' he says. 'Let's get front row seats.' I've no idea what's going on but I play along and stay with him. We're nearly running by the time we get to registration.

'Good morning boys.' Miss Green is smiling.

We repeat good morning back to her and then Dean sits down near the front of class which confuses me. There are no given seats in registration, you sit where you like and wait until the bell rings for the first class of the day. He's sitting bolt upright, watching everyone enter the room and he reminds me of a caged tiger, weaving back and forwards. Bored. Frustrated. Waiting for the action to begin. Waiting for his prey. Soon everyone is here and Miss Green switches off the lights. The smart board on the wall whirrs into life as she presses the green button on the remote control clutched tightly in her hand. The image on the screen comes into focus and I nearly die.

A man and woman are holding hands smiling for the camera. But here's the thing. They're both naked.

I try to speak but only manage a tiny squeak. Holy fuck. Miss Green is about to give us a lesson on sex. I don't know where to look.

'Okay,' she says, 'I explained all of this yesterday but to anyone who wasn't here.' She's looking at me, I'm sure of it. Keep staring at your hands, keep staring at your hands. 'For those of you who were absent let me go over the ground rules one more time. You're about to see some pretty straight forward and frank videos which will show you a few things that might help you out as you approach adulthood. On the video you will see naked men and women.' The class erupts into laughter and she raises her voice and continues. 'You will see a clip showing you how to put on a condom, and can I suggest to all girls that you pay attention at this point as this is a skill you might need one day too.'

Keep staring at your hands. Don't look up in case she's looking at you. I clasp my hands together. Please stop talking, please stop talking.

But she doesn't stop. 'As well as contraceptives, you will learn about wet dreams, periods and the video also mentions masturbation.'

A ripple of embarrassed laughter breaks out around the room. I don't believe this. Miss Green used the word masturbation. I think I might die any minute now.

'Finally, please wait until the end of the video before you ask any questions.'

Oh Jesus, now she's telling me there's a question and answer section at the end.

Miss Green takes a seat at the back of the class and I can feel her watching us as the couple on the screen chase each other around the bedroom with a feather duster. What the fuck has a feather duster got to do with sex? The voice over tells us that sex can be a positive, fun experience. But really, a feather duster! My gran has one of those and I swear she told me it was for cobwebs. I'll never be able to look her in the eye again.

'Okay everyone, settle down.' The video has finished and I look at the clock. It's only ten to nine. That was the longest twenty minutes of my life. Miss Green stands up straight in front of the class. 'We still have five minutes left if anyone has any questions?'

Please God, don't let there be any questions. Just let me out of here.

'I've got a question Miss.' It's Jamie. 'How many times a week do you have sex with your boyfriend?' What a dickhead.

She ignores the question and turns off the smart board.

Jamie stands up and grins at everyone. He throws Dean a wink and turns back to face the front of the class. 'Didn't you hear my question Miss? I asked how many times a week do you have sex?'

Miss Green lays the remote control down beside her laptop. 'I did hear you, but you'll have to give me a minute.' She looks up and smiles, 'I'm still counting.'

The class erupt in laughter and Jamie slinks back down in to his seat. His face is beetroot. Well done, Miss. Well done.

Now Callum stands up. Oh Jesus. The hands on the classroom clock are moving painfully slowly. I gaze longingly at the door. Let me out of here. Please.

Miss Green leans back against her desk and folds her arms. 'I hope this is going to be a sensible question.'

'I wondered if you could give me some advice for a friend.'

She's not taking the bait. 'Go on.'

'You see I've got a mate who's kinda shy and doesn't want to ask you himself.' Callum looks straight at me. It's only for a fraction of a second but I'm sure everyone else in the room saw it. Shit, now they all know he's talking about me. Stop him Miss Green, please stop him now before he says another word. But she's not noticed what he's up to. I squirm further down into my chair but there's nowhere else for me to go. Rachel's sitting behind me and I pray she didn't notice Callum's glance in my direction.

'And what does your friend want to ask?'

Stop, stop, stop.

'He's got a bit of a problem, and I thought maybe you could give him some advice.'

The bastard's looking at me again and ripples are starting to spread out across the room. The whole class is hanging on his every word.

'Miss,' I shout out. 'I've got a question.' Shit, what am I doing? What the hell am I going to ask her?

'Robbie.' Miss Green stares at me with disapproval. 'Wait your turn.' She doesn't realise what Callum's doing and now she's going to let him continue to embarrass me.

'What's up with you?' Dean hisses in my ear and for a split second I wonder if I'm wrong. Maybe this isn't about me.

Callum is still standing. 'This mate of mine,' he says and for the first time ever his speech is totally clear, he's not bloody mumbling a bit. He's talking as if he's on the fucking stage for *Britain's Got Talent* and he pauses to make sure everyone is listening before finishing his sentence, but I've already got a good idea that I know what he's about to say. 'This mate of mine cannae get an erection.'

Jamie is clearly over his embarrassment and the bastard slaps me on the back, 'Alright there, Floppy?'

The bell for next lesson rings and I get up out of my chair. As

I leave the room I hear Miss Green tell the class that we'll continue with questions tomorrow.

It's lunchtime and we head out into the courtyard and find Jamie and Callum hanging out by the bike shelter.

'Great news,' Jamie says as we approach them. 'We're getting football in PE this afternoon.'

Shit. Just when I thought this day couldn't get any worse. We haven't had football yet in first year and I've been dreading it. So far I've managed to stick to being the goalie when we kick the ball around at break time but the teacher's bound to put us in different positions during lessons.

'About time,' laughs Dean. 'I don't think I could stand another badminton lesson.'

'What are the girls doing?' Callum asks.

Dean punches him on the arm, 'Christ, is that all you ever think about?'

'Have you seen the shorts that Grace wears?' Callum laughs. 'And her t-shirt's so tight you can see her nipples.'

'Shut it,' Jamie cuts in. 'That's my cousin you're talking about.'

Callum doesn't say another word, but nobody answers about what the girls will be doing. I can't stop thinking about Rachel. Yesterday, she was in the badminton court next to us and every time her partner hit the shuttlecock too hard she came across into our court to get it back. I can still see her smile as she apologised for interrupting our game. I couldn't stop thinking about her last night and I've been hoping she'll be in the court next to me again. I imagine handing the shuttlecock back to her, our fingers touching briefly as I pass it to her. She smiles. But then her smile vanishes and she's laughing at me. *Floppy, Floppy, Floppy.* If she didn't know my nickname before today she definitely does now.

The bell rings and I follow the others down to the PE block. The stink of deodorant comes out to meet us, but it doesn't quite disguise the smell of stale sweat and cigarette smoke. I hold my breath as I make my way through the fug. I push open the door to the changing room and the room erupts with a loud cheer. A pair of boxers fly in my direction and I bat them away. What the fuck is going on? And then I see it. Some wee bastard has raced down before I could get here and scribbled my name across the mirror in black marker pen. *Robbie has a limp dick!* I'd have sworn it was Jamie and Callum except they were with me the whole time over lunch. The pair of boxer shorts lie abandoned at my feet and I step over them. I don't want to think about how they ended up here or what happened to the poor bastard they belonged to. The shouting dies down and I get changed in the corner as quick as I can before anyone can comment on my skinny, hairless legs or my white y-fronts. The other boys all wear boxers or trunks but Mum still buys me a five pack from Marks and Spencer every year in the sale. She says they wash well! How am I supposed to ask her to buy me different pants?

TJ bursts into the changing room and everyone quietens down. Nobody's sure what TJ stands for but there are some rumours that the initials are for Tall Jesus. Don't know about the Jesus bit but he's well over six foot tall and the man is a total legend. 'Get a move on,' he yells, 'I want you all ready to go in two minutes.' I'm ready but hang back, pretending to put my stuff away until most of the class have lined up. Suddenly, TJ is standing in front of me. 'Limp dick,' he points to the mirror, 'is that you?'

I shrug my shoulders surprised he knows my name.

'Well, get it wiped off.'

What the fuck? Shouldn't he try and find out who wrote it? I look around for something to wipe it off with but all I can see is the abandoned pair of boxers in the corner.

'What are you waiting for?' he shouts.

I pick up the boxers and start scrubbing.

'Is it true we've got football?' Dean asks TJ.

'Not today,' he says. 'There's been a mix up with the timetable. It appears we've got one last day of badminton.'

There's an almighty groan as all of the boys express their disappointment in unison. I join in but nobody cares what I think anyway so I give up and wait on everyone to settle. The mirror is clean and I join the end of the line.

TJ keeps talking, 'I have spoken to the head of department though, and he has agreed to let any boys from the school football team practise a small team game out on the astroturf.' A cheer goes up and TJ is grinning. He's back to being the most popular teacher in the school once more and he loves it.

Dean nudges me in the ribs. 'Tell him you fancy trying out for the team and he'll let you come up to the astroturf.'

I'm running out of excuses but there's no way I'm going to embarrass myself in front of the whole school. I'm crap at football, can hardly kick the ball in a straight line. Dad used to take me to the park every night for a kick about and then when I was old enough he took me along to a club. But I was never good enough. Couldn't pass, couldn't dribble, not fast enough, not got enough power. He stopped taking me to the park and gave up coming to watch me play in our junior league games. In the end, the coach came up to have a word with me. Turns out my dues hadn't been paid for a couple of months. He'd tried phoning my dad but never got an answer. 'If your folks can't afford the fees,' he'd said, 'you can still come along to play. You're a great wee keeper.' The coach didn't look me in the eye when he said this and I knew he was lying but at least he was being nice. I thought about sneaking a couple of pounds out of Mum's purse each week, but my boots were getting too tight and there was no way I could ask her to buy me a new pair. Besides, what was the point if I wasn't any good? That was round about the same time that Dad stopped taking me to the Hearts matches.

TJ saves me from answering. 'Right, lads,' he says to the small group of us at the back of the line. 'You head to the girls' gym. The badminton nets are all set up.'

Dean looks at me and I shrug my shoulders and quickly follow the others before he gets any ideas about asking Tall Jesus himself if I can join. Only three of us make our way through to the girls' gym and the other two are real geeks. Guess that makes me a geek too.

One of the geeks turns to me. 'Just wanted to say that we didn't do it.'

I look at him and at first I don't know what he's talking about. Then I get it and I try hard not to laugh in his face. Does he honestly believe that I might think for even a nanosecond that he was brave enough to graffiti school property? Geek number two starts to talk to me now. 'We think what they did was really mean and we don't believe what Callum said about you this morning.'

'Whatever,' I say and push past them.

The girls' gym hall is right next to the girls' changing room but other than that it's no different from the boys' gym. Several badminton nets divide the hall in two and a box of racquets and shuttlecocks waits in the corner. We sit down on one of the benches and wait too. I realise I don't even know the names of the other two boys. We don't say a word to each other and sit in silence. The noise of shrill laughter coming from the girls' changing room sounds like a pack of hyenas and I'm suddenly nervous. I look at the two boys sitting next to me. Are we the prey?

The door to the changing room is thrown open and we're allowed a glimpse into the unknown world behind it. I try to memorise the picture so I can brag to Dean and the others later on. The walls are candy floss pink and I'm sure I can smell some exotic perfume. The girls tumble through the door blocking my view, giggling and laughing, and hanging on to one another. I hold my breath, searching the small crowd for Rachel but my heart sinks. She's not there. Miss Carter leads the girls into the hall. All the boys fancy Miss Carter. She's one of the youngest teachers in the school and the fact that she walks about in a pair of tiny fluorescent pink shorts probably helps. But her screeching voice irritates me and she laughs like a donkey. Oh well, another reason to make Dean jealous. At this rate he'll be wishing he'd come to badminton too.

'Get yourself a partner and collect a racquet from the box.' Her voice echoes around the gym hall and I'm wishing I'd gone home. The geeks quickly pair up. Great, now I'm going to have to play with one of the girls and they'll probably beat me. But as the girls sort themselves into pairs my fate becomes clear. I'm going to be partners with Miss Carter. I keep my head down and try to think of an escape plan.

'Do you mind being my partner?'

I recognise her voice straight away and open my mouth to answer but only a strangled, gurgling sound comes out. I look at my feet and nod like a right idiot.

'I'll get us a racquet each,' Rachel says and bounces off before I can speak, which is probably just as well because I seem to have lost the power of speech. I pray it's temporary and try to think of something witty and smart to say before she gets back. I fail.

She hands me a racquet with a smile. 'You weren't in maths yesterday,' she says.

She noticed? OMG! Rachel noticed I wasn't in maths yesterday morning. 'Someone died,' I say.

'Sorry,' she says and I feel bad for lying to her. She doesn't mention this morning's sex ed' lesson.

Turns out she's not a bad player and I'm soon sweating, running back and forth to return her serve. Just as well we're not keeping score. She picks up the shuttlecock and comes forward to the net. 'Just need a minute to catch my breath,' she laughs and I laugh back but it sounds like I'm strangling a chinchilla. I don't know where to look. I'm desperate to look at her but I know I'll blush.

'So, what do you think of the book?' she asks me.

'The book?'

'*Animal Farm,*'

'It's okay,' I say. Okay! God, that makes me sound intelligent, witty and interesting, doesn't it?

'Wait 'til you get to the end,' she says, 'You'll love it.'

'I've already read it.' Great, now she'll think I'm a geek.

'Don't you love it when they look through the window and can't tell the pigs from the men,' she says. 'I thought that was brilliant.'

So did I, so why am I finding it impossible to talk about. I want to ask her if she's started *Tom Sawyer* yet and what she thinks about people wanting to ban the word nigger from new editions, but my lungs are squashed into that tiny space behind my ribcage and my tongue has transformed into rubber. I hold out my hand and she gives me the shuttlecock. It's my turn to serve.

She laughs when I miss my own serve but it's an okay laugh and I join in. If I could invent a machine to freeze time this is when I'd use it 'cause I wish this game could last forever. But it doesn't and before I know it, Miss Carter is screeching at us all to stop. The girls are told to go and get changed but us boys have to stay behind and put away the nets and the stands. If that's not sexual discrimination then I want to know what is.

I rush getting changed and the bell rings just as I pull on my shoes. The others aren't back from football yet and I don't wait to be dismissed. I run out into the corridor but the girls have already gone. Rachel has gone. I lean back against the wall and replay her smile over and over again in my head.

Twenty

Tracey gets to the house early and waits. She sees him leave for work and knows Robbie will come out soon to catch the school bus. And then he appears and he's so close that it takes all of her strength not to reveal herself to him. She watches as he glances back over his shoulder, searching for a figure at the window, but this morning there's no-one there to wave goodbye to him and she feels guilty. She stands at the street corner and sees him close the garden gate before crossing the road and heading in the direction of the bus stop. It's raining but as usual his jacket is unfastened and his hood flaps free around his shoulders. She wants to shout out to him, tell him he'll catch his death of cold if he's not careful. But he's a big boy now. She watches the bus pull away, taking her boy with it.

The house is empty, she's sure of it, but still her throat tightens as she slowly pushes the front door open. She can't believe she's doing this. What if he comes home while she's still here? She stands in the hallway and lets the sense of familiarity sweep over her like a wave of nausea. She's got to be quick, just grab her things and go. Grab and go. She takes a deep breath and puts her foot on the bottom step. She can do this.

She heads straight to their bedroom and finds his dirty clothes scattered across the floor and a couple of empty cans lying crushed on the bedside table. A porn mag peeks out from under his side of the unmade bed and she nudges it back under with her toe. Maybe he's missing her after all. She grabs some underwear and a couple of t-shirts from the chest of drawers without stopping to look at the photograph sitting on top. She doesn't need to, she knows its every detail. It was taken on Robbie's first day of school and it's her favourite picture of him. He looks so young and his face is filled with pure excitement. He couldn't wait to start. And when she picked him up at the end of the day he came running out with a great big smile and a dripping wet painting. His first day at school had been a success. She lifts the photograph and moves to put it in her bag but then stops. She can't take it with her. Can't let him know she's been back.

Her phone is sitting on the bedside table and she wonders if he's been checking it, trying to find out where she's gone, but she was careful to make sure she'd deleted any contacts that could lead him to her. She picks it up but it's out of charge. She checks her watch. It's already been five minutes. Long enough. Time to go. She lifts up her bag and closes the bedroom door behind her. Wait. Was it open or closed when she came up earlier? Open or closed? Think! But she can't remember. Would he bother to close the door behind him? She doesn't think so. She opens the door and leaves it ajar.

She needs to hurry up. Every extra minute is a risk she shouldn't take. She stands at the top of the stairs. Could he have sneaked in while she's been up here? Maybe he's been watching the house waiting on her to return. He knows she'll have to come back for some things. She tries to listen for noises downstairs but all she can hear is the drumming of her own blood in her ears.

The phone rings and she screams. Shit. He knows she's here. The door to Robbie's bedroom is open and she creeps through and waits for the ringing to stop. The phone rings off without the caller bothering to wait for the answering machine. She's sure it was him hoping to catch her out. She tries to relax a little. If he's just called then that means he's not inside the house. She wonders how often he calls home on the off chance that she'll answer.

Robbie's room is in darkness. He hasn't bothered opening his curtains. She gets up and pulls them open, surveying the mess in front of her. She scoops up his dirty pants and socks, and piles them by the door like she always does. His jeans are lying inside out in a heap by his bed and she picks them up and pulls each leg through until they're the right way round, searching his pockets for tissues or any rubbish that could clog up the washing machine. She stuffs a pile of empty chewing gum wrappers into her own pocket and grabs hold of his bedcovers. The bed doesn't look like it's been made in days. She stops herself. What is she doing? She's slipped into autopilot and it feels strangely good. She stands by his bed holding a corner of his Star Wars duvet and it's the happiest she's been in days. She knows she should get out of the house as quickly as possible but this is the closest she's felt to her son in a long time and she's enjoying spending a moment in his world. There's a pile of books stacked by his bed and she has a quick look through them. *To Kill A Mocking Bird* is on the top of the pile but she can't remember if she's read it or not. She picks it up and looks at the blurb but it all sounds a bit too clever for her and so she puts it back down. The only books John owns are detective stories and she can't get past the first chapter of any of them. She spots a battered, old copy of *The Adventures of Tom Sawyer* beside the pile and she smiles. Her teacher read it to her class when they were about Robbie's age. She picks it up and adds it to the t-shirts and underwear in her Tesco bag. He probably doesn't even know the book is there and it'll be nice for her to read it and feel close to him when she goes to sleep at night.

She throws the chewing gum wrappers across his bedside table and pulls the curtains shut again. Then she tries to toss his dirty clothes in a random pattern across the floor but it ends up looking like a snake weaving its way across the room. She shuffles the clothes around a little with her feet and hopes he won't notice. An empty tin of peaches sits on his desk and she resists the urge to wipe the bottom of the tin. At least he's eating fruit.

Twenty-One

I can't face going straight home after school so I head to the wee swing park, only to find it's full of little kids and their parents. I sit down on a bench and take out my copy of *Animal Farm*. I turn to the last chapter and think about what Rachel said about the pigs and the humans. She's way too smart to be interested in me, especially after this morning's sex ed' lesson. I'll kill that Callum if I ever get the chance. All day everyone's been laughing at me behind my back. *Floppy, Floppy, Floppy.* I bet the teachers have been having a good laugh too.

I put the book back in my bag and wander over to the swings to see if any of the kids want a push, but as I get near one mum scoops her wee boy off the swing and drags him to the climbing frame. I turn to the other parents and they're all looking at me as if I'm some sort of a paedo. 'Fuck yous,' I shout and head off towards the canal. There's no wee kids down here, just the odd jogger and an old guy walking his dog. The joggers never look at you, they're always listening to something on their iPod, focused on the path ahead, determined to beat their last time. I take the can of beer out of my bag and take a sip. It tastes better than I remember and I drink some more. I was going to share it with Dean but the bastard didnae stick up for me this morning when that wee prick Callum called me Floppy in front of the whole class.

I hold my can in the air and make a toast. 'Fuck yous all.' I picture Rachel in that tight t-shirt and shorts. 'Not so Floppy now,' I shout. The beer's making me a bit light-headed and it feels kind of nice. I rub my cock through my polyester trousers

119

and imagine Rachel's tits as she bends down for the shuttlecock. She's so fucking gorgeous. She stands up in front of me and I'm touching her tits and she joins in. I rub harder and harder and I'm coming, coming, coming.

Oh fuck, I've come in my pants and it's a right mess. Jesus, what did I do that for? I toss the can into the canal and make my way home.

As soon as I walk through the front door I smell dinner cooking. She's home!

'Mum,' I shout. 'It's me. I'm home.' I rush through to the kitchen but it's empty. She must be upstairs. She's probably unpacking. I wonder what she's brought me back this time. I hope it's a new book. What am I thinking? I don't care what she brings me. She's home. I stop and smile at the handbag on the kitchen table. I can hear water running upstairs and I sit down and take in the smell of dinner in great big breaths. My stomach growls but I don't care. This is going to be the best dinner ever.

I realise I'd better get changed before she sees me so I grab my PE kit from my school bag and lock the toilet door. Jeez, what a mess. I try to wash my dick under the sink tap but I'm not tall enough so I clean myself as best I can with wet toilet paper but it keeps breaking into tiny bits and getting stuck in my pubes. Upstairs, the water is still running and I hurry up. I roll my y-fronts inside my school trousers and shove them into my kit bag. I can wash them later. I've no other pants to put on but it'll not matter. I pull on my trackie bottoms and shove my kit bag under the stairs for now.

Dinner smells amazing and I set the table for the three of us, putting the fork on the left and the knife on the right like she taught me to do. There's no juice in the cupboards so I fill the jug with water and pour us each a glass. I'm guessing Dad would rather have a beer but maybe tonight he'll forget. The water upstairs stops running, she'll be down in a minute. I run out into the garden with a pair of scissors. The buddleia bush isn't flowering yet so I cut a stem from the foxglove which has beautiful purple flowers on it. I fill an extra glass with water and place the flower in the centre of the table. She'll be pleased that I remember it's her favourite colour and I imagine her hands around me, holding me tight. 'It's beautiful, Robbie,' she says, 'Thank you.'

The mince in the pan is piping hot but it smells amazing and I'm starving. Nobody will notice if I have one small mouthful. Carefully, I lift the wooden spoon to my mouth.

'What are you doing?'

I drop the spoon and bolognese sauce splatters everywhere. I spin round. 'Gran?'

'Get a cloth and wipe your school shirt,' she snaps, flapping her arms at me. 'Quickly, before it stains.'

'What are you doing here?' I ask.

'Take it off,' she says and starts unbuttoning my shirt. 'I'll dip it in soda water, that'll do the trick.'

I pull away. No one's undressed me since I was a boy. 'Where's Mum?'

Magically, she's already got a bottle of soda water in her hand and she's pouring some onto a cloth and dabbing my chest with it.

'Where's Mum?' I ask again.

She stops attacking me with the cloth and looks at me. 'I came to ask you the same thing. I've tried phoning several times but she's never in.' She pauses. 'It's been weeks since I last heard from her.'

I look at the floor but she places her hand under my chin and lifts my face up towards hers. 'I think it's time you tell me what's going on.'

'She always comes back,' I say and she waits for me to tell her more. 'She'll be back soon.' Do I really believe that? I'm not sure anymore. There's a part of me that knows she's not coming back this time.

'Where is she?'

'She doesn't tell us where she goes,' I say, 'but it's okay because she always brings me back a present.'

'Who feeds you when she's not here?' Typical Gran. As long as there's food on the table, life's okay.

'We do okay,' I tell her. 'Mum showed me how to make scrambled egg and Dad cooks dinner.' I'm not really telling any lies, Mum did show me how to make scrambled egg once. I fake a big smile. 'There's always plenty of food in the cupboards.'

Gran opens the fridge and lifts the milk out of the door. 'Look,' she says, pushing the carton in front of my face, 'it's out of date.'

I wonder why she'd put it back in the fridge if it's out of date but I don't dare say a word.

'You make scrambled eggs?' she says. 'How do you do that when there aren't any eggs?'

I don't know what she wants me to say, so I don't say a thing. Why am I the one getting shouted at? I'm not the one who walked out. I feel sick and I'm wishing I hadn't had that can of beer.

She's still talking. 'I've checked every cupboard and unless you're planning on making a jam sandwich with mouldy bread there's nothing else to eat. And what the hell is that on the table? It looks like a weed.'

'It's a foxglove.'

'A foxglove? Don't you know they're poisonous? Quick.' She grabs the vase and throws opens the back door.

'Wait,' I shout, but I'm too late. The flower has been tossed on to the garden path where it lies on the mossy slabs. Broken. I clench my fist around the front door key in my pocket and the sharp metal digs into my palm.

'Your poor father is at work all day and he doesn't even come home to a cooked meal.'

She stirs the mince with her back to me and I imagine the metal key piercing the base of her neck.

'It's about time you did something useful and learned how to cook.'

Blood and bolognese splattered across the tiles and kitchen units. Would you be able to tell which was which?

She tastes the sauce with a teaspoon. 'Well, he's going to be well fed tonight,' she says. 'I've slaved all afternoon making this.'

'Dad said he was treating me to a chippy tonight,' I say.

'Treating you?'

'For making the school football team.' Why did I say that?

She puts down the spoon and shrieks. 'Well done,' she says and wraps me in a tight hug. The smell of her perfume mixed with bolognese is suffocating me. 'Oh, your dad must be so proud. I'm surprised he didn't phone to let me know. That's brilliant news. What position do you play?'

I have no idea what to say.

'Of course,' she says, 'you're a defender. Just like your dad was. He always wanted to be a striker but he wasn't fast enough. Don't be too disappointed though,' she says. 'Everyone in the team is as important as the other.' She looks pleased with her advice and nods her head. 'All as important as the other,' she repeats.

'In fact, can I have my dinner now because I've got training tonight?' I need to get out of here before Dad comes home. What the fuck did I say I'd made the team for?

Gran serves me a huge plateful. 'And when you've finished this you can have some more,' she says. 'You need lots of energy before a training session.'

I take my second helping and lick the plate clean. Every time I look up at Gran she's smiling at me. It makes me feel kind of uncomfortable but I guess it's better than her usual disappointed look.

When I'm finished I go up to my room and pull on my red hooded top. I stand in front of the mirror. Do I look the part? I'm not sure but it's the best I've got. I grab a plastic bag and throw a towel and a spare pair of trainers in.

'Time for me to go,' I shout downstairs. I'm hoping to sneak out before any more questions but she's waiting at the bottom of the stairs.

'Got everything?' she asks. I nod and hope it's not a trick question. I throw my bag over my shoulder and head for the front door. 'Wait,' she shouts. I turn around and she takes me by the shoulders. 'Well done,' she says. 'I know this must mean a lot to your dad.'

My mouth fills with saliva but I can't swallow. I can't speak.

She gives me a gentle pat on the back. 'Go on,' she says. 'Knock 'em dead.'

I don't look back as I leave.

Out on the street, I don't know where to go. I check my phone to see if I've got a text from Dean but the battery's dead. I'm fairly sure I know where he lives and I start walking in that direction. I pass through the park on the way and stop at the swings to have a fag. Everyone's gone home now and the park's empty. The cigarette tastes good and I wonder why I didn't smoke sooner. Dad will be home any minute now and Gran's going to tell him about the school team before he even gets the chance to take his jacket off. Why the hell did I tell her that, it must have been the beer talking. He's going to be livid with me for lying to her but I had to say something. She wouldn't stop going on and on about what we were having for dinner and how poor Dad never comes home to a cooked meal. A decent cooked meal. I imagine her face if I told her I was going to steal us a couple of fish suppers. 'Do you want a pickled onion with that?' I'd ask.

I'm just getting ready to leave when a mum and her wee boy arrive. She's got her hands full with bags of shopping and she looks done in. No wonder. Her wee boy is running with his arms outwards, pretending to be an aeroplane. 'Neeyum,' he shouts as he makes his way in and out of the obstacle course.

He looks up at me and grins and I see that one of his front teeth is missing. He sticks his tongue through the gap and runs straight to the swing beside me.

'Lift me up,' he shouts to me. 'Lift me up.'

I get up from my own swing to give the boy a hand but his mum comes running.

'Oi!' She drops her bags. 'Leave him alone.'

'It's okay,' I say, smiling. 'I can get him.'

She ignores me and holds out her hand to the boy. 'Come on, Mark,' she says. 'We need to get home to Daddy.'

Mark looks at his mum. Go on, I will him, tell her you don't want to go home. Tell her you want to play with the nice boy on the swings. I look at him and he looks at me. He shrugs his shoulders. There's no tantrum. Little Mark takes hold of his mother's hand and walks over to help her pick up her bags of shopping. I wonder if there's a bar of chocolate in one of the bags. Or maybe a jammy donut for his supper. I hope there is.

Mark looks back over his shoulder and smiles at me. I give him a wave and decide to make a move too.

Dean's house is in the middle of a terrace block. There's no doorbell so I knock gently and step back to wait. No one comes so I try knocking a little harder. A commotion breaks out inside and next door's dog joins in and starts barking.

The door opens and Dean's standing there with a Pot Noodle in his hand. 'What the fuck are you doing here?'

There's a shout from inside. 'Who is it?'

'It's nobody, Mum, go back to your programme.'

'If it's the man wi' the book, tell him we'll pay next week.'

'It's okay, Mum,' Dean shouts.

'Don't you go buying any raffle tickets or air fresheners.'

'I won't.'

'We don't want to buy anything.'

Dean leans forward. 'Give me a minute,' he whispers and goes back inside, closing the door behind him.

The dog next door stops barking and the street returns to its original silence. I stand on the doorstep, aware that someone next door is having a good nosy at me through their lace curtains. I turn and give them the middle finger. They disappear.

I'm left standing on the doorstep and it's starting to feel cold. Maybe Dean's not coming back out. Did I mishear him? I think about giving up and going when Dean comes out, carrying a jacket. 'What you up to?' he asks.

'Nothing. Just thought we could maybe hang out together.'

He accepts this and we walk back towards town. 'Hungry?' he asks, laughing.

'What do you fancy,' I say. 'A fish supper?'

'No chance,' he laughs, 'I'm not letting you anywhere near the chippy ever again.' We walk a little further. 'What's in the bag?'

I'm prepared for this. 'Picked some stuff up from my gran's,' I say and he doesn't ask anymore.

We end up back in the same park where I'd met Mark. I hope he's getting that jammy donut.

'Has Rachel asked you out yet?'

'Shut it.' I blush and turn my collar up. Dean has got it in his head that Rachel fancies me and he won't stop going on about it.

'I'm telling you, she spent the whole period of maths looking over at you.'

'Probably because Johnson kept picking on me to answer his fuckin' stupid questions.'

'You did alright,' Dean says. 'I didn't know half the shit you did.'

There's no way I'm going to let Mr Johnson make me look stupid in front of the class, in front of Rachel, so I've been cramming some maths revision every night but I don't tell Dean this. I wait until he's playing a game on his phone. 'So was she really looking at me?'

Dean jumps off the swing and turns to me. 'Knew it,' he says. 'I fuckin' knew it. You fancy her.'

I don't deny it. I'm sweating, waiting on the ridicule and the teasing. Dean's always going out with a different girl. Not me. I've never even asked a girl out before. I'm kind of hoping Dean might help me out. I rub my hands up and down the rusted metal links of the swing's chain and my palms are slowly turning orange. I wish he'd hurry up and say something.

He slips his phone into his pocket and sits back on the swing beside me. 'What are you going to do about it?' he asks.

I don't know what to say.

'You've got to ask her out; she obviously fancies you too.'

Does she? How does he know this? I've replayed the afternoon in the library over and over so many times in my head but always without Jamie and Callum making an appearance. Rachel doesn't drop her book. Doesn't walk on by. In my version, she sits down beside me and asks me what I think of *Tom Sawyer*. Naturally, I give her an intelligent, mature and witty answer (it gets more intelligent, more mature and definitely wittier every time I replay it) and she laughs along with me, raising her head just enough for me to see down her top to her bra. I ask her if she wants to study the text in more depth after school and suggest we meet for a coffee (I hate coffee but a coffee shop seems more grown up than meeting in McDonald's).

'Why don't you ask her out now?' says Dean.

'What d'ya mean?'

'Don't you know anything?' He laughs. 'It's easy. You can message her on Facebook.'

He's got to be kidding. Facebook? Not exactly what I'd dreamed of. 'She's probably not on Facebook,' I say.

'Everyone's on Facebook,' he says. He takes out his phone and I watch over his shoulder as he logs in. He clicks on the pages of some faces I recognise from school and then searches their list of friends. Within a minute, he's on Jennifer Weir's page. How is Dean friends with Jennifer? 'There,' he says. 'She's friends with Jennifer.' I watch as he clicks on Rachel's name and her photo fills the screen. I can't breathe. The picture looks like it's been taken on a beach and she's wearing a skimpy, purple dress. Purple. The same colour as her boots. I know Dean's watching me but I can't take my eyes off the screen. Sand clings to her wet skin and she's grinning into the camera lens.

'Not bad, eh?' says Dean.

I can't say a word. I've never seen anyone so beautiful.

'Now all you need to do is message her.'

I can't take my eyes off her picture. 'I'm not on Facebook,' I tell him.

'You really are a fuckin' weirdo,' he says. I ignore him, I've been called worse. 'All we need to do is make you an account and add a few pictures.'

He closes his phone and I want to grab it from him so I can see her picture again. If I'm on Facebook, I can look at her picture whenever I want. 'So how do I make an account?' I ask.

Five minutes later it's my face that fills the screen on Dean's phone. He took some pictures of me on the swings and I made him take a few until he finally got one that didn't show up my spots.

'Right,' says Dean, 'what should we put for your status?'

I shrug.

'It needs to be something funny. The girls love it when you write stuff that makes them laugh.'

I can't think of anything funny.

'Got it,' says Dean and he starts typing in the box under my picture.

'What are you writing?' I ask.

'Trust me,' he says.

This is all happening too fast and I want him to stop. I stand up. 'Come on,' I say, 'I'm hungry.'

'Wait a minute.'

'I'm going to get a bag of crisps,' I say. I don't know what he's typing on my page but I wish he'd stop. When I get home I'll change my password. 'You coming?'

'Nearly done,' he says.

'What are you doing?' I ask, trying to sound like I don't care.

'There.' He snaps his phone shut. 'You've sent some friend requests.'

'Who to?'

'Just some kids in our year.'

'Who?'

'Callum, Jamie, Rachel.'

'You've sent Rachel a friend request?'

'Calm down,' he says. 'Everyone does it.'

'You've sent her a friend request from me?' Shit. I wish I'd never mentioned her. What the hell has he done? 'Now she'll know I fancy her.'

'Relax.' He laughs. 'Everybody says yes to friend requests, half the time nobody even bothers to look at who it is. Look,' he shows me her page again, 'she's got three hundred and seventy-two friends. D'ya think they all want to get into her knickers?'

I think they probably do, they'd be mad not to.

'Just chill, she's not gonna think you fancy her and so what if she does, she'll be flattered. Now come on,' he says, 'I'll treat you to a packet of pickled onion.'

I don't want anything to eat. I want to go home and look at her face on my computer screen in high definition. Home. Shit, Dad will be back by now and if he's found out I lied to Gran he'll be in a foul mood. Oh man, what have I done?

Football... Facebook... Total fuck up!

Twenty-Two

Margaret MacFarlane feels like she's been transported back in time when she watches her grandson leave the house with his kitbag. He's the double of her own boy at that age. He used to spend every spare minute down the park kicking a ball about. Like father, like son, she thinks and smiles to herself as she goes back through to the kitchen to save dinner.

The front door is thrown open. 'Tracey?'

'Only me, son,' she says, 'are you hungry?'

She instantly knows he's had a drink but she also knows better than to mention it. Besides, he can't have had much, it's only just after five, time enough for a pint and maybe a wee whisky chaser on the way home from work.

They eat dinner in silence and she watches him closely as he shovels huge forkfuls of food into his mouth. This man clearly hasn't had a decent meal in a long time and she decides she should pop by more often.

She clears the dishes from the table and has a proper look around her. Dear God, the place is filthy. And his wife has the bloody cheek to call herself a cleaner. She fills the basin with hot water and plenty of soapy liquid. Once she's done the dishes she'll wipe down the kitchen benches and the tiles, and if there's time she might even get the skirtings done.

'Just leave it, Mum, I'll get it later.'

She looks at the heaped pile of dirty dishes and takeaway cartons next to the kitchen sink. 'That I doubt very much,' she mutters under her breath and then breezily sings, 'No problem, no problem at all.'

'I said leave it.' The anger in his voice delivers the words like a punch, echoing the voice of the man she buried twenty years ago. *You stupid bitch, now look what you made me do. I told you to leave it.* He's painting the hall a lovely, bright shade of yellow and she thought it'd be nice to make him a cup of tea because he'd been working so hard. *You've made me paint yellow across the fucking gloss.* Won't it wipe off if we catch it straight away? she thinks, but doesn't say out loud. Wouldn't the yellow paint have stayed in a straight line if you weren't so fucking pissed? she thinks, but she doesn't say this out loud either. What does she do? She does the same thing she always does. She looks down at the floor and apologises, although by now the apology is too late. *What fucking good is sorry?*

She stares into the soapy bubbles in the basin and sees the tiled floor of their old hallway. Through the cloudy water, she catches a glimpse of him stepping down from the ladder, still carrying the paintbrush. Droplets of yellow paint fall on to the black and white floor tiles. She sees him put down the paintbrush and lift his fist.

'I'm sorry,' she whispers and squeezes her hand around something sharp.

'Mum.' She hears her boy calling her but where is he? 'Mum, your hand!' He snatches her hand out of the soapy water. It's bleeding and he wraps the dish cloth round it and holds it tight with one hand as he rakes around the soapy water with the other. 'It's a breadknife, you must have gripped it in your hand. Didn't you feel it?'

She looks at her son. 'I'm sorry,' she says again.

The funeral was on a Tuesday morning and it was raining. His body had finally had enough of the booze and he'd collapsed in the street from a heart attack. As she stood by his coffin she vowed to bury his memory along with his body. The service was short, unfeeling and without emotion, just like his life had been. And in death, the bastard was just as miserable. He had no life insurance or savings and all he'd left her was a mountain of debt.

She turns and faces her son and finds him cradling a newly opened bottle of beer. 'I'm sorry if I shouted at you, Mum, it's just you've already done enough for us by making dinner.' He wraps her cut with a clean, white tea towel and sits her down with a cup of tea. Her cheeks burn with shame. Did she really believe her own son could ever hurt her?

She sips the tea and changes the subject. 'Great news about Robbie.' He looks at her blankly and she wonders how many drinks he managed to squeeze in on the way home. 'Robbie,' she repeats, 'making the school football team.'

'Fucking hell. That's brilliant news. Absolutely fucking brilliant. I always said he could do it, eh? Just goes to show that he's got some of his old man's genes in him after all.' He jumps out of his chair and shouts on Robbie.

'He's not in.'

'Where is he?'

'He said he had a training session.'

'Of course.' He sits back down and lifts his bottle. 'He'll probably have training most nights from now on. I wonder if they'll need any help, you know, like any coaches. I'm sure I can still remember everything I knew, and he'd love that, wouldn't he? His dad helping out.'

She looks beyond the bottle to the man. Is it possible her own son has a problem? No, she shakes her head firmly. She of all people would be able to spot it. Wouldn't she?

Twenty-Three

I take a deep breath and push my key into the lock. The front door slips opens and I sneak into the hallway. Without stopping to take off my shoes, I head upstairs, knowing to avoid the third step up which creaks every time. I'm almost at my bedroom door when he shouts on me.

'Get downstairs. Now.'

I freeze.

'Did you hear me?' he shouts from the bottom step.

I breathe a small sigh of relief. He sounds sober. Thank God. 'Coming.' I throw the plastic bag onto my bed and look up at the signed shirt above my bed. If only I'd had John Robertson's talent, things would be very different. Dad wouldn't be angry and Mum would still be here. Dad would come home every night from work and drag me out to kick the ball about instead of going to the pub. He'd go in goals and get me to take penalty kicks and he'd pat me on the back and tell me how brilliant I am.

But I don't have John Robertson's talent and I was never good enough for my dad. When I missed a goal he'd get me to try again. And again. And whenever he managed to stop the ball he'd shout at me to stop kicking like a girl. *Maybe if you try harder they'll pick you to play next week.* But I was never chosen for a game and eventually he stopped asking me to come out for a kick around. I remember sitting on the edge of my bed waiting for him to come and get me, and when I finally gave up waiting and went downstairs I found him sitting in front of the television with a beer.

I leave the plastic bag on my bed and go downstairs. He's waiting for me and I look down at my feet.

He leans forward and punches me on the arm. 'Well done, son,' he says. 'I'm so proud of you.'

Shit. He believed Gran when she told him I got picked for the team. I smile. 'It's just the school team,' I say.

'Nonsense,' he says. 'Today the school team, tomorrow Hearts of Midlothian. This calls for a celebration. Grab your jacket.'

'Where are we going?'

'For a quick pint,' he says.

'But I'm not old enough,' I say.

'Well, you can have a pint of cola,' he says. 'But if your gran asks, you've to say we were at the cinema.'

'What did we see?' I ask him.

'How should I know,' he says. 'Just make it up. The old bat won't know any better.'

'We haven't been to see a film in ages,' I say, hoping that he might take the hint. He doesn't hear me. 'Maybe we could take a look and see if anything good's on.'

'Come on,' he says. 'If we leave now we should catch the last ten minutes of the match.'

The match is finished by the time we get there and the pub is nearly empty. Dad nods at a couple of regulars standing at the bar. The room smells of warm beer and stale sweat. He stands me by the pool table and tells me to wait. I watch as he speaks to the woman behind the bar and I get the feeling she's not happy that I'm here but in the end she nods her head and pours my dad a pint of beer. Then she hands him a small glass of cola and points to a table in the corner of the room.

'You're alright as long as you sit over here,' Dad says as he puts my drink on the table in the corner. 'I'll be back in a minute after I've caught up with Big Steve.'

And then he's gone and I'm alone. I take a seat like I'm told.

The seating is supposed to look like leather but it's cheap plastic and my jeans stick to it as soon as I sit down. The television's right above my head but no matter what way I turn, I can't see it. I give up and look around the room instead. Dad and Big Steve are by the door, and by the way my dad's moving his hands about I can tell he's talking about the game. Two men next to me are playing a game of pool and by the way they keep missing the white ball I reckon they've been in here all day. One of them catches me watching and I look away before he can say anything.

I finish my cola and manage to find my own way to the toilets by following the smell. A crusted bottle of bleach sits on the windowsill but it's been a long time since any bleach was used in here. I hold my breath and try not to throw up as I pee into the trough. Fag ends float in the puddle of urine and an empty condom wrapper blocks the drain. I don't stop to wash my hands and make a quick exit. The stench of piss follows me back into the bar and I wish I could go home.

'What's your name, son?' The woman behind the bar has been waiting on me to return.

'Robbie,' I tell her. 'After John Robertson.'

She raises a painted eyebrow.

'The best striker that ever played for Hearts,' I add.

'Oh,' she says, but she doesn't look impressed. 'D'ya want another drink?'

I shove my hand deep into my pocket and bring out my loose change. I don't know how much a glass of cola costs and I panic.

She laughs and it's a gentle laugh. A bit like Mum's. 'Put your money away,' she says. 'This one's on the house.' She pours me a drink. 'Here,' she says, handing me a bag of ready salted, 'they're a bit out of date but I'm sure they'll be fine.'

'Thanks,' I say and I mean it.

'No bother,' she says. 'This is no place for a boy to spend a Monday night.'

'We're celebrating,' I tell her. 'I qualified for the school football team.'

'That's nice,' she says but I can tell she doesn't care. She picks up her drying cloth and takes a glass from a sink behind the bar. She rubs it as if it's a magic lamp but no genie appears to grant me three wishes.

'Thanks for the juice and crisps,' I say but she's already turned away. I slope back to my seat in the corner and sip my juice. It's flat. I check my phone again but of course the battery's still dead. What if no-one's accepted my friend request? What if Rachel doesn't accept it? Will everyone know that I asked her? Shit, I wish I knew how it all worked. I never should have mentioned it to Dean. Dad and Big Steve are making their way over and I pick up my glass and pretend to be watching the game of pool. I swear those guys haven't potted a ball since I got here. Dad sits beside me and throws his arm around my shoulder. 'This is my boy,' he tells Steve and gives me a squeeze.

Big Steve reaches across the table and grasps my hand so tight it hurts. 'Well done, son,' he says, pumping my hand up and down. 'Well done.'

'I always knew he had it in him,' Dad says. 'Takes after his old man. You wait and see, he'll be playing in Tynecastle one day. Wait and see.'

'You never know, Robbie,' Steve says. 'Maybe you'll get to play in a cup final.' He turns to my dad. 'Best day ever, eh?'

Dad raises his glass. 'Best day of my fucking life,' he says and drains his pint. 'Get you another?'

Steve nods.

'Wee chaser?'

'Go on then.'

Dad goes up to the bar and I'm left alone with Steve.

'Shame you missed the game,' Steve says. He's still talking about the cup final.

I stare at my fingernails.

'I know my boy will remember it forever. He'll be able to tell

136

his own boys about it one day.'

I feel my stomach tighten. 'My dad tried to get me a ticket,' I say.

Steve looks at me, 'What you talking about?'

'He promised to take me if there was a spare ticket.'

Steve lifts his glass. 'But I offered him a ticket the day before the game.' He takes a sip and says, almost to himself, 'I'm sure I did.'

The knot in my stomach tightens. My head hurts and I need fresh air. I turn to Steve. 'Tell him I'm not feeling well so I'm away home.'

'Wait a minute,' says Steve, 'I'm sure he'll want to go with you.'

I watch Dad smile at the barmaid as she pours him another pint. 'It's okay,' I say. 'Tell him not to rush, I've got a key.'

Outside, I can think more clearly. Am I really surprised that he didn't want to take me along with his friends. I imagine the conversation on the supporters' bus. 'This is my boy, Robbie. Named after the best ever striker Hearts signed. What's that? What position does he play? No, no. My boy doesn't play football. He's a fucking pussy and spends all day in his bedroom reading books.'

I kick an empty can of Tenant's into a shop doorway, but I even miss that and it bounces off the overflowing bin. Fuck. I slam my fist into the steel window shutter and it rattles in mock applause. 'Loser, loser,' it says and the cars and buses rushing past join in the chant. I stick to the shadows and slink home, head down.

Twenty-Four

The boy picks up his jacket and walks out the door without looking back at his dad. She wonders for a second if she should follow him, check he's okay, but she's worked here long enough to know to stay out of other people's business. But she's never had to worry about a kid before, and he reminds her of her own brother at that age.

The boy's father has been a regular in here since before she took the job on, and she remembers the night the boy was born. It was her first Saturday night shift and the place was packed with Hearts supporters. There'd been a game on, hell, isn't there always, and everyone was knocking back the drink like it was their last day on the planet. She'd been gobsmacked at how the money kept spilling out of their wallets. *Keep the change, darling. Get one for yourself.* Her pay might have been minimum wage, and barely enough to cover the rent on her pokey student flat, but the tips were amazing. That is, the tips were amazing when Hearts won. She leans against the bar and tries to work out how many years ago she started working in here. It was her first year of uni which must make it about thirteen years ago and it was supposed to be a temporary job, just some extra money to help her get by. She was training to be a teacher and this area was as close to the college as she could afford.

The door opens and she looks up, hoping the boy has returned, but it's just another regular and she goes back to remembering the night he was born. 'It's a boy,' his dad announced as he walked through the pub doors. A huge cheer erupted inside and there was lots of back slapping and congratulating going on and she remembers wondering if the reaction would have been the same had he announced that it was a girl. 'Drinks are on me,' he'd shouted and the whole bar went crazy. She had barely learned how to pour a pint at the time and suddenly there was a flood of people demanding drinks. 'Keep a note of what you give out,' Jerry whispered in her ear, 'and try to watch that you don't serve the same person a free drink twice. They're good at that.'

Jerry works weekend and evening shifts behind the bar so that he can pay off his gambling debt but he's been working here longer than her and he's still never moved on. She's often wondered whether he's married or has kids but he keeps himself to himself and she respects him for that. He's the kind of guy that doesn't take any crap and he saved her bacon that night because when the dust settled and it was time for the bill to be paid, she discovered that the proud new father didn't have enough money on him. 'If they don't pay for their drink it comes out of our pocket,' Jerry hissed in her ear, 'and there's no way I'm losing money because of a prick like him.'

Like she said, Jerry doesn't take any shit from anyone and in the end Big Steve stepped forward with the cash to save his friend's neck, which at that point in time was held up against the door to the men's and was being slowly squeezed shut. It turned out she got some of her best tips ever during that shift and she'd gone shopping the next day and treated herself to a whole new wardrobe. After that night she always made sure someone paid up front before offering to buy everyone a drink.

She hopes the boy is safely home by now and wonders what sort of mother would let him come here in the first place.

Twenty-Five

The blue bar's not shifting and I'm in a hurry! The bus leaves in ten minutes but I want to check if she's accepted my friend request. When I got home last night I found loads of holiday photos on her Facebook page and there's even one of her in a bikini and I swear you can see her nipples. I tried wanking off but it felt like she was watching me and I couldn't do it.

I keep one eye on the screen as I scoop up yesterday's shirt from the floor and give it a quick spray with deodorant. It's impossible to fasten buttons when you're in a rush and I keep putting them through the wrong hole. I can't find my school trousers anywhere and if I'm not quick, I'll miss the bus. I've got English first period today and Rachel sits in the seat in front of me. I picture her long hair tied back in a ponytail, her perfect skin with the tiny mole under her left ear. My cock starts to swell and I blush as I remember my trousers are still in my gym bag in the cupboard under the stairs. I'll deal with them later. I grab an old pair from my wardrobe and pull them on. They don't really fit me and there's a hole in the knee but they'll do. At last the computer has loaded and I go straight to Rachel's page. She still hasn't accepted my friend request but that's okay, maybe she hasn't seen it yet. I have another quick look at the bikini photo and I picture her leaning backwards in class as she asks me to help her with a question on *Animal Farm*. She smiles at me in wonder as I explain the parody of Snowball being exiled from the farm just as Leo Trotsky had been exiled from Russia in 1929 during the revolution. 'Maybe you could come back to my house and help me with my homework,' she whispers, 'we could go upstairs to my bedroom.' Oh, fuck, I wish I had another five minutes before the bus comes.

I grab my school bag and shove my tie in my pocket. I'll tie it when I'm on the bus. My heart plummets as I leave my room and see the mess at the bottom of the stairs. I step over the broken photo frames and try to forget what happened last night. He's probably sleeping it off but there's no way I'm going to try and waken him. It's not my fault if he doesn't make it in to work today. He's big enough to look after himself.

There's nothing in the cupboard for breakfast so I nick a fiver from his wallet and pray he doesn't notice. I open the front door just as the school bus drives by. Jamie and Callum are sitting up the back and they flip me the bird as the bus disappears round the corner. Shit. Now I'm going to have to walk.

Miss Green is leaning against her desk, reading aloud from a copy of *Animal Farm* as I enter the classroom and I hope she doesn't ask me for another note. She smiles at me as I sit down so I figure I'm okay. 'Chapter three,' she says and tosses a copy of the book to me. 'We're discussing the section where the pigs have painted the commandments on the barn wall.'

She continues to read aloud and I sit back and let the slow rhythm of her voice wrap around me like a warm, woollen blanket and I wonder what life would be like if she was my mum. I imagine us cuddling up in front of a warm fire. It's snowing outside and she's made me a hot chocolate to drink while she reads *Tom Sawyer* to me.

'Robbie?'

Miss Green is looking at me. She's clearly expecting an answer but I don't know what the question was. Everyone in the room is waiting on me to speak. I stab at a wild guess. 'Orwell was signifying the socialist ideals behind Soviet communism,' I say and the class burst out laughing.

Her face is filled with disappointment and I know I've let her down. She turns to the rest of the class. 'Can anyone else answer my question?'

Rachel's hand shoots up and I squirm further back into my chair. Behind me, Callum and Jamie are sniggering. The end of a ruler pokes me in the back but I ignore it.

Rachel explains the metaphor perfectly to the class and Miss Green beams at her with pride. 'Thank you,' she says, 'I couldn't have explained it better myself.' I watch Rachel drag her fingers backwards through her hair as she shifts in her seat, embarrassed by the praise. I knew the answer to the question and I'm sure Miss Green expected me to.

She starts reading again but I've heard enough. I shift my attention to what's going on outside where a group of sixth years are playing football on the astroturf. Their shouts can be heard through the open window along with the distant sound of a lawnmower. I let my eyes watch the blur of blue move backwards and forwards across the green pitch. Team strips aren't allowed in school but that doesn't stop some of the older kids, and in our school that means Rangers. You'd be crucified if you even joked about supporting any of the fenian teams. If the rumours are true then Dean's the only Hibs fan in the whole school but I think they're nothing more than Chinese Whispers. I've never seen him wear green.

A bluebottle flies lazily in through the window and lands in front of me. Christ, even the flies here are blue. I swat it with my copy of *Animal Farm* and watch it move on. It zig zags across the room as if chasing its own imaginary ball, and then lands on Rachel's desk. She flicks her hand and it's off again.

The bell rings. Shit, I've got maths with Mr Johnson next. Dean was right, though. Nobody has questioned me about the note. Seems a death in the family is too awkward to talk about. Maybe Johnson will go easy on me today. I stand up and push my chair in. Better get the next lesson over with.

I join the end of the line and shuffle my way towards the door. They insist we walk around the school in single file, and even though the maths department is in the same corridor they make us walk around the whole school to get there. It takes forever to get from one class to the next which is fine if your teacher doesn't care that you're late. Not fine, if your teacher is Mr Johnson, the biggest prick in the school.

'Robbie.' Miss Green is standing by her desk, waiting for me to walk past. 'Can I have a word?'

Jamie is standing behind me in line. 'Maybe she wants to give you a blow job,' he whispers. 'I've seen the way she looks at you.'

I step away from him and walk over to her desk. 'I've got maths next,' I say and look up at the clock on the wall.

'Don't worry about that,' she says. 'I'll explain to your teacher.'

I wonder if she knows who my teacher is. I can hear Jamie and Callum giggling and whispering and I look up to make sure they're leaving. Jamie turns in the doorway and winks at me. He blows me a kiss and disappears. Good riddance.

'I noticed you seemed tired in class this morning,' Miss Green says.

Tired? Christ, so would she be if she'd had the night I'd had. Usually Mum's there to meet him when he comes in from the pub but I'm on my own now. He was so pissed when he got home that he literally fell through the front door. 'Where are you?' he yelled and I knew he didn't mean me. 'Where are you bitch?' I crawled inside my wardrobe. He's never actually hurt me before, but... I covered my ears with my hands but I could still hear him. 'Bitch,' he shouted, 'Fucking bitch.' Then there was a smash and I squeezed myself in behind my jackets and tried to remember a song Mum used to sing to me when I was scared.

'Hush, little baby, don't say a word,'
Mum's arms were around me,
'Mama's gonna buy you a mocking bird.'
She's smiling at me and I can't hear him anymore.

143

'And if that mocking bird won't sing.'

I closed my eyes,

'Mama's gonna buy you a diamond ring.'

I woke up cold and cramped in the corner of my wardrobe. My legs hurt, my arms hurt. I was sore all over. I slid the door open and listened. Nothing. I climbed out of my small cave and from the top step I could see the splinters of glass standing upright in the wooden floor.

'Robbie?' Miss Green looks worried. 'How are things at home?'

Why is she asking me this? 'Everything's fine, Miss,' I tell her.

She waits for me to say more.

'Honest,' I say, 'nothing's wrong. I stayed up a bit late playing on my computer, that's all. Please don't say anything 'cause I had the volume down. Mum and Dad hate me playing it before bed, they always like me tucked up sleeping by half eight but I'd die if the boys in class found out.'

It works. Miss Green smiles at me. 'I understand,' she says, 'but don't be too hard on your parents. They're only doing what's best for you.'

I pick up my bag. 'Thanks, Miss,' I say. 'I'll try to have an early night tonight.'

'Sorry for holding you back,' she says, 'you'd better get along to your next class.'

The corridors are empty and I make my way towards the maths department. There's no point in running because I'm already late. I take my phone out of my pocket and check for messages. There's none. Why doesn't she get in touch to check how I am?

I freeze outside Mr Johnson's room. The door's shut but his voice carries out into the corridor and I hear him yelling at some poor kid for something. I sneak a look through the narrow window in the door. Stacey Burton is standing with her hands by her side and Johnson is shouting at her from the other side of the desk. Poor Stacey looks like she's about to burst into floods of tears. I look around the room. Everyone's watching in silence, glad that it's not their turn today. Johnson moves closer to her and you can almost hear the rest of the class hold their breath, willing her not to cry. He loves it when he makes a kid cry. Stacey blinks and a single tear rolls down her cheek. The bastard. I clench my fist. If I was bigger I'd make him pay. Make *him* cry. One day. I unclench my fist and turn away from the window.

Dean meets me in the dinner hall at lunchtime.

'Where the fuck have you been?' he asks.

'I had a message to do for Miss Green.

'For a whole fuckin' period?'

I shrug my shoulders.

'Johnson's after your blood,' he says. 'He knows you're in school.'

'How?'

'He picked on Stacey, made the poor girl cry. She told him you'd been in English.' He sees the look on my face. 'You can't blame her,' he says. 'I wouldn't risk lying to that bastard either.'

'I guess you'd better write me another note,' I say.

'No way,' Dean says, 'not after the mood he was in.'

I put down my slice of pizza. I'm no longer hungry. 'What should I do?' I ask.

'Keep your head down and stay out of his way.'

A couple of teachers enter the dinner hall. They ignore the long line waiting to be served and walk to the front of the queue. They don't even look at the kids they've pushed past in line. Too busy laughing at some shared joke. I hate them. I look around the room at the beige plastic chairs arranged around beige circle tables. The walls are beige, the floor is beige, our lives are beige. The only colour in the room comes from the posters telling us to eat five fruit and veg' a day, telling us to drink milk because it's good for us, telling us to put our rubbish in the bin. They'd tell us how to wipe our arse if they thought they could get away with it.

I get up from the table and leave my plate with its half eaten burger on it. Fuck it. Somebody else can put my rubbish in the bin.

'Where are you going?' Dean's following me.

'I'm not hanging around here waiting for Johnson to come and get me,' I say. And then I see her. I stop dead. She's laughing with some girls from our class but I don't know their names. Her tie is pulled low and her top buttons are undone and I can see her bra strap. I picture her in her gold bikini and my hard-on returns immediately. It seems my dick needs no encouragement to perform these days. I can't breathe. She stretches up and pulls her hair together into a ponytail and a flash of skin shows for a brief second. Oh God, I'm actually dying here. Is this what it feels like to be in love?

She looks across the dinner hall and I'm still staring at her. I know I should look away but I can't seem to look in any other direction. She smiles at me and I've got a horrible feeling I'm grinning at her like a fucking idiot but I've lost control over all parts of my body. She says something to her friends and they all giggle at some shared joke. She looks back to me again and then... And then... Oh God, I can't breathe. I actually can't breathe. She's winding her way through the tables and chairs and I think she's walking over to me. I'm gulping for air. Breathe, breathe.

'Robbie,' she says with a smile.

Oh God, she remembers my name. She actually remembers my name.

'Erm,' I try to say hi but I sound like a strangled cat. Please let me retrieve the power of speech.

She stands closer and I can smell her perfume. It's nothing like Palmolive soap. 'I wondered if you fancied hanging out with me tonight,' she says.

I can't speak, I think she's asking me to go out with her and I can't fucking speak. Am I drooling?

She doesn't care that I haven't answered. 'Let's say six o'clock at the new play park on Balgreen Road.'

Is it me she's speaking to? I look around for someone else but there's only me.

She smiles, 'Great, I'll see you at six.' Then she leans forward and touches my bare arm and I swear I'm gonna come in my pants right here, right now if she moves any closer. 'And remember,' she whispers, 'it'll be just you and me.'

I stand and watch as she snakes her way back to join her friends in the dinner queue. Her hips wiggle from side to side as she sways between the jumble of table and chairs and I know every boy in the room is watching her. Her friends huddle around her, giggling and looking across at me. Holy shit, Rachel Jones asked me out on a date.

'What the fuck just happened?' Dean looks pissed off.

'Nothing.'

'Didn't look like nothing,' he says. 'Looked like she wanted to suck your fuckin' dick.'

I grin. 'We're meeting tonight.'

'Ya jammy bastard.' He laughs and slaps me on the back and I wish he wouldn't do that because it's beginning to get on my nerves. 'Better make sure you've got a condom on you.' He winks and pats my jacket pocket.

Twenty-Six

Anna Green is determined to do something. She knows Robbie was lying to her this morning when he said everything was fine and she wants to find out what's going on. Right now, she's standing outside Derek Johnson's office waiting for him to call her in. He knows she's here but it's all about control with him. He likes to show you who's the boss. Wanker. Eventually he calls her name and she steps inside and finds him sitting behind his desk, pretending to be busy on his mobile phone.

She doesn't wait for him to speak. 'I'm worried about one of the boys in my first year English class.'

'Go on.' He doesn't even look up. The wee prick's probably playing Bejewelled or Candy Crush.

'I'd like to note a cause for concern. Officially.'

Johnson puts down his phone and leans forward. She's got his attention.

'I think some of the other boys in his class are bullying him.'

'Well, that's easy. You deal with that kind of thing all the time. Have you spoken to the boys that are involved?'

'It's a bit more complicated than that.'

'Complicated how?'

'He seems to be friends with the boys who are doing the bullying.' She remembers Johnson's comment about Robbie becoming best buddies with Dean straight after Dean grassed on him for smoking. 'Or at least he thinks he's friends with them and he doesn't really have any other friends.'

'What's wrong with him?'

'What do you mean?'

'Most students his age have got plenty of friends so why doesn't your boy?'

She pictures Dean, Callum and Jamie and wonders why a bright kid like Robbie hangs about with them. 'I was thinking it might be a good idea if I speak to his parents. Might get a picture of what life's like at home.'

'Why do you want to do that?'

God, this man is such an arse. 'I don't know,' she says calmly. 'I get a feeling that maybe things are tough for him at home. He seems really tired in class and he's easily distracted.'

Johnson lets out a small squeak. 'You've just described three quarters of our students. Most of our boys are up past midnight playing those nasty video games and God knows what the girls are getting up to.'

She doesn't argue back. If she's going to help Robbie she needs Johnson on her side. 'I still think it might be worth going to speak to his parents. Now that I've raised it with you it would be terrible if we miss any signs of abuse or neglect.' Her sentence hits home straightaway and she knows she's won. Johnson wouldn't dare let a boy like Robbie ruin his career. 'I can arrange a home visit for this week.'

This time he doesn't try to conceal his laughter. 'A home visit? You must be mad. I'm sure a phone call will do just fine.'

'But I feel...'

'I'm not discussing it any further. A home visit would be far too dangerous for one of my members of staff. No idea what you might be walking in to. Besides we need you in school in case we need you to cover a class.'

Anna knows this is bullshit. He doesn't really think a home visit could be dangerous, nor does he care about her safety, and as for covering a class, well, there's plenty of staff available.

Johnson interrupts her thoughts. 'No, I think it would be much more sensible if you speak to his parents over the phone.' He turns his attention back to his game. 'Much more sensible,' he repeats.

She sighs. Surely it would be easier to talk to Robbie's mum face to face. Parent's night for first years is already past and she can't really remember what his mum was like. She'd only had the class a few weeks and was still getting to know them. Had the dad come too? They sometimes do but it's usually just the mothers. 'Thank you Sir,' she says, 'I'll try and phone them during my free period.'

'No problem,' says Derek Johnson, 'glad I could be of help.'

Anna gets up to leave the room.

'Before you go,' he says. 'You never did tell me the name of the child.'

'It's Robbie,' she says. 'Robbie MacFarlane.'

Twenty-Seven

I see her at the end of the day as I'm going to catch the bus. I'm sure it's her. An umbrella hides her face but I'd recognise her red coat anywhere. She got it in the Boxing Day sale last year and when she brought it home she wore it in the house for the rest of the day, that's how much she loved it. Even Dad laughed at that one and for once there was no argument over how much she'd spent. I think he knew how much she loved it. We bought her a pair of matching red gloves for her birthday and I can still see the look on her face when she opened the wrapping paper. She hugged me so hard it hurt.

She's standing on the other side of the main road. Watching me. I try to wave but a van drives past and blocks her from view. I run up to the traffic lights and press the button to cross. Cars and buses rush past and the red man tells me to wait but I keep pressing, sure that the lights will change quicker. I pray to the tiny god that lives inside the box with the button and beg him to flick a switch. My prayer is heard and the lights turn to red. The green man flashes at me, telling me it's safe to cross and I run across the road and back to where she was standing. I stop. She's gone.

Why?

Why didn't she wait to speak to me? I want to tell her that he's drinking more than usual. I want her to know that I spent last night hiding in my wardrobe. And I want to know why she doesn't come home and make everything alright again. If she's forgotten about us then why is she watching me come out of school? My head hurts and I wish I had a can of beer.

Dad's standing at the front door when I get home from school. I stare at him. He looks different but I don't know what it is. The broken frames and shattered glass have been cleared away but if you look closely you can see pockmarks in the wooden floor. I think I can smell dinner. 'How was your day?' I ask him. It's only four o'clock which means he hasn't gone in again today and I'm beginning to wonder if he's still got a job.

'Never mind that,' he says, avoiding the question. 'I've got something for you.'

'For me?'

He grins. 'Come on through to the kitchen.'

I throw my jacket over the banister and don't even bother to take off my shoes as I follow him through to the kitchen. I can do what I like now there's no mum around to give me a row. Dad's whistling as he produces a bag from behind his back. 'I've got you a present,' he says and hands me the white plastic bag. 'Bought it off Big Steve in the pub last night. Sorry it's not wrapped but I was never any good at that kind of thing.'

Is it an early birthday present? I take the bag and lay it down in front of me.

'Open it,' he shouts.

I lift the bag and slip my hand inside. I can feel the soft, silky material and I know what it is. I can't believe it. He hasn't bought me my own Hearts strip since I was in primary school. I take it out and hold it up.

'Look,' he says and grabs it from me. 'There's the badge to show we won the cup. Special edition.' He holds the shirt up to my shoulders. 'I always said you were their lucky mascot. Maybe that luck's starting to rub off on you now that you've made it into the school team.'

I take the shirt and put it back in the bag. 'Thanks Dad,' I say.

'Put it on,' he says. 'Now you're a real footballer it's time you look the part.'

'A real footballer?'

'That's right. Now you're in the school team it's time we got you some proper stuff so I'm taking you to the shops today to get you a decent pair of boots. What do you say, eh?'

'Thanks, Dad.'

'Jesus Christ. Is that all you've got to say? That shirt cost me a bloody fortune, never mind the fucking boots.'

'Really, I mean it Dad. I love my shirt, I just can't believe it, that's all.' My wee speech has nearly got him in tears. Maybe we don't need Mum after all.

'Go and get ready, son. We'll go into town and get you your new boots.'

'But I've got training tonight.'

'Training, eh? Oh well, you'd better not miss that.' He looks disappointed but there's no way I'm not meeting Rachel at the park. I've been counting the hours since lunchtime. 'How about I meet you straight after school tomorrow and we'll go and get you a pair that'd be good enough for Robbo himself. We'll soon have you playing for Hearts.'

'I don't think I'll ever be that good.'

'Don't speak such rubbish,' he says, 'of course you will. You just need to practise, and that means you need the right gear.' He slaps me on the back and I take my shirt upstairs to my room and send Dean a quick text.

guess what?

I pull the shirt on over my head. It's a bit of a tight fit but it'll do.

My phone beeps.

what's up?

I message him back straight away.

my dad got me a new football shirt!

I wait by my phone for his reply.

lucky bastard

shame it's the wrong fucking colour

I smile. Another message follows straight after.

u fucking tart

I grab the maroon scarf from my drawer and wrap it around my neck. Dad's gonna be so pleased when he sees me wearing it with my new shirt. I can't stop grinning. Championees, championees. It's almost time to meet Rachel and I can just tell it's going to be a great night.

The church bells chime loudly as I run along Slateford Road, telling me I'm late. As if I didn't already know! Nobody told me that getting ready to meet a girl was so stressful. First off, I didn't want Rachel to think I'm like all the other boys and only interested in football so I wanted to wear something cool. But I couldn't find anything cool to put on that was clean, so I rummaged in the dirty basket 'til I found my Kermit the frog t-shirt. I hope she'll find it funny. I sprayed it with half a can of deodorant to make sure it smells okay and put it in a sports bag with my jeans so I could smuggle them out of the house. Then I borrowed some of Mum's hair mousse but it went sticky and looked like I hadn't washed in weeks so I had to have a shower. My hair's still a bit wet but at least I don't look like a hobo. The last straw was when Dad stood and waved to me from the front door and I had to pretend I was walking in the direction of the school playing fields, the complete opposite direction of the park. For a moment, I was sure he was gonna suggest coming with me.

I duck into the toilets of The Diggers Bar and quickly get changed out of my football gear. What if she's already left? Girls don't like being kept waiting. I hide my bag behind the toilet cistern and rush back out into the daylight. I've got a stitch in my left side and it's screaming at me to slow down but I'll die if I get there and she's gone. Maybe she never came in the first place. What if the whole thing is a set up? I'm gonna look a right dick arriving out of breath only to find a bunch of her pals lined up to point and laugh at me. The stitch in my left side forces me to slow down. What if they've all got their phones, ready to post a picture of Floppy on Facebook. I mean why would a girl as gorgeous as Rachel ever ask me out?

I'm almost at the park and I spit out my chewing gum and sort my hair in a shop window. If she's not there I'll keep walking and maybe shout on a pretend dog or something. That'll work. God, I wish I'd nicked one of Dad's fags.

She's sitting on the swings when I arrive, her long legs pushing back and forwards, her heels digging into the dirt. She sees me and waves and I wave back in a trance.

'Sorry, I'm late.'

'That's okay, I knew you'd come.'

Hers is the only swing that's not wound round the top bar. I think about trying to unravel one of the others but I play safe and lean casually against the metal frame, hands in pockets, trying to look cool. I don't feel cool.

She continues to sway back and forth in her plastic seat. Neither of us speak and I'm confused. Is she waiting for me to say something? Is that how it works? The hard-on I had on the way here has gone and I'm wondering if this is a date or not. I'm wishing I hadn't told Dean now. He's going to want all of the details on the bus tomorrow.

She leaps out of the swing and wanders over to a wooden bench on the edge of the play area where she sits down and takes out her phone. What the fuck am I supposed to do?

My phone beeps.

sit beside me

I look over and she's smiling at me and my hard-on is returning. I walk over and sit down beside her. 'How did you get my number?'

'Dean gave me it the other day when he told me you fancied me.'

I jump up from the bench. 'Is that what this is all about, everyone having a laugh at me. I suppose it was all his idea. Wait 'til I see him.' I should have realised this whole thing is a wind up. What an idiot thinking she might actually fancy me.

'Tell him I'll get him for this.'

She's laughing but it's not unkind. 'Sit down,' she says and pats the wooden seat beside her. 'I'm the one who asked you out. I've noticed you in class and then yesterday in PE,' she looks down at her hands and I notice her fingernails are all chewed.

'Go on,' I say, 'in PE?'

She blushes. 'I asked the other girls if I could partner you.'

'You did?'

She touches my hand. 'I thought we made a pretty good team.'

Everything around me stops moving and time stands still and I know I'll remember this moment forever. This is the moment I fall in love. She shuffles closer to me and I smell her perfume. And then we're kissing. We're kissing and I'm praying. Praying that I'm doing this right. Her mouth pushes against mine and I push back. Her eyes are closed and I try closing mine but I'm worried I'm going to fall off the bench so I open them again. Our teeth clatter and I try turning my head sideways, then suddenly her tongue is inside my mouth and my heart feels like it's going to explode. Or maybe I'm mistaking my heart for my dick. It certainly feels like something's about to explode.

I try slipping my own tongue into her mouth but I meet her braces on the way and decide it's safer to withdraw for now. In my head I'm screaming, 'Look at me, look at me. I'm kissing a girl,' and I'm really having to concentrate on what I'm doing.

We're kissing forever and the smell of her perfume is beginning to make me feel a little queasy. I hope we come up for air soon.

She takes her tongue out of my mouth and pulls away. I wonder if I've done something wrong but she says nothing. She checks her phone, sorts her hair and then comes in for another go. This time I'm prepared and I sneak a deep breath before she reaches me.

I can't wait to tell Dean in the morning. Maybe I should text him when I get home but what will I write. After all we're only kissing and Dean's probably kissed dozens of girls. If I make a big deal out of it he'll probably realise Rachel's my first proper girlfriend. I don't suppose holding hands with Rebecca in the nursery counts.

We come up for air again.

'Is this your first time?' she asks.

'No,' I say, probably a little too quickly.

We go in again. Why did she ask that? Am I doing it wrong? I close my eyes and ignore the feeling that I'm falling. I open my mouth wider but our teeth keep clashing and my lip nearly gets caught in her braces. So we sit and hold hands on the bench for a while. We talk a bit about some of the teachers at school and she tells me that Jennifer Weir fancies Dean.

'Do you think you could get him to come here one night and I could just happen to be here with Jennifer.'

'I guess so,' I say but I know I won't. I don't want Dean around when I'm with Rachel; he'll only mess things up.

'It'd be great if they got together,' she's saying. 'We could go on double dates to the cinema and stuff. It'd be fun.'

I look at her and want to kiss her again. So I do. And this time it's perfect. I'm definitely in love.

She doesn't let me walk her home and I get the feeling her mum and dad don't know she was meeting me tonight. We say goodbye at the bridge but this time she doesn't let me kiss her and I wonder who she told them she was with.

I go back into the toilets at The Diggers. The pub's not actually called that but that's the name everyone around here gives it. It comes from the nearby graveyard and legend has it that this is where all the grave diggers came to drink at the end of a day's work. Legend according to my dad that is. The pub's a lot fancier than his local and the toilets are a lot cleaner. There's only one cubicle in the men's and I left my bag tucked out of

157

sight behind the cistern. I have to wait because someone's using it just now but that's okay, I'm in no hurry to go home. My phone beeps and I yank it out of my pocket hoping it's her. Maybe she's missing me already.

The message is from Dean. One word.

Well???

The guy in the cubicle must be constipated 'cause he's taking forever. I put the phone back in my pocket and cough loudly to let him know I'm out here. There's a rustle of toilet paper and it sounds like the cheap, waxy stuff that you get at school. The stuff that smears the shite further up your arse.

My phone beeps again but this time I don't recognise the number. The message is a single *x*. A kiss. What should I do, should I text her back? But what if it's not her? What if it's Dean texting me from his mum's phone. Or Jamie, or Callum. They're playing with me, waiting to see what I text back so that they can show everyone at school tomorrow. The bastards. But what if I'm wrong and it is her? Aw man, my head is spinning. Then I remember that she texted me earlier at the park. I check the message she sent me and compare the numbers only to discover that the kiss didn't come from her phone. I'm gutted and I think about phoning the number to see who answers, but what the fuck would I say? The guy in the cubicle flushes and I put the phone back in my pocket for now. I'll decide what to do when I get home.

When the guy finally comes out he looks like crap, pardon the pun! He's sweating real bad and looks like he's about to pass out. 'You alright?' I ask, not really wanting any details but I feel I should check. He looks me up and down with bloodshot eyes, 'I'm not fuckin' queer, you know.' He shoves his shoulder against the door and heads back to the bar. Without washing his hands.

The smell coming from the cubicle is toxic and I cover my mouth with my t-shirt before heading in. The toilet has no lid and the remains of what couldn't flush away are floating about in the pan daring me to look at them. I focus on the corner with the heating pipes where I stuffed my bag. The pipes aren't on and I reach my hand down, ready to grab the bag and go. I feel around blind with one hand but there's nothing there. The stench in here is killing me and I need to get out. I have one last grope around but the bag's definitely not there. I run out of the cubicle and gasp for fresh air. Where the fuck's my bag? It must be in there, no-one could find it unless they knew it was there. I mustn't have reached round far enough. Here goes again...

I don't believe it. My bag's fucking gone and so is my new shirt. The shirt my dad gave me, the one he expects me to wear to training every night. It can't be gone. Can't be.

'Fuck.' I bang my fist on the cubicle's partition and it shakes. 'Fuck, fuck, fuck.'

Twenty-Eight

She knew she wouldn't be able to concentrate on the film but John insisted they have a night out together. 'A date,' he called it. The box of popcorn sits wedged between them but she hasn't touched it. She has no appetite. Every couple of minutes he reaches in for a handful, snorts his way through his pile and then reaches in again. The woman in front turns and stares at him every time but he doesn't notice.

Tracey had hinted at going to see a romantic comedy but John just laughed and said he'd pick a film they'd both enjoy. Then he ruffled her hair. She doesn't remember him doing that before. The film he chose is supposed to be a 'gripping' thriller but she's lost track of who's chasing who so she closes her eyes and tries to remember the last time she came to the cinema. She remembers bringing Robbie to see the last Bond film. He kept pestering her to take him because he was the only one in his class that hadn't seen it yet. She can't remember what it was called or what it was about, but then, aren't all Bond films the same? They'd brought their own sweets and sat in the very front row and he didn't fidget or talk over it once. He'd loved it. On the way home he'd tried to explain to her what the film was all about but she didn't care, she'd just enjoyed being with him and doing something kind of grown up together. She wonders what he's doing just now. Right this minute. He's probably curled up on the sofa with a book. He's a bright boy, much brighter than most of those teachers realise, and he loves reading. He'd have his nose in a book every minute of the day if she let him.

The credits roll and the lights fade up.

'What did you think?' John asks and reaches out for her hand.

She quickly picks up the empty popcorn box with two hands. 'Great.'

'Told you we'd both like that one,' he says and ruffles her hair again. What the hell is it with the hair?

The cinema is quiet and they follow the small trail of people out of the rows, down the steps and through the door out into the bright lights of the foyer.

'Give me a minute, I just need to visit the little boy's room.' John hands her his jacket and she steps back in case he wants to touch her hair again. She leans back against the wall and watches the last dribs and drabs of people leave. Then she spots Robbie's English teacher walking out of the same screen and she steps forward, hoping she'll see her. The young teacher said great things about Robbie at parents' night, and she even thanked Tracey for taking him to the library when he was little. It was kind of embarrassing when she said that but also kind of nice to hear. His dad used to try and get her to take Robbie along to the football clubs when he was a toddler but instead she used to take him to the library and they'd sit amongst the cushions and bean bags and read story after story. She didn't want him to grow up like his dad. Didn't want him to live his life around Match of the Day and Saturday afternoons in the pub where the only important things are match results and referee decisions.

She looks across at the woman and wonders if she'll even remember who she is. Maybe she should say hello. She could ask how Robbie's getting on. He's probably doing much better already since the yelling and arguing has stopped and he can concentrate on doing well at school. She knows he's going to be really clever one day, probably go to university like his English teacher said he could. She tries to remember her name.

'Ready to go?' John is back and lifts his jacket with one hand and grasps her firmly by the arm with the other.

Robbie's teacher looks across at her but before Tracey can smile or say hello she looks away.

'Who was that?' John asks as they walk towards the exit.

'One of Robbie's teachers. Can't remember her name but she says he's her top student, reckons he'll go to uni one day and come out some sort of literary genius.'

'She didn't seem to like you very much.'

Tracey stops and looks at him. What does he mean? Why wouldn't she like her? Maybe she exaggerated about the genius bit but she really did say great things about her boy.

John stops outside the cinema doors. 'Change of plan. Let's go for a bite to eat. Celebrate our first official date together.'

She lets him guide her through the door to the Pizza Hut that's next door to the cinema. Why wouldn't Robbie's teacher look at her?

The pizza restaurant is full of teenagers and students and they're the only couple in the place.

'Let's get a large pizza to share, cheese and tomato okay?'

She nods but she's not really listening. Is his teacher angry because she's left him, is that why she wouldn't look at her? The waitress comes over and John orders a beer for himself and a glass of white wine for Tracey. She didn't really fancy wine but he's paying so she keeps quiet. There's a young lad in the corner that reminds her of Robbie. His hair is hanging over his eyes and he keeps sweeping it away with one move, trying to tuck it behind his ear but it's not quite long enough. He's watching the others laughing around him and she wonders if that's what it's like for Robbie. Is he on the outside of life watching everyone else taking part?

Twenty-Nine

I couldn't sleep last night, too busy trying to think of a way to get some money so I can replace the Hearts top before Dad notices it's missing. He'll go mental if he finds out I've lost it. I grab a seat on the school bus and check her Facebook page. Again. I've just missed her. She was active five minutes ago and I look to see if she's posted a comment about me or, even better, changed her status from being single to in a relationship. It turns out she's posted a video of a cat falling off a table. Too cute, she's written above it. Several of her friends click *like* almost straight away and I recognise most of them from school. They're all girls. I hate cat videos but I press the thumbs up sign anyway and try to think of something clever to say. I vaguely remember a joke about nine lives and as I'm fine tuning it in my head a comment pops up beneath the video. PMSL. Michael Smith. Who the fuck is Michael Smith? His profile picture is Papa Smurf. So the man thinks he's funny. I click on his name and up pops dozens of photos of him either in an action shot on the football pitch or posing with a trophy. Should have known. There's a picture taken straight after he's scored a goal and he's showing off a tanned six pack and shaking his long hair. Thinks he's Fernando Torres. I try tensing my muscles but it makes no difference.

And then I see it. A photo of the two of them together. It looks like it was taken at a party and he's got his arms around her and she's gazing into his eyes like a love sick puppy. I try telling myself that he's in the past, but then why is he commenting on her post of a cat falling off a table. And now she's liked his comment. PMSL – pissing myself laughing. What kind of stupid comment is that? No thought or brains went into that one. My joke about nine lives is gonna be much better. But what if she doesn't 'like' it?

I stare at her picture. I can't stop thinking about her. Her perfume, her smile, her kiss. There's no braces in the photo with the golden bikini. Maybe she had them removed for going on holiday. I check again and she's still single. I think about changing my own status but maybe I should wait until she changes hers first. In a relationship. Sounds good. I bet if Mum sees it she'll get in touch straight away.

'Fuckin' hell, look at her tits!' Dean is leaning over my shoulder. I never even noticed he'd got on the bus. I shove the phone into my pocket and turn around in my seat.

'Alright?' I hope I sound casual.

'Well?' He's grinning at me like the Cheshire Cat.

'Well what?' I ask.

'Still got that condom in your pocket?'

'None of your fuckin' business.'

'I'll take that as a yes. So did she turn up?'

'What the fuck do you mean? Of course she fuckin' turned up. Jesus Christ.'

'Keep your knickers on.' He leans back in his seat. 'And did she text you night night?'

I stare at him. 'It was you that sent me the text last night, the one with the kiss.'

The bastard laughs and slaps me on the back, 'It was worth a try.'

There's a loud cheer as the bus hits a speed bump and everyone's thrown into the air. Same time, same place, same fucking cheer every morning of my life. We're coming up to her stop and I don't know how I should sit. What should I do when she gets on? Should I smile and say hi or should I pretend I'm talking to Dean and then notice her at the last second and flash her a surprised smile like I didn't know she gets the same bus as me. We're nearly there and I still haven't decided what to do. In my head she gets on the bus and walks up the aisle to where I'm sitting. 'Anyone sitting here?' she asks and I move my bag to let her sit down. We talk the whole way to school and I ask her a string of amusing questions and she throws her head back and laughs, and everyone's watching us, the new couple, and we meet at lunchtime by the bike shed and add our names to the hundreds before us.

Robbie + Rachel

She draws a heart around our names and we kiss. This time we don't clash braces.

Shit. I see a flash of her turquoise jacket as the bus slows down. She'll be on the bus in less than a minute and I still don't know what to do. I wish Dean wasn't sitting behind me. How am I supposed to talk to her when he's there? I think about moving seats but the bus is pretty full and besides Dean would probably follow me. I sit back in my seat and try to look casual.

Her friend, can't remember her name, gets on first and they're giggling and whispering about something. I wish I knew what. I move my bag on to the floor at my feet and wait, ready to smile. Dean had better be nice to her friend when she sits beside him. Rachel can't find her bus pass and she's searching her pockets. At last she finds it and shows it to the driver who waves them both on.

I stretch my arm out across the back of the seat, waiting on her to walk towards me but she doesn't. She stops at the bottom of the steps and heads upstairs to the top deck. What the fuck! She doesn't even look down the bus once.

'I'm bored.'

We're sitting on a wall outside the PE department. We're meant to be in maths but the older kids are still on study leave and none of the teachers seem to be bothered about us first years and I can't stand being ignored by her another minute. I don't understand. Last night she was all over me like a rash and today it's like I don't exist. She hasn't looked at me once this morning and every time I try to catch her eye she's surrounded by her giggling friends. I give up.

'We could head to the park,' says Callum.

'We did that yesterday.'

Dean jumps down from the wall and spins round, arms outstretched like a ring master at the circus. 'I've got a plan,' he says and sweeps his arms in an overdramatic performance. 'A way to get back at Johnson.'

Jamie and Callum are listening as if he's God.

'I've been watching him closely during his lessons and he's a creature of habit.'

'So?' I ask and Callum flashes me a look warning me to keep my mouth shut.

'So,' repeats Dean, 'have you noticed he always takes his phone out of his jacket pocket at the start of a lesson and puts it on his desk?'

'He's never off his fuckin' phone,' says Jamie. 'I swear he's probably hooked up to all sorts of porn sites. Girl on girl action.'

Callum hits Jamie in the ribs. 'Let the man speak. Go on,' he says to Dean. He's rubbing his hands together. 'This sounds interesting.'

Sounds fucking stupid I think, but say nothing. I'm as keen as Dean is to get my own back on Mr Johnson. I can still see the smile on the prick's face when he gave me detention.

'Jamie's right. Johnson's always on his phone and that's what makes my plan so fuckin' amazing.' He grins, knowing we're hanging on his every word. 'That's why it's gonna hurt him.'

'What is?' I ask. I still don't see where this is going.

'Stealing his phone,' says Dean.

'Excellent,' shouts Callum and he leaps off the wall and pats Dean on the back. 'Fuckin' excellent.'

'Steal his phone?' Am I the only one whose brain is still working? 'We'll never get away with it.'

'Why not?' asks Callum. 'Dean's plans always work. Don't they?' He slaps him on the back again and Dean looks like if he does it once more he'll slap him back.

'The minute he sees it's gone he'll know it was us,' I say. 'And he'll demand to search our bags. There's no way we'll be able to get his phone out of his room without him noticing.'

'Aw fuck,' says Callum.

Dean's still smiling. 'Where's your faith? I thought you said my plans always work?'

'Yeah but Jamie said it. The man's on his phone all the time. He's on it when we turn up for class and you've seen the bastard. He sets us work to do then spends all his time playing on the fuckin' thing.'

Jamie can't resist interrupting. 'I'm telling you,' he grins, 'he's watching porn.'

Something clicks. 'Imagine if there is porn on his phone,' I say.

'Watch out,' laughs Callum. 'Floppy wants the porn.'

'Shut it,' I say. Dean's plan is beginning to come alive in my head. 'What happens if a teacher gets caught with porn on their mobile? Can you imagine the front page of the papers?'

'He'd have to quit.' Dean sees what I'm getting at.

'And he'd never get another teaching job,' I say.

'Genius,' shouts Dean, grinning at me. 'Fuckin' genius.'

Callum's pissed off. 'Yeah, but how are we going to get a hold of his phone, genius? You said yourself we'll never get it out of his room without him noticing it's gone.'

'Not if he's distracted.'

Dean's still grinning at me. 'Any ideas?'

'I was thinking fire alarm.'

'Some plan,' says Callum. 'As soon as he hears the bell he'll reach for his phone. You're gonna need a better idea than that, Spiderman.'

Thinks he's funny, taking the piss out of my sleeping bag. He'd better watch himself, I'm gonna get him back one day. 'By the time he notices it's missing we'll be out of class and long gone in the chaos,' I say

'Who's gonna hit the alarm?' asks Dean.

Callum jumps in and says he'll do it. Typical, he's offering to take the easy bit. Dean and I argue over who gets the pleasure of taking his phone. My seat's nearer his desk so I win the argument.

Dean's quiet and I can see he's still thinking. At last he says what's on his mind.

'I've been thinking,' he says.

We're all waiting to hear what he's got to say.

'Hitting Johnson is great but are we thinking big enough?'

Big enough? Shit, if we get caught stealing a teacher's phone we'll be excluded for good.

Dean pauses for maximum dramatic effect and then continues. 'What if we get them all back?'

'Love it,' shouts Callum, 'Who else can we get?'

'How about we take one each?' says Jamie.

'Love it,' shouts Callum again. 'Who?' That wanker is really getting on my tits.

'We each pick one who's given us a hard time,' says Dean.

'Bagsie Miss Clark,' says Jamie.

'The art teacher?'

'Cow told me my picture was shit.'

'Fair enough,' says Dean.

'She doesn't have a phone,' I say.

'Everyone's got a fuckin' phone,' says Callum.

'Yeah, right wise crack but have you ever seen her use it?'

Jamie interrupts us. 'I don't want her phone. I want that wee wooden model that sits on her desk.'

I cannae stop myself from laughing. 'What the fuck do you want that thing for?'

'Cause it gives me the creeps. She sits and plays with it when we're working. Twists its arms and legs like it's a voodoo doll and I'm sure she pretends it's me.' He stands up and dances around on the top of the wall like a puppet on strings. 'When I get it I'm gonna tear its arms and legs off and burn the fuckin' thing 'til it's nothing but a pile of ashes.'

We all laugh as he collapses on to the wall in exhaustion.

'Do you want to stick with Johnson?' Dean asks me.

I nod. I've already pictured the bastard's photo on the front of the local paper. 'Don't know how I'll do it by myself but I'll come up with something. What about you?' I ask. 'Who are you going to choose?'

He grins at me and taps the side of his nose with his finger. 'You'll have to wait and see,' he says, 'you'll have to wait and see.'

I put my hand into my pocket and find there's a small folded piece of paper that wasn't there earlier. I casually turn my back on the others and take it out. It's a torn page from a jotter and it's been folded carefully several times into a small square. It must be from her. I check no-one's looking before I open it.

Meet me on Sunday night.
Same time, same place
x

She finished with a kiss! Fucking hell, she was just playing it cool in front of her friends, probably doesn't want any of them to know we're getting serious. At last, my luck is changing.

The front door is unlocked and Dad is standing staring out of the kitchen window. He promised me we'd go for boots when I got home from school today.

'Dad?'

He doesn't turn round.

'Has something happened?' I ask. I stand, frozen to the spot. Something's happened to Mum, I know it has. He still won't look at me. 'Dad?' I'm scared to ask. 'Is everything okay?'

Giant sobs shudder through his body and his shoulders shake uncontrollably. The sound is terrifying. Alien.

I stand in the middle of the kitchen, not knowing what to

do. If Mum was here, she'd put the kettle on but it doesn't seem right. I'm too young to be offering cups of tea. So instead I do what he trained me to do - I go to the fridge and get him a beer.

'Here,' I say and hand it out towards him.

'Thanks, son. I can always rely on you.'

I stand and watch him drink. After a couple of sips his shoulders relax and he seems more like his usual self but I'm guessing he's forgotten about my new boots. The can is soon empty and this time he gets himself the next one from the fridge. 'Have you got training tonight?' he asks, as if everything's normal.

'Not tonight,' I say. He'll expect me to wear my new top to training. I need to be careful, he'll soon realise there's no routine to my nights out.

'Got a game soon?'

'An away game,' I say hoping that it'll be too much effort for him to come along. 'But I'm not sure the coach will pick me to play yet.'

'Do you fancy coming along to the pub with your old man tonight?'

'I've already arranged to meet a friend down at the park tonight.' Please God don't ask for any details.

He looks away and I feel bad. Maybe he would have sat beside me tonight or played a game of pool with me.

'No bother,' he says. 'We can do it another night.'

I go to leave the room but when I reach the door I stop. Maybe he's missing Mum too and I wonder if I should tell him that I saw her outside the school yesterday, but something stops me.

'Have you heard from her?' I ask quietly. I can feel him staring at me and I tense every muscle.

'No, son,' he says and his voice is shaking.

Thirty

Margaret MacFarlane gets off the bus at the bingo hall. It's Thursday night, big money night, and her luck is in, she can feel it. She's got her lucky bag, her lucky purse and her lucky bingo dabbers.

'Yoo hoo, Margaret.' Sadie waves to her from the front. 'I've got your seat.'

Margaret is a regular at the Bingo Hall in Wester Hailes and rarely misses a night. 'Keeps me young,' she tells people.

'Keeps you skint,' her husband used to say when he was alive. He only ever allowed her to go to Bingo on a Thursday. Pay day. He was always in a good mood on pay day, but then he would wake up bad tempered and with a hangover on the Friday morning. Then the next Thursday he'd be cook-a-hoop all over again, only to be a bad tempered bastard the next day. The man's mood swings were like clockwork but she never tried to change him, just took her tenner on a Thursday and enjoyed her night at the bingo. He was always too drunk to get it up by the time he staggered home from the pub so it was a great night all round.

'Y'alright, Sadie.'

'Grand, hen, just grand.'

Sadie's man died last year and she's finally worked her way up to five nights a week as well. She can be a bit tiresome at times and Margaret gets sick fed up of hearing about how smart her grandchildren are. Still, it's nice to have some company and Sadie always keeps her a seat near the front of the hall which means Margaret can catch the later bus.

171

The two women sit down with their card and their dabbers and wait for everyone else to settle down to play. There's a hen party at the back of the hall and they're making a lot of noise but Margaret's not too worried because she sees Nell and Isobel are sitting in front of them and they'll soon get them to quieten down. Big money night is serious business and this is no place for giggling wee lassies.

'So my Sophie got her first foster kid today, a wee boy called Zak. I mean no wonder the wean's got problems wi' a name like that. Who'd call their wean that? Jesus Christ. I mean what's the world coming to.'

Margaret can't remember Sadie mentioning her daughter fostering before but maybe she wasn't listening. 'What age is the wee one?' she asks politely.

'I think he's eight, or maybe nine. Somewhere about that age. A bundle of trouble if you ask me, but she gets a load of help for doing it. Gets a cheque to help pay for his food and clothes and stuff. She'll probably end up better off having him.'

'Is he from round here?'

'Other side of Edinburgh but he still gets to go to the same school. Taxi will pick him up and bring him home. They say it's important his schooling isnae interrupted so the council are gonna pay to take him back and forth. Sophie says he'll settle in real quick. Had a terrible home life apparently, and the woman from the council says some time in a stable house with proper meals and a proper bed will do him the world of good.'

'How long is he going to be with her?'

Sadie rolls her eyes. 'Nobody's sure yet. Could be a few weeks, could be a few months.'

'A few weeks could help him?'

'So they say.'

A plan begins to form in Margaret's mind.

'Look,' Sadie says, 'I've got my money spider with me tonight.' She holds up a jam jar and Margaret can't believe it. There's a bloody big spider in it.

'What the hell?'

'Daniela says it's guaranteed to bring me some money.'

'Daniela?' Margaret laughs. 'That girl opens her mouth and lets any old shite tumble out. Makes it up as she goes along.' Daniela is Sadie's new Polish friend who lives in the flat below.

'She says she always has a spider with her when she wins.'

To be fair, Margaret does remember that Daniela won a big pile of money a few weeks back. 'Will any spider do?'

'She never said.'

'Why don't you pop it on the table in between us,' Margaret says, 'just in case.'

The hen party are still making a racket and tempers at the back of the room are becoming frayed.

Keep the fucking noise down.

Shut it, granny!

Just as the bouncers are being called, the screens around the room start flashing.

'This is it.' Sadie grips Margaret's arm and squeezes tightly. 'It's big money.'

Margaret's heart starts thumping. She's dreamt of winning big money since her husband died leaving her stony broke, and she's always imagined blowing it all on some big fancy holiday. Sadie's sister went on a cruise round the Caribbean last year and Margaret remembers how jealous she was when she saw all the photos. But now she's beginning to think she's got a better idea of what to do with the money.

The room holds its breath, and even the girls from the hen party have fallen silent. Margaret picks up her lucky red dabber. She changed to red after reading in the *Daily Mail* that it's a lucky colour in China, especially when it comes to money. She reaches out and touches the jam jar, and then focuses on the rows of numbers in front of her.

Sadie gets off to a flying start and her card is quickly covered with spots of blue whilst Margaret is still waiting on her first number. If Sadie wins because of a spider in a bloody jar she'll never get over it. *Fifty-six.* Another splodge of blue. They've never actually spoken about what they'd do if the other one won big money but surely they've been friends long enough that they'd split it two ways. It would be the decent thing to do. *Forty-two.* Sadie reaches over and points to a square on Margaret's card. Damn, she nearly missed it. She dabs it red and listens carefully for the next number. *Twenty-one.* The key to the door and another dab of red, maybe it's her lucky colour after all.

Her numbers keep coming and she can't breathe. There's only one box left on her card and it's the number thirteen. Unlucky for some. She thinks of her grandson, Robbie. It's his birthday soon and he's going to be a teenager. He's going to be thirteen. She's got a feeling this is going to be her lucky night. She stares at the last number on her card. If she wins tonight she's going to buy him something special to celebrate. The tension in the room is electric as everyone waits for the next number. Margaret grips her red dabber and whispers a quiet prayer to the spider...

Fourteen.

One away, she can't believe it.

'I've won,' screams one of the silly wee lassies from the hen party. Her friend leans forward and whispers in her ear. 'I mean house,' she shouts as she climbs on to the table and flashes her knickers at the bouncer who is trying to persuade her to get down. 'House,' she squeals waving her card in the air, and everyone in the room is praying it's a wrong call.

But it's not, and soon their whole table is celebrating. Three thousand pounds, that's how much she's won. Three thousand pounds. And all Margaret was waiting for was the number thirteen.

Sadie squeezes her hand. 'Never mind,' she says and looks down at the pattern of red splodges. 'Maybe next time.'

Thirty-One

Shit. It's Father's Day and I forgot all about it. I'm thinking I'd better buy him a really special card to put him in a good mood in case he finds out about the shirt. He doesn't know I've lost it yet but he's soon gonna ask why I've not worn it. I search through all of my pockets and even check underneath the cushions on the sofa until I manage to scrape over two pounds together. I'm not sure how much a card is gonna cost me but I hope that's enough. I think about looking in his wallet but he's still sleeping and I don't want to waken him before I'm ready. Besides, he probably shouldn't pay for his own card. Mum always bought it before, but this year he'll know that I've chosen it myself so I want to get one that he'll really like.

I count my money again and then head for the card shop at the other end of Gorgie Road. It's a bit further away but Mum says the cards are miles cheaper. As I pass the corner shop I catch the smell of frying bacon and my mouth waters. The chalkboard outside has a list of prices and I've got enough for a bacon roll but I shove my hands deep into my pockets and keep on walking until I get to the card shop. I stop and stare at the banners in the window. There are pictures of golf clubs and fishing rods, cars and yachts. Dad's not into any of these things and I cross my fingers there's a football card. He'll love it if I get him a football card. The coins in my pocket feel light and I'm scared I don't have enough.

It turns out I'm not the only one who's forgotten it's Father's Day and the shop is heaving when I get inside. Everyone's squashed around the half empty rows of cards near the door.

Mum always bought him a card with wee cutesy pictures before but I'm going to be a teenager soon so I'm thinking I'll choose something more grown up. I squeeze between a small group of women and manage to make it to the front but the cards say things like for a dear husband, a darling husband, a devoted husband! What's going on, I thought it was supposed to be Father's Day, not darling, devoted husband day. What's being a husband got to do with being a dad?

I duck and ignore the loud tuts as I fight my way further up the row. This time I'm even more confused because these cards are for granddads, grandfathers and papas. Isn't there a different day for grandparents, why the hell is everyone trying to take over a simple thing like Father's Day. And now I see a card for step-dad and one for being 'like a dad.' What's so fucking complicated? I mean, doesn't the name tell it as it is.

I feel like giving up but I imagine his face when he finds out it's Father's Day and I've not even got him a card. I'll go home and make him breakfast in bed like Mum used to do and I'll put the envelope on a tray with a cup of coffee and a slice of toast, and then later I'll ask him if we can go down the park for a wee kick around and then, fingers crossed, he'll suggest we go out somewhere for lunch. Me and him.

And wouldn't it be great if she walks by and sees me and Dad sitting having lunch together, laughing over some shared joke, probably about Hibs, and then she stops to watch us (I see her out of the corner of my eye but I don't look up) and she sees that we're fine without her. We're a team. Then she walks away but she can still hear our laughter drifting out of the open window and she knows. Knows that she should never have left us. But it's too late now 'cause we're doing fine. Dad and me.

I finally find the Father's Day cards, with no mention of being a step-dad, an adopted dad, or a granddad, just regular 'to my dad' cards. There's hardly any left and it looks like the small ones down the front are the cheapest, but they're all crap so I look at the next row and spot one with a photo of a chimpanzee dressed in a football strip and holding a ball. I turn it over. Eighty-nine pence. Result. I've got plenty of money. There's a joke inside about me inheriting his good looks and talent and I know this is the one to get him. It's perfect, it's funny and it's got a football on it. It's a shame the chimp's strip is the wrong colour, it's blue. But it could be worse, it could be wearing green. I pick up the card and count out my change. I've still got one pound fifty-two left to spend. Not enough for a bacon roll but maybe I can get him a present to go with the card, something that he can keep.

There's a big wire basket of soft toys near the tills and a shelf with Father's Day mugs, keyrings and photo frames squashed together on it. Everything looks cheap and I'm getting excited. I never thought I'd be able to afford to get him a present.

I put the card down on the shelf and rummage through the basket first, but everything's too girly or too babyish and my dad would hate most of it. I'm not too disappointed though 'cause I've still got the stuff on the shelf to look at.

'You okay there?'

I look up and there's this gorgeous girl standing in front of me. Her dyed red hair is tied back in a pony tail and I can make out the edge of a tattoo behind her ear. I think it might be a butterfly. She's wearing the shop's uniform and her name badge tells me she's called Fiona. I wonder if she gets called Fi for short. Fi's looking at me, waiting for me to answer.

'I'm looking for something for my dad 'cause it's Father's Day.'

Fiona (I've decided that's more sophisticated than Fi) laughs and I can't believe I just said that out loud, in here, with all the banners and posters. I'm such an idiot.

'What does he do?' she asks kindly, realising my embarrassment.

'Works in a factory.'

'What about in his spare time?'

'Not much,' I say. I don't think telling her that my old man spends his days drinking or falling asleep in front of the telly is going to impress her.

'Has he got any hobbies?'

I bet she's wishing she never started speaking to me now. 'He likes football,' I say and she smiles. Her smile is amazing and my dick thinks so too.

'Don't all men,' she says and I swear she winks at me. Holy crap, I'm dying here. Could she really fancy me? 'I think I might have the perfect gift,' she says and stretches up to the top shelf on her tip toes. As she reaches up, her blouse rises up too and I see that she has another tattoo at the bottom of her back. My eyes follow the trail of yellow stars down towards her bum and I imagine where they might end up. I'm sweating.

She's holding a small cardboard box in her hand and she's looking at me with this weird look. 'Are you okay?' she asks.

'Fine,' I say, 'it's just hot in here.' I can't shake the image of the stars leading down her arse and in between her legs. 'I like your tattoo,' I say. Fucking hell, what am I doing?

'Thanks. It's called a painted lady. I loved the irony of having a painted lady tattooed behind my ear. Most people haven't heard of them.'

'It's my Mum's favourite butterfly,' I say. I look at her and take a chance. 'But that wasn't the tattoo I was talking about.'

She giggles and I've made her blush. Oh man, this is going so well, any minute now she's going to ask me to meet her after the shop shuts. Or maybe I should ask her. I wonder if she'll let me see where the tattoo ends.

'Here,' she says and opens the box. 'We've got hardly any of these left, they've been so popular.' She holds out a green mug with the words *for a footy-mad dad* painted on the side. 'Will this do?'

'Almost, except the colour's all wrong. My Dad's a Hearts supporter.'

'A Hearts supporter, eh?' She laughs. 'Just like my boyfriend.'

Boom. There it is. She's got a boyfriend.

'I can see if we've got it in a different colour?'

Not even the thought of seeing her reaching up on her tiptoes can cheer me up. 'Don't bother,' I say and I pick up my card and walk to the till. The stupid chimp is laughing at me. I put the card on the counter and hand over my pile of copper coins. The girl with the tattoo groans.

Thirty-Two

Tracey can't afford to buy proper flowers at the supermarket but it felt wrong to come empty-handed so she picked some in the park on the way here. She remembers the day Robbie brought her daffodils home from school and she sent him to his room to punish him. She can still hear his words as he stormed upstairs in floods of tears. 'I picked them for you 'cause they're your favourites.' Before that day she used to always celebrate spring with a giant bunch of daffodils in a vase at the kitchen window, but she's never bought them again since. She kneels down and lays the flowers on the fresh turf.

'I've done it,' she whispers. 'I promised you I'd get out and I have. It's not quite the way we planned it but it's a step in the right direction. He hit me hard last time. *Really* hard. Almost as bad as the time, well, you know, and so I didn't have a choice. If I hadn't left I might never have got another chance. But...' The tears come before she can finish her sentence and she changes the subject. 'Robbie's hanging about with a boy called Dean Thomas and I don't know what to do about it. I don't want him hanging around with boys like that. Dean's dad walked out on his mum when he was just a wee boy and she turned to drink. Drink and men. She's always got a man staying, another uncle for Dean.' A seagull lands nearby and she shoos it away. She still has more to say. The words don't want to come and they feel heavy in her mouth but she forces herself to continue. 'I had to leave Robbie behind. I keep telling myself that it was the best thing for him, that he'll be better off without me.' She wipes away the tears. 'But what if I'm wrong?'

'I watched him come out of school the other day. He didn't know I was there but I wanted to see that he's okay. I wanted to see his face. If I'm really honest I think I wanted to check that he's got no bruises, although the bastard used to be clever about that and only ever punched where people couldn't see. But you noticed.' She spreads the flowers out across the grass. 'Robbie looked happy when I saw him, and I think he could maybe hide the black and blue bruises on the outside but I don't think he could hide the hurt that's on the inside. Not from me. He was laughing and fooling around with the other boy and I know I should feel happy about that. I mean, I am happy, of course. I'm glad to see that my boy's doing okay. But...' *Get over it*, she tells herself, *you were the one who walked out on him, why should he be missing you. Is that what you want? For your wee boy to be miserable without you.*

'It's his birthday soon and I've got just enough money for something special. He's turning thirteen. Thirteen. Can you believe it? The wee boy who used to play in your front garden.' She sits without speaking for several minutes. They could always sit comfortably in each other's silence. 'I'd never have done it without you and I know you can't hear me, but, well, I wanted to come and tell you. You'd be proud of me. I think.'

She hears footsteps on the gravel path and turns to see Angela, Mrs Carmichael's daughter. Tracey recognises her from the countless photographs she dusted over the years. Angela's graduation photograph sat pride of place on the mantelpiece where any visitors could see it. But hardly anyone ever visited Mrs Carmichael. The picture was later joined with a baby photograph of her grandson, Drew's boy. Mrs Carmichael rarely saw her grandson but she liked to pretend she knew everything about the boy. She'd always be asking Robbie what kind of toys he liked to play with and what TV programmes he liked to watch so that she could buy something for her grandson.

Tracey gets up to leave but there's only one path leading away from the grave and there's no way to avoid Angela.

'Please stay,' Angela says. 'Don't leave because of me.'

'I was going soon anyway. I just wanted to bring some flowers.' She blushes as Angela looks at the unwrapped spray of snapdragons, so obviously plucked from the earth.

'Please,' Angela says and holds out her hand towards her. 'I thought I could do this alone but now that I'm here...' She doesn't finish her sentence. She doesn't need to. Tracey nods to let her know she'll stay.

'I think I saw you at the funeral?'

The funeral had been a quick service in a local church and then a whistle stop visit to the grave side. Mrs Carmichael hadn't wanted a church service, she'd told her so herself. She said she'd stopped believing in any god a long time ago.

'It was a lovely service,' Tracey says.

'It was hideous,' snaps Angela, 'and Mum would have hated it but Drew insisted, said it was proper that the service was local. He didn't bloody care, just wanted somewhere quick and easy so he could get back down to London again. Made sure he took what he wanted before he left though.' Tears are running down her cheeks but she's still talking. 'He was always Mum's favourite. Couldn't put a foot wrong. And of course as soon as his boy was born, well, that was everyone else forgotten. Nobody was more important than her grandson.'

She's trying to light a cigarette but her hands are shaking too badly. Tracey gently takes the lighter from her and holds it towards the cigarette with a steady hand.

She smiles at her and Tracey can see the same little girl from the photographs. 'Thanks,' she says, 'and sorry for shouting. I'm a bit of a mess today. Father's Day is always difficult.'

Tracey had forgotten it was Father's Day. 'It's my wee boy's birthday tomorrow and I've bought him a remote control helicopter,' she pauses, 'He's going to be thirteen.' What is she doing? The woman's mum is dead and here she is telling her about her boy. If only she could explain how much Mrs Carmichael loved Robbie then maybe she'd understand.

Angela takes a long drag on her cigarette. 'Tell him happy birthday.'

Tracey wishes she could.

They sit in silence for a minute. She's thinking about her boy and she guesses Angela's thinking about her mum.

'I didn't think to bring her flowers.'

'You can bring them next time.'

'Maybe.'

'She loved primroses,' Tracey says.

'What?'

'She loved primroses. I think.' She doesn't say anything more and wonders if she should go.

'Come on,' Angela says. 'Let's get out of this place.' She stands up and brushes herself off. 'Let's grab a coffee. My treat.'

Thirty-Three

I sneak in through the back door when I get home from the card shop but I needn't have bothered because he's still in his bed. I take a pen from the kitchen drawer and try scribbling on an old envelope. It doesn't work. I try another but it doesn't work either. Why doesn't anything work in this house? I go to my school bag and take a felt tip from my pencil case. It'll have to do. Sitting at the kitchen table, I don't know what to write. I chew on my pen and wait for inspiration.

I hear his footsteps upstairs and panic. I quickly write *From Robbie* and seal the card inside the envelope. The upstairs loo flushes and I scribble *Dad* across the front of the envelope and jump up and flick on the kettle. I was planning to make him a cup of coffee and toast for his breakfast but there's no bread and I'm too late anyway. I can hear him coming down the stairs.

'Good morning,' I shout at him as he walks into the kitchen.

He scowls at me.

'Would you like a cup of coffee?'

He shakes a sachet of dissolving aspirin into a glass and runs cold water from the tap.

'Got a sore head?'

'What the fuck's it got to do with you,' he snarls at me.

I hide the card under my jumper and go up to my room to wait a while, hoping that the aspirin will put him in a better mood. I check my phone but as usual there are no messages. I think about texting Rachel. Her note told me to meet her tonight at the swings. Maybe I could ask her to come back here. I look around me at the mess. It shouldn't take too long to tidy.

I stand in the middle of the floor and imagine that the clothes are all back in the wardrobe, then I picture all of the empty wrappers and cans being swept into a giant bin and the dirty dishes all scrubbed and clean and neatly stacked in the kitchen cupboard. I sigh. It all seems like too much effort.

I look for Miss Green's copy of *Tom Sawyer*. Maybe I can have another go at trying to work out what the inscription on the inside cover says. I hunt through the pile but I can't find it which is strange 'cause I'm sure I left it beside my bed. I wouldn't leave it lying around downstairs in case Dad found it. He's always going on about how books are for girls. I try remembering when I last had it and I'm sure it was by my bed but it's definitely not there now. I check my school bag but it's not there either. I panic. Miss Green insisted that I look after it and I got the feeling it was special to her. She trusted me with it and now I've lost it. Shit, shit, shit. I can't bear to tell her that I've lost her precious book. It's not that I can even replace it because of the writing on the inside and she'll hate me forever when she finds out.

I turn my whole room upside down and now the place looks even worse, but I can't find the book anywhere. Where the fuck did I leave it? I go downstairs in a foul mood. Dad's been to the corner shop and now he's in the kitchen reading the sport section of the Sunday paper. He's made himself a cup of coffee and he's finishing off a bacon roll. My stomach growls at the smell.

'Smells great,' I say.

He doesn't look up from his paper.

'Did you get me one?'

'Haven't you had your breakfast?'

'I'll just have some toast,' I say, but then I remember there's no bread so I grab a packet of ready salted instead. 'Here.' I hand him the blue envelope.

'What's this?'

'Happy Father's Day,' I say.

He actually puts down the paper and smiles at me, and for a wee second I'm on top of the world. I don't exactly forget about losing Miss Green's book but for a moment it's not the most important thing in the world. He opens the card and laughs out loud at the picture of the chimpanzee.

'Brilliant,' he laughs, 'fucking brilliant.' And I think he's maybe talking about me. He stands the card up on the kitchen table and looks at it. 'Listen, son,' he says. 'I'm sorry if I snapped at you earlier. My head was killing me and I didn't mean to shout at you.'

'It was my fault,' I say. 'I should have brought you breakfast in bed for Father's Day. Sorry.'

'Apology accepted,' he says and goes back to his paper.

Thirty-Four

Angela drives Tracey to a garden centre on the edge of town. The sun is shining and the place is busy. They wait in line for coffee, hardly saying a word and she's wishing she'd made some excuse not to come.

Angela stops to grab some sugar and napkins while Tracey chooses a seat by the window, so if they've nothing to talk about at least they can watch what's happening outside. They sit opposite each other and stir their coffees in silence. Tracey tries to think of something to say.

'So your brother lives in London. Do you see him often?'

Angela looks at her. 'Not if I can help it.'

Tracey is surprised by the bitterness in her voice.

'Did Mum ever tell you about our father?'

She shakes her head. Mrs Carmichael had only mentioned her husband once and she told her that he'd died when her children were young. She'd always thought it was strange that there were no pictures of him in the house but had assumed it was too painful for her to be reminded of her loss.

'Dad was a doctor, and in our village that made him close to a god, and whenever we were out everyone in the street would stop and say hello to him. Even as a little girl I could see he was an important man.'

Tracey's tired. It's been a long day and she doesn't know if she can bear to hear this romantic tale of a daughter remembering her hero.

'Sometimes he would take me into his surgery and I'd get to sit at reception and watch the ladies answer calls from people who wanted to see him urgently. It was always urgently. Nobody ever wants to see a doctor tomorrow, it always has to be today. He was always busy. If he wasn't at the surgery, he'd be out on house calls and by the time he got home I'd be in bed. But I wasn't sleeping. I never was. I would lie and pinch myself to keep myself awake. And then I'd hear him. He shouted at her. Called her all sorts of names, words I didn't understand but I knew they were bad. Drew was a baby at the time and sometimes they'd shout so loud that he'd waken and I used to sneak through to his cot and take him through to my room. I'd play with him to get him to stop crying and then we'd cuddle in together until he'd go back to sleep. Sometimes when they were shouting I'd go through to Drew's room even if he was still asleep just so I wasn't alone. I suppose you think I was daft, deliberately staying awake to hear him come home. If I went to sleep then I wouldn't have heard what was going on. But you see, I was scared. Scared that one night he'd hurt her so bad that she'd die, and I wanted to make sure I'd be there to help her if it ever got that bad.'

Tracey sits in stunned silence. Has Robbie ever pinched himself to stay awake?

'I knew I couldn't stop him myself, after all I was only a little girl. But Dad had shown me how to dial 999 if I ever needed help and that was my plan.' Angela looks out of the window. 'Sounds stupid now, doesn't it? My great plan.'

'What age were you?'

'Drew was just a baby so I must have been about six or seven. He remembers none of it.'

Outside, a little boy helps his mum lift a conifer into a trolley. The tiny tree is almost the same height as the boy and he's beaming as he manages to get it high enough to go in. His happiness and the normality of the scene through the glass is hard to bear and Tracey is filled with a sudden urge to run and get her own boy.

'Then one night things got worse.' Angela pauses and

Tracey's scared to hear what she's got to say. 'He'd been out on a house call. I found out later it was to visit a young boy with asthma that he'd seen at the surgery earlier the same day. He'd told the boy's mum that there was nothing to worry about and that he would be fine. She called him back later, saying the boy's breathing was worse but instead of calling an ambulance Dad said he'd make a house call. By the time he arrived at the house it was too late. He called an ambulance but the boy died before it arrived and it was my dad's fault. That night he went back to the surgery before coming home. You see, my dad never went to the pub, as the local GP in a small village that would be frowned upon. And I never really saw him drink in the house. As far as I can work out, he only did his drinking at work. I'd like to think that he waited until he'd seen his last patient but I don't know for sure. Maybe he'd already been drinking that day.'

'What happened when he came home?'

'There was shouting as usual and I think he hit her. I think he hit her a lot but I never saw it. I was never brave enough to go downstairs. Drew woke up crying like he sometimes did and I went through to his room and lifted him out of his cot. I brought him through to my room and lay him down beside me. I could hear lots of yelling and stuff being thrown around but that wasn't too unusual. And then I fell asleep.'

Angela stops but Tracey knows there's more to come. Outside, the boy and his mother are choosing some bedding plants and he picks up a tray of summer pansies. She smiles at him and puts the pansies in the trolley next to the conifer. She then walks him over to the pallet of lavender and shows him how to rub the leaves between his fingers. She raises his hand up to his nose. He grins and rubs it again.

'When I woke up it was still dark. Drew was crying and my nightshirt was wet. His nappy was leaking and I was covered in my baby brother's pee. I couldn't get him to stop crying and I was scared that either Mum or Dad would hear him. I'd get into huge trouble for lifting him out of his cot. But nobody came. The house was silent so I took Drew through to his bedroom and changed his nappy in the dark. I knew how to do it because I'd helped Mum lots since he was born.'

Tracey could picture the little girl changing her brother's nappy in the darkened room. She'd often wondered what kind of brother Robbie would have made.

'I put Drew back in his cot but he started crying again. He was wide awake now and wanted fed. There was nothing else I could do. I needed to take him downstairs with me to get him a cup of milk. If I left him lying he'd scream the house down and waken Mum and Dad.'

The boy through the window doesn't want to leave the lavender plants and his mum is trying her best to persuade him to follow her. He's not listening.

'I carried Drew downstairs and let him down onto the floor. Seems a silly thing to remember but I can still see him crawling in to the kitchen as I switched the light on. The memory is frozen in black and white. A photograph.'

Suddenly, Tracey sees all of the photographs on Mrs Carmichael's dressing table. A happy family smiling for the camera. One picture is clearer in her mind than all the others. Angela is sitting on a tartan rug in the garden. She must be about seven years old and her baby brother is laughing as he clutches a football.

'You don't have to go on,' Tracey says. She's not sure she's strong enough to hear this out.

'Drew crawled across the lino towards a small plastic container which was lying beneath the kitchen table. He squeezed his way between the chair legs and sat himself down amongst the pills which lay scattered across the floor. He tried to pick one up but his chubby little fingers couldn't quite grip the coated shell. I stood and watched as he rolled them across the floor, desperately trying to clutch hold of one. I shouted on him to come but he thought it was a game and laughed when I shouted at him to leave the pills alone. "Come here Drew," I called. "Come and get a drink of milk." The promise of milk got his attention and he started to fuss again and was soon out from under the table and pulling on my nightshirt. I scooped him up and held him close. I think I scared him because I remember he started screaming again. But I didn't let go. You see, he hadn't spotted Mum and Dad. I'd left it too late with my plan to dial 999. I can't remember much that happened afterwards. There were the lights of the ambulance bouncing round and round the ceiling in the living room and a young police officer asking me questions and making me a drink of warm milk and I was thinking, "Why is she giving me milk? I'm not a baby." And then a man in a suit was telling me that my mum was going to be okay. But I don't remember anyone telling me that my dad was dead. I know they must have but I really can't remember. I suppose there must have been an inquest and a funeral. You see, being a doctor, he knew exactly how many barbiturates to take and I think he maybe tried to get Mum to take them too. I don't know because we never spoke about it.'

Tracey can't believe what she's hearing. She'd known Mrs Carmichael for twelve years and thought they shared everything. But now she sees. She was the one who shared and that was okay. That was the way Mrs Carmichael wanted it. She'd made her own escape years before when her children were still young and she wanted Tracey to do the same.

'We moved away from the village that year and I remember some things like starting at a different school, and making new friends, but I don't remember being sad without my dad. Drew was too young to remember him but he won't hear a bad word said against him. I tried talking to him after Mum died but he refuses to listen and says I'm making it all up. He even tried to suggest that maybe Mum provoked him. Sometimes I look at my brother and see my father and it terrifies me because I think Mum always hoped she got us out when we were still young enough.'

Tracey can tell Angela's thinking about her brother. If Drew was just a baby when the Carmichaels started a new life then why has he still turned out to be like his father? She thinks of Robbie. Is it possible that he'll turn out to be like his dad? She pictures him finding his dad dead at the kitchen table, pills scattered across the floor. Is it possible? She sees the picture again but clearer this time. Robbie is screaming. It's not pills that lie scattered at his father's feet but empty cans and bottles. She feels sick. What is she doing, leaving her boy with that man?

Angela interrupts the nightmare. 'I'm so sorry,' she says, 'I invite you for a coffee and then bore you with my life story. Tell me about you. Did you say you have a little boy?'

Tracey looks at her. 'His name's Robbie,' she says. 'Maybe next time you can meet him.'

Thirty-Five

The park's empty when I get there and I take a seat on a bench and wait for Rachel to arrive. She turns up pretty soon after me and she looks so amazing I'm hard straight away. We smile and say hi and then we're kissing. No messing about. I've been practising on my arm and I think it's helped 'cause we don't clash braces once. She keeps pushing her tongue against my lips and I open wide to let it in. It flickers against the roof of my mouth and my dick is so hard it's throbbing. Please God, don't let me come. I try picturing boring stuff but I keep seeing the photo of her in the gold bikini and I'm dying here.

And now she puts her hand on the inside of my thigh. Aw, man. Quick, think of something boring, think of anything but Rachel in that bikini. I try to picture Mr Johnson, sure that'll deflate any hard-on but she's slipping her hand up towards my cock. Aw, fuck. I cannae let her touch me.

Just as her hand reaches my balls she lifts it off. Thank Christ. Wait. Now she's taking hold of my own hand and she's moving it towards her. She's pushing it up inside her jumper. Inside her bra. Nipples, that's all I can think of. Nipples in a gold bikini.

She's pushing her tongue deep inside my mouth and I can hardly breathe. Her tit feels so soft in my hand but her nipple is brick hard under my fingers. Should I squeeze or rub? I've no idea.

Her hand is back on my leg and she's moving it up towards my zip. Squeeze or rub? Rub or squeeze? I try rubbing her nipple but she gives a yelp so I go back to squeezing but I don't

193

know if I'm doing it right. She's fumbling around and I wonder what she's doing down there when suddenly I'm free. My button's undone, my zip's down and she's slipped her hand inside my y-fronts and before I know it her fingers are brushing against my dick. I forget about the tit in my hand and I hear myself groan as she bites down on my lip. Aw fuck, I cannae help it, I'm going to come. She circles her hand round me and I'm groaning again. Her hand grasps me and she begins to slide it up and down. Up and down. I'm coming and there's nothing I can do to stop it.

I come in her hands and she's staring at my dick. She's smiling.

I'm not sure what she expects me to do. I take my hand off her tit and pull my zip up. I'm really gonna have to learn how to work the washing machine. She's trying to be discrete but I know she's wiping her hand on her jeans and I feel like I should say sorry or offer her a tissue or something.

Already I think of texting Dean. I almost laugh out loud, wait 'til I tell him about tonight's hand job.

We sit in silence and I don't know what to do next. We try kissing again but my dick's totally spent and she doesn't seem too bothered either.

'D'ya fancy going for a walk down by the canal?' I ask.

She shrugs her shoulders and we start walking away from the park. I try to work out which one is her clean hand so that I can hold it, but I'm not sure so I try not to think too much about it. We hold hands and walk under the tunnel in silence. I blush as I remember wanking off down here as I imagined squeezing her tits. I'm not sure tits are everything they're made out to be. I mean they felt alright but what are you supposed to do with them?

We make our way back up towards the road again and I try to remember some of the witty things I'd planned on saying to her. Here goes, this is the intellectual bit, the bit where we laugh and stay up half the night talking. This is when she leans her head on my shoulder and I tell her about the afternoon in the library when I noticed her for the very first time. I wonder if she'll blush and admit that she's secretly fancied me since our first day in high school. 'So, what do you think of *Tom Sawyer?*' I ask her.

She doesn't even look at me. 'It's alright,' she says, 'a bit boring. I mean it's not exactly *Twilight*, is it?' I stare at her but she doesn't even notice. She's too busy biting her nails and I really hope to God that's not the hand I came in. 'Is it?' she asks again.

'I don't know,' I say. 'I've never read *Twilight*.'

'Don't know why Miss Green gave it to me; she must think I'm some kind of nerdy geek. I gave her it back and told her I couldn't read it, said it was too hard, too old-fashioned. I hope she gets the message and stops giving me stuff to read. Thank God we'll get a different teacher next year.' She let's go of my hand. 'Come on, let's head to the school and see if anyone's about.'

I watch her walk away. What does she mean a different teacher? 'Wait up,' I shout. 'What do you mean we'll not get Miss Green?'

'Haven't you heard?' Rachel asks and I have no idea what she's on about. She laugh. 'Boys! You know nothing.'

I'm getting impatient now. 'Why aren't we getting Miss Green next year?'

'Because she's pregnant.'

'She's having a baby?'

'Jeez, you're smart. Yes, she's having a baby. Haven't you noticed she's gotten awful fat lately? Now get moving and try and keep up.'

I let her walk ahead. Pregnant? Miss Green?

Rachel stops. 'Look,' she points to the playing fields, 'there's some of the gang.'

I don't know who "the gang" are, so I squint and try to make out who she's pointing to. 'Come on,' she says and drags me by the wrist.

We cross the road without looking, and make our way over to the football pitch. Great! A bunch of boys from the year above are playing a team of first years and the only ones watching are girls. Now what am I supposed to do? I'll look a right fanny if I just stand about watching. I'll tell her I'm not feeling too well, that I'm going to head home, but I look up and she's gone. She's been absorbed into the crowd of girls and there's no way I'm gonna get a chance to speak to her now. Not that I'm bothered. Boring? How can she say *Tom Sawyer* is boring? Was she kidding me on? A couple of girls from our class drag her squealing and giggling to a corner of the field and they keep looking over to me. Aw man, this is so fucking awkward.

'Hope you didn't think you had any secrets?'

I look behind me and there's a girl from my English class standing there but I can't remember her name.

'I'm Susan,' she says as if she can read my mind. 'But people call me Susie.'

Now I remember who she is. Everyone at school calls her Weird Susie. Apparently she's into stuff like black magic and the occult. I'm rather disappointed because even out of uniform she looks kind of normal. 'Hi Susan,' I say.

'You do know that whatever you got up to with Rachel Jones is now public knowledge, with the girls anyway. And once Jen knows she'll tell John, and once Becky knows then Richard will know, blaa de blaa...'

'Who's Richard?' I ask.

'Becky's boyfriend. He's a second year.'

I look at the team of second years on the football pitch.

'Most of the girls go out with a second year. You're lucky Rachel so much as looked at you. Usually first years are considered way too immature to go out with. I hope you knew what you were doing.' I haven't got a clue what this girl's going on about and she can see it on my face. 'You did kiss her?' she asks me. I nod. 'Did it go any further?'

'None of your fuckin' business.'

She laughs in my face. 'It's everybody's business, didn't you hear about Ruth?'

'Everybody's heard about Ruth,' I say. 'She's the slapper that sleeps with any guy that tries.'

'Get my point?' Susie says. 'Pretty soon everyone in our school will know every detail of your wee date with Rachel but don't fret, I'm sure it went fine.' She shuffles about and I know she's dying to ask me something.

'Go ahead,' I say. 'You might as well ask. By the sounds of things you'll know what happened pretty soon anyway.'

She's not brave enough to look me in the eye as she leans forward. 'I was wondering if you were, you know, if you were able...'

'Just fuckin' ask,' I snap.

'Okay, okay. I wondered if you were able to get it up?

'Jesus fuck.'

'You told me to ask.'

'I didn't think you'd ask that.'

'Oh come on, with a nickname like yours, everyone's gonna want to know if Rachel could get you to have a hard-on.'

I look across at Rachel. She's standing with a group of girls and they're all laughing and chatting and I know they're talking about me. 'Okay,' I say. 'You asked me a question, now it's my turn to ask you. Is that the only reason she asked me out, to see if my nickname was true or not? Was it some kind of bet or dare?'

Susie shrugs her shoulders and looks away.

Oh, this is great. So the only reason Rachel went out with me was to find out if I could get a hard-on. I feel like such a fucking idiot. No wonder she was so quick to squeeze my fucking dick.

Bitch.

Thirty-Six

It's his birthday tomorrow and Tracey's bought him something special, something he's always wanted. It cost her most of this week's wages but he's turning thirteen and it's important that she gets him something he'll remember for becoming a teenager. It flies by remote control and the man in the shop showed her how it works and helped her pick out the right batteries. Robbie'll love it, she knows he will. She's hidden it in the top drawer tucked in between her t-shirts where John won't see it. He doesn't like her to talk about Robbie, says she'll never be able to move on unless she forgets about both of them. But she can't forget his birthday.

The forecast for tomorrow is sunshine and this makes her smile. It was a glorious sunny day when her boy entered her life and she still remembers it like it was yesterday. The birth was straightforward and within a few hours she had pushed her baby boy out into the world and was cradling him in her arms. She didn't sleep a wink the night after he was born because she couldn't take her eyes off him, couldn't stop looking at him. Over and over again she counted his ten perfect little fingers and his ten perfect little toes and she couldn't believe that she'd created this gorgeous little human being.

She lifts his present out of the drawer and admires it. She tries to picture his face when he opens it. The sheet of wrapping paper is metallic blue and it cost her a pound but it's worth it and she carries it through to the kitchen with the remote control helicopter. The dishes from lunch are washed and away and the kitchen table is clear. John likes everything to be in its proper place. When she first moved in she planned to clean the house for him when he was out working, make herself useful and help her feel like she was paying her way. But his house is spotless and there's never anything to clean. He washes his cup every time he uses it, hoovers each morning before he goes out to work and puts bleach down the loo every night.

The blue foil shimmers as she unfolds it and spreads it out flat across the table. She smoothes the paper carefully with her hands and goes in search of scissors and sellotape. She finds a pair of scissors in the cutlery drawer but she can't find a roll of sellotape anywhere. She searches each of the kitchen drawers methodically, which isn't difficult because each one she opens is organised and tidy. Neatly folded tea towels, matching utensils and a set of plastic chopping boards stacked according to size. She finds a collection of takeaway menus and bets that if she looks closely she'll find they're arranged alphabetically. But where's the sellotape? Her kitchen drawers at home are the complete opposite of these, filled with assorted junk like old supermarket coupons, used batteries and pens that no longer work, but at least they contain all of the necessary equipment for wrapping a child's birthday present.

She continues her search in the living room where she opens the drawers under the coffee table only to find the same neatly organised piles, only this time it's National Geographic magazines and a pile of what she assumes are birthday cards (organised by size of course!). What she wouldn't give to discover a messy cupboard or drawer, something...normal. She can't resist having a little look through the birthday cards and removes the elastic band that's holding them together. She doesn't stop to question what she's about to do, expecting to find that they're from his mum or some great aunt who lives down south. They're not. Every card is signed from the same woman. Stacey. She laughs. Stacey, Tracey; maybe he chooses his women according to their name.

'What are you doing?'

She hadn't heard the front door open. 'You're home,' she says which is a stupid thing to say.

'Mum isn't feeling too great so I thought I'd come home early and surprise you but it seems you're the one surprising me.'

John takes his mum out for dinner every Sunday night. Just another part of his routine. 'I was looking for sellotape.' She throws the cards back into the drawer, the elastic band that bound them together still dangling from her wrist. 'I need to wrap a present and...' Shit. Robbie's helicopter is on the kitchen table.

'I thought we agreed you're never going back.'

'But I can't forget his birthday. I've always left his presents at the end of his bed so that when he wakes up everything is there for him to open. If I don't get him something he might get nothing and that wouldn't be right, would it?' She waits for him to speak. 'He's going to be a teenager tomorrow. Don't you remember when you were thirteen?'

John picks up the box and the sheet of wrapping paper and carries them to the bin in the corner. 'It's up to his dad to buy him a present now,' he says and lifts the lid.

She looks away before she can see him throw it in the bin.

He ignores her tears. 'Have you eaten?'

Without waiting for her answer he opens a tin of tomato soup and heats it slowly over the hob as they stand in awkward silence. She knows he's angry and he avoids looking at her as he sets the table, complete with table mats and coasters. She pours them both an orange juice and sits down at the table and waits for him to serve the soup. Anyone watching would think they've been married for years. He puts the bowl in front of her and places his hands on her shoulders. 'I'm sorry if you think I'm being hard,' he says and kisses the top of her head. 'But I need you to trust me. Give it a couple of days and you'll see I'm right.'

They hardly say a word over dinner and he doesn't mention it again. He pecks her on the cheek as he heads out to the gym (after washing the plates and returning them to their correct place in the cupboard, cup handles facing outwards in a perfect row) and she waits five minutes until she's sure he's not going to return. She knows he'll see the helicopter is gone but she'll worry about that later.

Half an hour later, Tracey stands beneath the lamp post and stares up at his bedroom window, gripping the parcel tightly in both hands. The metallic blue paper stinks of vinegar and is covered in tea stains, but she managed to cover the worst of it with the birthday card. The card has a picture of a t-rex on it. Robbie loved dinosaurs when he was growing up and t-rex was always his favourite. She wrote a message inside the card, nothing too sentimental but she wants him to know she's thinking of him. Her boy turns thirteen tomorrow and she needs him to know that she remembered.

Before coming over, she rang the house from the phone box several times and each time there was no answer but she still waits to check there's no movement inside the house or any lights on. Maybe they've gone out for Father's Day. Finally sure no one's home she walks up the path, surprised that it feels so unfamiliar and strange. It's like she's watching this through someone else's eyes.

She takes out her key and slips it in the lock but it sticks. She looks around but none of the neighbours are in their gardens and the street is quiet. She tries again to slide the key into the lock but it stops halfway. She doesn't understand. Has he changed the locks? This thought takes her by surprise. How dare he? It's her house too. She tries one last time to push the key into the lock and she realises too late what's going on.

The door swings open and he's there in front of her.

'What the fuck do you want?' He's drunk.

'I've come to leave a present for Robbie.'

'He's not fucking here.'

He sounds like he's been drinking all day. Where's Robbie? She tries to see over his shoulder but he moves to block her view.

'You don't fucking live here anymore,' he says.

She tries to push past him. 'I just want to leave this for him.' she says.

'Are you fucking deaf? I've told you the boy's not here.' He grips the door frame to stop her getting past but he's slow and she ducks under and runs in to the house.

'Robbie,' she screams. 'Where are you?'

The door slams shut behind her and even his laughter is slurred. 'Where are you going to run to this time?'

He's got her trapped but all she can think of is Robbie. 'Where is he?'

'What do you care?' he says. He takes a step closer and she stands her ground. 'You're the one who walked out. Left your boy.'

'I know he's here,' she says. She tries to get to the stairs but he throws his fist out and it meets her square in the face. The blow stops her and she drops the present to the floor. 'Robbie,' she screams, 'it's me, Mum.'

'He's not your boy anymore.'

Warm blood is running down her face and into her mouth. The pain is excruciating but she needs to get Robbie out of here. She looks around the hall for a weapon but there's nothing. She's too slow.

He forces her back against the wall and she can feel him press against her. He grabs her hair and leans in close, and she remembers every time he's ever hurt her. Every slap, nip, punch and cut. Terror rushes through her body and she fights to stay upright. His hands move to her breast and she has nowhere to go. She feels his erection push hard against her pelvis. 'Missed me?' Spit sprays over her cheek.

She needs to start using her brain and focus because she knows that if she tries to fight him he's going to kill her. He's drunk and that means she's faster than him. If she can get to the front door she can get away but what if Robbie is lying hurt upstairs? What if he needs her?

'Where have you been, bitch?' he growls in her ear.

This might be her only chance. 'I've been fucking another man.'

If she thought the element of surprise would buy her some time she's never been more wrong. He grabs her so tight she knows her wrist will snap is she tries to struggle free.

'You little slut,' he pants and he's unbuckling his belt. 'Slut,' he yanks her leggings down. She tries to move but he tightens his grip on her wrist. 'Slut,' he forces himself in. She bites down to stop her screams. Please don't let Robbie be in the house. Please let him be far away with his friends. She feels herself rip as he pushes his way inside her. 'Dirty little slut.' Tears run down her face. Where is her boy? 'Slut... slut... slut...'

He shudders and it's over. He pushes himself off her and without looking back he disappears upstairs.

Thirty-Seven

A grubby, battered parcel is lying in the hallway when I get home and I guess it's my birthday present from him. I don't bother trying to sneak a look at what's inside. I'm surprised he remembered.

My head's been spinning the whole way home and it feels like someone keeps changing the channel in my brain. Rachel didn't even look my way when I left the football pitch tonight. Bitch. And Miss Green is leaving me to have a baby. She's leaving and I've got a hundred questions, like when is she having the baby, and how long will she stay off work for after it's born? And where has her copy of *Tom Sawyer* disappeared to? And where's Mum? If Mum was here I could ask her about these things. I need to find Miss Green's book soon or she might not want to teach me again. I wonder if Dad's been in my room and taken it, but why would he take *that* book? And then the channel in my head changes and I'm thinking of Rachel again. I picture us kissing and touching, and her touching me, and then it changes again and I see weird Susie telling me that Rachel only asked me out to see if she could make me get a stiffie. I feel hot inside. Raging.

Dad is lying passed out on his bed with his trousers around his ankles and the room stinks of piss. A bottle of beer sits untouched on his bedside table and I help myself. It goes down quick and my head starts to clear. I'm feeling brave and I switch on my computer and watch the cold, blue glow come alive. I log into Facebook and go straight to her page and find the picture of her in the gold bikini. I stare at her tits as I unzip my jeans. This won't take long. I'm ready for her this time.

'Bitch. Fucking, teasing, little bitch.' It's over quickly and I pull my jeans back up and stare at her wall. Her last post is a photograph of her painted nails. Loving life! Smiley face. Twenty-six likes.

I click my mouse on 'write post' and start typing.

Rachel Jones sucks pussy!

Let's see how many likes this one gets.

I switch off my computer and sit in the darkness. It's my birthday tomorrow and Mum's still not here. She always sneaks into my room and leaves presents at the bottom of my bed for me to open in the morning. Last year I got Fifa for the X-box. 'Might as well see if you can play it on your machine,' Dad said, 'because you sure as hell can't play any worse than in real life.' That started a row and I turned my television all the way up to drown out the shouting. It didn't work. We were supposed to go out for a pizza but Dad stormed off to the pub so Mum and I sat at the kitchen table and ate cake instead.

'I'm going to be thirteen tomorrow,' I announce to the empty room. 'A teenager.' A ripple of excitement shudders through me. Me and the boys have got big plans for tomorrow. We'll show the teachers what we think of them. My cock starts to stir again. The bottle is empty and I head downstairs to get another one from the fridge. Dad's so drunk, he'll never notice that one's missing. I stand at the kitchen window and lift the bottle to my lips. Her yellow, rubber gloves still hang over the draining board. They've been there since the night she left. Since the night she walked out. She hasn't been back, not even once. I could be dead and she wouldn't know.

Mrs Carmichael's butterfly sits on the windowsill and watches me. Mum never let me hold it. Said it was too precious. Fragile. I pick it up and hold it in two hands. 'She's forgotten about you too,' I whisper. I open my hands to let it fly and it falls to the ground and shatters into a thousand pieces.

Thirty-Eight

Margaret dips a custard cream in the hot tea and holds it there just long enough for the cream to soften. She's seen this episode of *Poirot* before but she loves his attention to detail and the way he uses his *little grey cells*. She wonders if Robbie likes detective shows. It's his birthday tomorrow and she plans to take his present over after school and then they can sit down and plan their future together.

A car pulls up outside the house and she pushes herself up out of her seat, just enough to see what's going on. It doesn't do well to stick your nose into other people's business around here, but still, she likes to think of herself as the neighbourhood watch. She peers out the window and sees the yellow roof light of a taxi. No-one round here ever gets a taxi, especially not on a Sunday night. She turns the TV down and watches to see who gets out the back of the car.

She's shocked to see Tracey and it looks like she's limping. Margaret holds her breath and waits to see if anyone else gets out of the car but no-one does. Tracey's alone and she breathes a sigh of relief knowing that Robbie's still not with his mum.

She's been thinking about the boy a lot lately, imagining what it'd be like if he came to stay with her. It's not such a daft idea. She'll need to tidy up a bit, but there's the spare room upstairs and she's checked to see he can catch a bus outside that takes him close to his school. When she's out at bingo in the evening he can stay in and play his video games. It's perfect. She'll make sure he's properly fed and wash his clothes for him.

At first she'd thought about moving in with them but that

wouldn't work. She'd be too far away from the bingo, and her doctors, and she'd have to find a new hairdresser. No, it's too complicated. The best idea is if Robbie comes to stay with her. She's gone over her plan several times and can't find a reason why it won't work, but as she watches Tracey step away from the taxi she feels her heart plummet. Could Tracey interfere with her plans?

The doorbell rings and for a split second Margaret considers not answering it but she knows Tracey will have seen her through the window. The bell rings again and she curses as her custard cream falls into the cup. She won't let the boy's mother interfere with her plans. She opens the door and stumbles backwards in shock. Blood is smeared across her daughter-in-law's face.

'Can I come in?'

Margaret opens the door and ushers her along the dark hallway and through to the kitchen. Tracey sits down at the table and Margaret switches the kettle on. The kettle soon starts to boil and the sound fills the awkward silence that sits heavy in the room. It hasn't quite finished boiling when Margaret lifts it and pours water into the chipped mug sitting on the bench. The teabag floats, bloated on top for a few seconds before she stabs at it with a spoon, plunging it downwards and then plucking it back out. She dumps it in the bin, ignoring the streaks of brown that dribble down the side.

She slams the mug of weak, milky tea in front of Tracey and stays standing. 'So, what happened?'

Tracey stares in to her mug for a minute before she speaks. 'A few weeks ago I left home.'

'I know.'

Tracey looks up at her. 'Oh.' Another minute passes before she speaks again. 'It's Robbie's birthday tomorrow so I went back to the house with his present.' She smiles into the mug. 'He's gonna love it. It's a remote control helicopter. Bright red. And you can even fly it inside.'

Margaret thinks of the goalie gloves that are already wrapped and waiting by the front door for tomorrow. Would he really rather have a helicopter? Isn't he getting a bit big for toys now? 'He's in the school football team, you know?'

'What?'

She smirks as she realises that she knows the boy better than his own mother does. 'He's been picked as goalie for their next away game.' A little white lie but it'll do no harm.

Tracey's hands are shaking as she lifts the mug of tea. 'That's great.'

Each passing second is marked by the slow, sombre beat of the kitchen clock. Tracey finally breaks the silence with three small words. 'He raped me.'

'Who did?'

'Your son.'

'Don't be stupid. He's your husband, how can he rape you?'

'I went back to the house to leave Robbie's present and *he* was there.'

'Of course he was there, it's his house.' Margaret can't believe what she's hearing but she needs to tread carefully, try and find a way to get Tracey to leave. Forever. She knew she was a trouble maker the first time they met and she's never trusted her. For years he did what she told him to, and they never visited, never came to see how she was. But all that's about to change. Things would be so much simpler if Tracey would disappear out of their lives. 'Sex isn't always about kisses and cuddles, you know. A man has his needs. You've been gone for weeks now. What did you expect when he's had to go without for so long?'

'He forced himself on me.'

'You're making this up.'

Tracey throws her arms outwards. 'Look at me.' Red marks circle her wrists where he gripped her tightly.

'So you like it a bit rough.'

'He pushed me against the wall, held me there, hurting me,

and then he forced himself inside me and fucked me as I cried.'

'Stop it,' Margaret screams.

'Your son raped me.'

Margaret slaps her. 'Shut up. Shut the fuck up.'

Tracey reaches up and grabs Margaret by the hand. 'Please, I'm begging you, I need your help. Let me stay the night.'

Margaret remembers the morning after her son's wedding when Tracey turned up on her doorstep, exactly like she did tonight, asking for help. Margaret had quickly put her in her place. What goes on behind closed doors is no-one else's business. It's between a husband and wife. God knows, she'd put up with enough herself and hadn't complained once.

'Please, just one night to let me think things over. I promise you I'll be gone in the morning. I've nowhere else to go.'

Margaret snaps. 'You little bitch. How dare you? You come into my house, accusing my son, and then you say you want to stay here and think things over. Do you know what I think? I think your new boyfriend did this to you. He's the one that likes things a little rough and you didn't like it. And then you have the fucking nerve to turn up on my doorstep asking for help.' She yanks the mug out of Tracey's hand spilling tea across the table and floor. 'It's time you were leaving.'

'Margaret, wait.'

'You've said enough.'

'I'm begging you to listen to me.'

'Enough.' She throws open the back door. 'Now get out.'

Thirty-Nine

I wake up but don't open my eyes. It's my birthday, but I don't want to get out of bed yet, I want to lie here for a few minutes longer and pretend everything's back to normal. Mum is downstairs making breakfast and Dad's in the bathroom getting ready for work. Any second now she's going to yell upstairs, telling me to get up or I'll be late for school. I lie still and listen but all I can hear is the rain battering off the pavement outside. My window is wide open and it's freezing. What a stupid, childish idea, hoping she might return through an open window on the second floor. What was I thinking? I'm thirteen now. I'm not a wee kid anymore. It's time I grew up.

I drag myself out of bed and stand in front of the mirrored wardrobe. I don't look different. I don't feel different. The door frame is graffitied with pencil marks up one side, a line for every year. I stand against the frame, heels back against the wood, feet flat on the floor and I reach up to put my hand on my head to mark the spot. But there's no-one to help me. No-one to show me how much I've grown.

There are no birthday cards waiting downstairs for me, no brightly coloured envelopes poking through the letterbox. Even the battered present that was lying in the hall has disappeared. I tell myself that she's not forgotten but I don't believe it.

I don't bother making myself any breakfast. I'm not hungry. I have a quick shower and get myself dressed and ready for another Monday at school.

On the school bus Dean sits behind me as usual. 'Today's the day,' he says but he's not talking about my birthday. This is the day we agreed to each take revenge on our chosen teacher. 'Let's meet at the old bike shed at the end of the day.'

'Can't,' I say. 'I need to get home early.'

'Why?'

'None of your fuckin' business.'

'Alright, alright.' He holds his hands up in surrender. 'We'll meet at lunchtime instead. Gives us less time to do it but hey, might make it a bit more exciting eh? Get the old adrenaline going and all that.' He peers through the grimy window. 'So how did your date with Rachel go? I saw her at the football pitch after and noticed you didn't hang around.'

'Had things to do.'

'Like what?'

'What is it with you and your fuckin' questions this morning? I'll say it again, slowly this time. It's none of your fuckin' business.'

'Fuckin' hell. Someone got out the wrong side of the bed.'

'Did you hear about Miss Green?' I ask him.

He slaps me on the arm. 'So that's what's wrong with you?' He laughs. 'You fancy our English teacher.'

'Fuck off.'

'Yeah, I heard she was up the duff. And she had the fuckin' cheek to stand up there and teach us how to put a condom on. Wish we'd know then, we could have had some fun.'

'The bitch doesn't give a shit about us.'

'Whoa, calm down big man. She's just a teacher. Wait and see who we end up wi' when she leaves. My money's on Hairy Harrison.'

'Who?'

'Hairy Harrison. Come on, you must have seen her. So hairy she looks like a man. I swear she's even got a beard. Callum reckons she has to shave every morning like a man.'

'What the fuck does Callum know about shaving? His face is as smooth as a baby's arse.'

Dean laughs and things are okay again.

'So, have you thought anymore about how you're gonna steal Johnson's phone.'

I look at my bag on the floor beside me. 'Not sure yet,' I say. I'm keeping my plan to myself for now, they'll find out soon enough. 'What about you? Who are you going to get back at?'

The prick laughs at me and taps the side of his nose. 'Wait and see,' he says, 'wait and see.'

We're coming up to Rachel's stop and I stay facing Dean, keeping my back to the front of the bus. I'm determined she's not going to see me looking at her. I try to think of something funny to say so she'll see us laughing. 'Callum's face is as smooth as a baby's arse,' I try again but Dean looks at me as if I'm off my fuckin' head.

He punches me on the arm. 'Oi, fuckwit. There's your girlfriend.'

I shrug my shoulders. 'Whatever.'

'You two fallen out?'

'Just ready to move on,' I say. No idea what I'm talking about, but it sounds good. Sounds mature. Like something a teenager would say. I say it again. 'Ready to move on.'

Dean moves closer. 'Did she not let you finger her?' I don't answer but he nods to himself anyway. 'I get it,' he says, 'I get it.'

The bus drives on.

Today is the slowest day ever and I wish it would hurry up and be lunchtime so I can get on with what I've planned to do. We've arranged to meet up at one o'clock and I know the boys are gonna be impressed. I just wish the clock would turn faster because so far my day has been shit. I've broken a beaker full of acid in science and told my new French teacher she looks like an enormous donkey. That one was Dean's fault. I'd missed last week's lesson on adjectives and let him whisper the answer in my ear. Madame MacDonald was furious.

'What's the big deal?' Dean asks. We're walking along the

corridor on our way to English.

'I could have got detention.'

'Come on, it would have been worth it to see the look on her face.' He laughs. 'Besides you've had detention before. It's no big deal.'

'I told you. I need to be straight out after school.'

'What's so fuckin' important?'

'I just don't need another detention.'

'Stop going on about it,' Dean says. 'You sound like a big baby.'

'You're the one that needs to fuckin' grow up,' I say and that's it. Dean storms off along the corridor in a big huff and doesn't even bother to wait on me when he gets to class. I try sitting beside him but he scrapes his chair out and moves to the table behind. A couple of the boys in the class slap me on the back and congratulate me on my "fantastique français". Or at least, I think that's what they say. I'm no good at French.

I sit down and sneak a wee look at Miss Green's belly but it's impossible to tell how fat she is 'cause she's wearing a baggy top. She catches me looking and I pretend to be busy getting my book out of my bag. I'm totally prepared for any questions she might fire out about the final chapters of *Animal Farm* but Miss Green doesn't even look at us as we settle down. 'Take out your jotters and copy from the board.' That's all she says to us and we do as she asks without any protest which is kind of unusual. I guess everyone can sense that something's up 'cause we all sit in silence and copy a long list of definitions for metaphors, similes and on and on. Boring, boring, boring. I want her to lean against her desk like she always does as we read from the book. I'm ready to discuss the importance of the change in the seven commandments but she doesn't say a word. She doesn't even look my way. She might as well have left us already 'cause she can't even be bothered to give a proper lesson today. I wish the bell would hurry up and ring.

Every class I've been in today has the date written in big

letters on the whiteboard. Monday, 18th of June. My birthday. But no one has wished me a happy birthday. I look at the clock on the classroom wall and count down the final minutes 'til the end of the lesson. At last the bell rings but as I get up to leave Miss Green tells me to wait behind. She stands by her desk as everyone else pushes to get out of the door. I try to catch Dean's eye as he leaves but he doesn't look my way.

Eventually everyone's gone and Miss Green pulls a jotter out from under a pile of folders. I recognise it straight away.

Without saying a word she opens the jotter to a page near the end and I'm faced with my own scribbled handwriting across the centre of the page. *Who Fucking Cares?*

'Did you do this?' she asks.

I think about making up a story but what's the point. She already knows that I wrote it. I nod.

She closes the jotter again. 'I thought you might want to chat.'

She thought I might want to chat. What does she care? She's bailing out on us anyway. Deserting us. 'There's nothing to talk about,' I say.

'How are you?'

I pull myself tall, look her straight in the eye and grin. 'Never been fucking better, Miss. What about you?'

I wait for her to blush and look down at the desk, but instead she reaches out her hand and touches my arm gently. She isn't giving up. 'What did you think of the book?'

I stare at the ground. 'It's a pile of crap.'

'Oh.'

I hear the disappointment in her voice and my stomach clenches in a tight fist.

'I thought you'd enjoy it. Especially the parody between the pigs and the Russian revolutionaries.'

'Who gives a shit about Stalin or Tolstoy?' I say. 'They're both fuckin' dead.'

She shrinks into the chair behind her desk. 'I thought you

wanted to learn, wanted to make something of your life.' She looks away. 'I thought you were different.'

I wait for her to say something more but instead she opens the first jotter that sits on the top of the sloping pile on her desk. She lifts a pen and begins writing in the margin.

'Miss?'

'You'd better get a move on,' she says without lifting her head. 'You'll be late for your next class.'

Forty

Anna slams the staffroom door. After everything she's done for him, all the extra books and encouragement, and then he treats her like that. What an idiot she's been. Thank God she's leaving soon and it'll be up to his next teacher, Mrs Harrison, to sort him out.

'Everything okay?'

'Fine,' she snaps. She can't believe *he's* in here; she only wants a cup of coffee in peace.

'How were your first years this morning?'

She ignores the question and snatches a tea bag from the box beside the empty biscuit tin. She's not about to tell Derek Johnson what just happened. He'll only say he told her so. She shuffles past him and reaches up to take her mug out of the staffroom cupboard. The three words painted on the side stare her in the face and she stops.

World's Best Teacher

She leaves the mug sitting on the shelf, drops the teabag in the bin and storms out of the staffroom. There's no way Derek is going to be right about Robbie. She's not stupid. She knows she's nearly lost the boy but a tiny part of her still believes she can reach out to him.

The school secretary is busy on the phone, and Anna tries her best to stay invisible as she slips into the office and slides open the drawer to the filing cabinet. She flicks through the manila files until she reaches the letter M and then slows until at last she finds the contact details for Robbie MacFarlane. A number for the house phone is listed along with a mobile number for both parents. She scribbles his address and all three numbers onto a yellow sticky but hopes she'll get through first time on the home phone. She hates catching a parent on their mobile because they're usually at work or in the supermarket. Either way they're always distracted.

She slips the file back into the drawer and pretends to concentrate on her registration folder as she heads back to her classroom, praying she doesn't bump into Derek Johnson on the way. She locks her classroom door and takes out her mobile. She dials the first number on the list but it rings out. Next she tries Mum's number but an electronic message informs her there's no connection. She looks at the eleven digit number for the dad but doesn't key in the numbers. A phone call won't make any difference. Instead, she knows she's going to ignore Derek's advice and visit the house. She's got a free period just now and then it's lunch break which gives her plenty of time to go round and see if anyone's home. If she doesn't act soon she's sure things are going to get worse for Robbie.

She scribbles a note and leaves it on her desk in case Derek comes looking for her. She smiles at her excuse. It seems you never quite grow out of telling little white lies.

At dentist, back by 1pm

She picks up the yellow sticky with Robbie's address on it and heads for the car park.

The house is in a street straight off Gorgie Road and sits in the middle of a row of tenements. It's taken longer to find the address than she expected but the road is quiet at this time of day and she manages to park straight outside. She takes a deep breath and reminds herself why she's here. There's no record of social work involvement and there's nothing in any of his reports from primary school to suggest violence or neglect but her gut instinct tells her that his behaviour is due to more than just hormones. He's pushing her away, stopping her from finding out what's going on.

217

She tells herself not to be judgemental as she walks up to the front door but she can't help notice that the garden's overgrown and there's an empty irn-bru bottle lying amongst the weeds. She presses the doorbell and takes a step backwards. No answer. Maybe the doorbell's not working. She puts out her hand and knocks three times on the wooden door. *One, two, three.* She waits. This time she hears someone moving around inside. She knocks again. *One, two, three, four times.* 'Come on,' she mutters, 'I don't have all day.' She steps up on to her tip toes and looks in the living room window. Flickering shadows from the TV dance around the room and she swears someone has just turned the volume up. It seems no-one wants to speak to her. She thinks about turning round and leaving but then she remembers the anger in Robbie's voice this morning. This is the same boy who loves reading Mark Twain.

This time when she bangs on the door she doesn't stop until someone answers it. She's speechless when the door is finally opened. The resemblance is so strong that it knocks her for six. The man in front of her is Robbie's double. Although that's not quite right, is it. She should say that Robbie is the double of the man standing in front of her. Of course Robbie's much younger, but the mouth and eyes are identical. Well, not exactly identical. She can't put her finger on it, but there's something unnerving about this man's eyes and she wonders if Derek Johnson could have been right and whether she should have taken his advice.

She's been standing here for what feels like a minute and he still hasn't said a word so she bites the bullet and starts the conversation. 'Mr MacFarlane?'

He puts his hands on his hips and nods once.

'Are you Robbie's father?'

Another single sharp nod.

'I was wondering if I could have a word with you about your son.' She waits for a response and realises she hasn't introduced herself. 'Sorry,' she stumbles over the words. 'I'm Miss Green.

From the high school. I'm one of Robbie's teachers. His English teacher.'

'You look like a teacher.'

She doesn't know what to say to this and tries again. 'Like I think I said, I was hoping to speak to you and your wife about Robbie.'

'I'm listening.'

Is he not going to invite her in? She really doesn't want to speak about one of her pupils on the doorstep. 'Is your wife in?'

'No.'

'Can I come in for a moment, maybe we could chat about Robbie over a cup of tea?' She tries smiling. 'I'll even offer to make it.'

'Listen, Miss whatever your name is, just say what you've come to say and then leave.'

She takes a moment to recall the first line of the speech she rehearsed on the way over here in the car. 'Mr MacFarlane,' she begins, 'I've noticed lately that Robbie doesn't seem to be spending as much time reading as he usually does.'

'About time he grew out of all that girly nonsense.'

His remark throws her for a second but she keeps going. 'I have some concerns about his class work. He's a bright lad but lately his mind has been elsewhere.'

'Football.'

She looks at him. 'Pardon?'

'The boy's into football, like the rest of the boys his age.'

She doesn't know what to say. Robbie MacFarlane is one of the least physical boys she's ever taught. From what she hears in the staffroom the boy couldn't even catch his own shadow let alone tackle a ball from someone.

'He's a great wee goalie.'

The man in front of her isn't listening to a word she's saying and it's time to get straight to the point. 'I was wondering if there could be anything that's worrying Robbie lately, he seems a bit distracted in class and hasn't been completing his written

219

work.'

He comes outside to join her on the top step but there's barely room for both of them and she's forced to move down on to the next step, making him tower above her and she wonders if that was his plan. To intimidate her. 'As far as I know Robbie's doing great. Things are really looking up now he's made the school football team and...'

'The school football team?'

'Yeah, like I said, he's a brilliant wee goalkeeper.'

'But Robbie's not on the school team.'

'What?' He sounds angry and she's suddenly very glad that they're standing outside in full public view. She doesn't want to be alone with this man. She seems to have hit a raw nerve and she's wishing she'd kept her mouth shut. 'Sorry,' she tries, 'just thinking aloud.'

'Are you saying my boy's not on the school team?'

'I'm not sure,' she says. 'You'd have to ask.'

'The wee bastard's been lying to me.'

'Mr MacFarlane.'

'Wait 'til I get my fucking hands on him. I went out and bought him that shirt, cost me a fucking fortune.'

'Mr MacFarlane, please.' Her heart races and the baby kicks her hard under her ribs.

'What's your fucking problem?' He looks her up and down once more. 'What are you here for anyway, eh? You didnae come to tell me my son isn't good enough for the fucking lousy school football team.'

The baby kicks again and she thinks she might be sick.

'I think it's time you left. And when you see Robbie, tell him I want that fucking shirt back.' He goes back inside and the door is slammed shut in her face.

Anna stands on the second step, staring at the closed door. What has she done? She slams the palm of her hand into her forehead. Damn it. Now she's only made things worse.

Forty-One

It's lunchtime and as usual all of the teachers have fucked off. They've probably gone for a sly fag or even a quick pint in the pub round the corner to help them through the afternoon. I think about the can of lager in my bag but I can't risk mucking this up so I push it to the back of my mind. For now.

The door to the classroom is shut and for a second I worry it might be locked. If I don't do this now the others will think I bottled out and they'll never let me live it down. We've agreed to meet at the abandoned bike shed at one o'clock.

After thinking about it I decided that stealing Mr Johnson's phone was a stupid idea. He'd probably just think he'd lost it and claim a new one through his insurance. Dad did that with his last one except he hadn't actually lost it, he'd gambled it with some guy in the pub over who'd score the first goal.

So I've come up with a better plan. The idea came to me in a flash of inspiration and it's perfect. Nothing can go wrong. Unless the fucking door is locked.

It's not.

The classroom feels creepy when there's no-one in it but I still close the door behind me in case anyone comes along the corridor and sees me. The clock on the wall counts down each second like a ticking bomb. I've got less than fifteen minutes until I meet the others so I'd better get started.

The spray can feels good in my hand. Real. As close as I've come to a loaded gun. Fucking teachers don't have a clue. They're always going on about the games we play, saying they mess with our head. Every time some nutter goes mental with a gun they blame computer games, saying we can't tell the difference between real life and fantasy. Well, I know the difference. This isn't a video game. This is real. Absolutely fucking real. They don't know what life is like for us. They spend all their time telling us what to do, what to think. It's bad enough that you've got someone at home nipping your head - make your bed, pick up your clothes, do your homework, but then you come to school and they're fucking worse. They'd tell you how to fart if they could. And none of them give a shit about you. None of them.

I squeeze the trigger and red paint bleeds down the wall and I know exactly what to write. Three words that will send my message loud and clear but they'll never be able to prove it was me. I grin. It's perfect. I lift the can and begin.

Forty-Two

Tracey gets off the bus and stares at the rows of tall hedges that line both sides of the road for as far as the eye can see. Enormous houses hide behind these leafy screens, set back from the road at the end of ridiculously long driveways. The address is scribbled on the back of a receipt but she remembers the house number she is looking for. Number eighty-one. But these houses don't seem to have numbers, instead they have names. Who the hell gives their house a name? She's not sure which way to turn and for a moment she considers trying eeny, meeny miny mo but in the end she stabs a guess at left and starts walking until she comes to an iron gate with a private post box secured to it. The post box has a brass plaque with the number fifty-three engraved into it. She congratulates herself on finding the odd side of the street but is she walking in the right direction? She keeps going, hoping she'll spot another number soon. Every part of her body aches and the bag in her hand is heavy. John was asleep when she got in last night and she climbed into bed beside him, keeping her clothes on. When he left for work this morning she pretended to be asleep and he didn't try to waken her. She doesn't intend to go back. All of her belongings are crammed into a Tesco bag for life.

She can't believe her luck when she spots number eighty-one a few minutes later. For once things are going her way. She tucks her bag of belongings behind a bush by the front door and rings the doorbell. She expects an old fashioned chime and is surprised when the doorbell delivers a lively *ding-dong*. Angela answers the door almost straight away and she's dressed in a pair of ripped jeans and a vest top which looks like it was once red but has now faded to a washed out pink. Her hair is tied up in a loose knot on the top of her head and she's not wearing any make up.

'Perfect timing.' She laughs. 'I was just about to start painting the garden fence.' She stops and her face turns serious. 'Come in and I'll pop the kettle on.'

Tracey has her story ready. She doesn't intend to tell Angela what happened but as she hears the kettle start to boil she knows she will tell her everything.

'The first time he hit me was our wedding night. We danced together all evening and everyone kept telling us how happy we looked. The perfect couple. He'd arranged for a taxi to come and pick us up and I couldn't believe it when it stopped outside one of the hotels right on Princes Street itself. The castle looked down on us as we stepped out of the taxi and I felt like a princess. I was still in my wedding dress because I loved it so much. It was white with dusky pink roses on the shoulders and a dusky pink sash around my waist. When we got into the hotel, the reception was full of Japanese tourists and they thought it was great. A Scottish bride. Anyway, they all started taking photos and I guess I got carried away, posing and stuff. Well, I hadn't noticed that he'd left until all of the tourists disappeared.' She sits back and twists the gold band on her finger. 'He'd gone up to the room without me.'

'What happened next?'

'I took the lift up to our room, still light-headed from all the champagne and I remember giggling to myself in the mirror, saying my new name over and over again.' She pauses for breath. 'And then I knocked on our door and I waited. I remember feeling excited and nervous about the night ahead. We'd slept together before our wedding night, obviously, but I wanted this time to be special. He'd said he wanted to carry me over the threshold to our room like they do in films.' She looks at Angela. 'I still remember the look on his face when he opened the door. The rage was oozing out of his pores. He dragged me inside and slammed the door. I tried apologising but before I could get the words out he struck me to the floor. Funny, how even then, he knew not to hit me in the face where the bruises could be seen.' Tears are running down her face but she doesn't care. Words describing his abuse flow as freely as her tears and she tells Angela details she thought she'd forgotten.

'And now I need to get my boy out of there but there's nowhere for us to go and I don't know what to do.'

Angela pushes herself out of her chair and walks across the room to an old desk in the corner. She sits back down a moment later, clutching a brown A4 envelope and slides the envelope across the table towards Tracey. 'I think this might be exactly what you need.'

Forty-Three

It's one o'clock and I'm the first one to arrive at the bike shed. I should have waited 'til the others were all here and then I could have made a big entrance. I check my watch. Where are they? Is it possible that they bottled out at the last minute? Lame pricks. I open a crushed packet of salt 'n' vinegar that I find lurking at the bottom of my bag but the crisps just leave me feeling thirsty. Fuck it. I open the can of lager and start drinking. A bunch of sixth years walk past and stop and stare. 'What the fuck are you looking at?' I shout and they shuffle away. I fold the empty crisp packet into a perfect triangle and watch the gang of sixth years disappear in the direction of the nearest chippy. Lucky bastards are out of here in a couple of weeks and can do whatever they like. I crush the empty can under my foot and kick it into the gutter. It starts to rain and if the others don't get here soon I'm leaving.

I'm finally getting up to leave when Dean and Callum come running round the corner. Callum looks scared which is kind of funny 'cause he's supposed to be the hard man of the group.

'Everything alright?' I ask sounding dead casual.

'Think Cameron saw us coming out of the science block.'

'Us? I thought we were supposed to get revenge on one teacher each.'

'Well, Dean needed someone to keep a look out,' Callum says.

'In other words you were too fuckin' scared to do anything yourself.'

'Scared, eh? Is that what you think?' Callum throws his

jacket to the ground. 'C'mon then,' he says, 'I'll take you on, show you I'm not scared.'

Dean picks up Callum's jacket and hands it to him without a word and Callum puts it back on like an obedient puppy.

'My job was going to take a long time so I asked Callum here to keep an eye out for any teachers coming,' says Dean.

'We could all have done with somebody keeping an eye out but that wasn't what we agreed.'

'Are you not going to ask what I did?' Dean's grinning at me, dead pleased with himself. 'I managed to get into the cupboards in the science lab and–'

'I thought they were locked,' I interrupt.

'Cameron keeps the key in his top drawer on a Scooby-Doo key ring. You never noticed?'

I haven't but I nod to get him to go on.

'I got into the cupboard where all the wee beasties are kept.'

I stare at him.

'You know,' he says, 'the cockroaches and the beetles and the stick insects and stuff.'

'What did you do with them?'

Callum jumps in. 'We set them all free so next time Cameron goes into his room...Aargh!' He leaps in the air and circles his arms as he pretends to be Mr Cameron. What a tosser.

I don't think our science teacher is going to be scared by a bunch of stick insects but I keep this to myself. 'Great plan,' I say 'cause if I say anything else they'll think I'm jealous. 'Can't wait to hear what his face is like when he finds them.'

Dean's grinning, 'Can you imagine it? He's gonna be hunting for the wee fuckers everywhere. It's fuckin' brilliant.'

'Fuckin' brilliant,' Callum repeats.

I'm getting ready to tell them my news when Jamie comes running round the corner out of breath. 'One of the second years just told me that Miss Clark has been crying all morning. He said that her fiancé gave her the wooden figure as a goodbye present before he went off to fight in Iraq where he was blown up by a landmine a week later when he was out on his first field trip.'

I don't know how someone knows all this but I keep quiet.

'You got it, then,' Dean asks.

'Nipped in and took it before registration this morning.'

I'm impressed. I'd never have had Jamie down as being the organised one. I pat him on the back. 'Well done,' I say. 'Well done.'

'Do you want to hear the best bit?' he asks us.

We do.

'I left a ransom note in its place.'

'A ransom note?'

He's killing himself laughing now. 'One million dollars or the wee wooden guy gets it.'

'Wee wooden guy.' I laugh. 'Love it. Did you cut it out of newspapers?'

He looks at me blankly.

'You know, like in Grand Theft Auto. The third one.'

'Don't be fuckin' stupid,' he says. 'I didnae have time, I just thought of it when I was in there.'

'So what?' Dean asks. 'You just fuckin' wrote it?'

'Aye.'

'Didn't you stop to think that she'll recognise your handwriting?'

Jamie's face falls. He turns to me and changes the subject. 'So did you get Johnson's phone?'

'Changed my mind.'

'Pussy,' Callum says.

I swear I'm gonna kill him if he doesn't shut his face. 'I did something better than stealing a phone,' I say, 'and way better than letting a bunch of insects out of their cage.'

'What did you do?' Dean asks me.

I look him in the eye. 'I sent Miss Green a message.'

'Miss Green?'

'Spray-painted her classroom.'

'Holy crap.'

'Jesus fuck. What d'ya do that for? She's the best teacher in the whole fuckin' school.'

'If she was the best teacher she wouldn't be leaving us,' I say.

'What did you write?' Dean asks.

I hold up three fingers, folding them down one at a time with each word. 'Who–Fucking–Cares?'

'What the fuck's that supposed to mean?' asks Callum.

'The bitch is leaving us,' I shout.

'Calm down, man,' Dean says.

'What's the fuckin' point in writing that?'

'Who fucking cares? That's the point, don't you get it?' The three of them stand and stare at me. 'Nobody,' I shout. 'Nobody fucking cares about us. We're on our own, 'cause nobody fucking cares.'

'What the fuck,' Callum says. 'I'm outta here before every teacher in the school turns up to find out what the fuck he's screaming about.'

'I'm coming with you,' says Jamie.

'Good fuckin' riddance,' I shout after them both.

Dean picks up his bag and looks at me. 'I can't believe you did that to her.'

I shrug my shoulders. 'Bitch deserves it,' I say.

'You're off your head,' he says and turns and walks away.

'Fuck you,' I shout but he doesn't look back.

I'm on my own again. Alone. I shake the can of red paint and picture their blood. All of them. I take off the lid and spray a red cross. That's for Mum for walking out on me. I spray another. That one's for Miss Green. The third cross is for Rachel for being a cock tease and a little slut. Three more for the boys that just walked away from me. The paint drips downwards and it looks like the bike shed wall is bleeding. They all deserve to bleed for what they've done to me.

Forty-Four

Tracey knows the contours of the iron gate well and remembers the exact angle the handle needs to turn through before it allows her to enter the small garden. The grass hasn't been cut in a long time but the flowers are in full bloom and she smiles as she watches a butterfly land on the clump of lavender by the front path. She's not supposed to have a key yet but Angela gave her the spare she keeps in her kitchen drawer. Tracey takes it from her pocket and holds it in front of her. He'll never look for them here but even if he does it's okay because they can lock the door. Their own front door.

Her hands are shaking as she slides the key into the lock and she looks back over her shoulder, feeling like an intruder. What if one of the neighbours spots her and calls the police? She has no right to be here. Not yet. Angela says Drew's fighting his mother's will but she insisted that there's nothing to worry about because Mrs Carmichael had it witnessed by her lawyer. Once the estate has been sorted, the cottage will belong to her. Belong to them. She can't wait to tell Robbie the news. She turns the key firmly and the wooden door swings open. She stands at the threshold and takes a deep breath. She can do this.

The house is cold and empty and she stands in the dark hallway like she's done a thousand times before, but this time is different. She has no duster or mop in her hand. She opens the door to the living room and looks inside. All of the furniture is gone and the beige carpet is threadbare beneath her feet. Orange and brown floral wallpaper is peeling away from below the windowsill. Funny how she never noticed the rundown state of the place before. It always had such a warm feeling to it with the countless knick-knacks and family photographs, photographs that in the end turned out to tell only part of the family's story. She runs her hand along the dusty mantelpiece where the china butterfly once sat. 'I wish you'd told me about your past.' Mrs Carmichael doesn't answer.

She walks through to the bedrooms where faded shapes on the walls mark the place where memories once hung. Robbie can have the smaller room that looks onto the front garden. That way he can look out on to the flowers anytime he likes. Tracey thinks she will paint it sunshine yellow once she has the money, and together they can make their own memories. Happy memories, untainted by the stench of alcohol and abuse. Mrs Carmichael believed in her, and now it's her turn to believe in herself.

Forty-Five

The school grounds are quiet because everyone is back in class after lunch. I walk along the gravel path and past the front door but no-one calls my name, no-one chases after me, and I'm allowed to walk free. I leave the school grounds and head towards the main road to the spot where she stood a few days ago. But she's not here today. A small group of people stand huddled together in the bus shelter across the road to keep out of the rain. I'm soaked right through to the skin and a large droplet of rain lands on my neck and rolls down the inside of my jacket. I look up to the sky and shout, 'Happy fucking birthday to me.'

'Watch your language, boy.'

I turn and face my accuser. The old man is dressed in a slate grey raincoat that matches the grey sky and the coat is so long it almost reaches his shins. He stands to attention, holding on to a wooden walking stick and I notice the part he's holding has been carved into the shape of a duck's head. Its painted eye is watching me.

I step towards him and pull myself up as tall as I can. 'What the fuck are you saying, Granddad?'

The old woman standing next to him places her hand on his elbow to warn him but he lifts it off and steps towards me. 'I'm telling you to stop using that foul language.'

'Or what?' I ask. 'Eh? What the fuck are you going to do about it?'

'That's enough,' Granddad says and now he's waving his cane in front of my face. Fucking cheek.

'Are you threatening me?' I laugh. 'You better watch it or I'll call the police.'

The woman grabs hold of Granddad's arm and tries to pull him back, away from me, but the old man's not budging. He's waving his cane like a fucking eejit. 'No discipline,' he's shouting. 'That's the problem. No discipline and no respect for your elders.'

'Shut it, Granddad.'

'Do you hear that?' A crowd is gathering around us and he's lapping up the attention. The bus has arrived but nobody's noticed. Nobody cares. There'll be another bus along any minute.

The old man points the tip of his walking stick into my arm and turns to his audience. He digs it in a little further and shuffles his feet to gain his balance, then he sweeps his other arm outwards in a wide circle and waits until everyone, including me, is hanging on his every word. 'I...' he pauses for effect, 'I blame this boy's mother.'

That's it. Something inside snaps. I grab hold of the walking stick with one hand and pull him towards me until we're eye to eye and I can hear his breath rattling and wheezing through his old body. He stares back at me with pale, watery blue eyes and I'm pleased to see he looks scared. My free hand clenches into a tight fist and I feel my nails dig into the palm of my hand. Blood is pulsing round every vein and artery in my body and every muscle is coiled, ready to spring. I've never felt so alive.

'Leave him alone,' someone from the crowd shouts and for a moment I think they're on my side. I look up but everyone's staring at me like I'm some kind of animal.

'Please help my husband,' the woman shouts.

'Where's the boy's mother?'

I force the walking stick away pushing the old man backwards. The sound as his head hits the wet pavement silences the crowd. I stand over his chest and look down on him. 'My mother's dead.'

233

Forty-Six

Tracey sits in the doctor's waiting room. Her appointment was for half three but already it's four o'clock. She picks up a magazine from the table in the centre of the room but she can't concentrate. She'd wanted to run straight to Robbie's school and tell him the good news but this was the only appointment they could give her and she can't put it off. She can't wait to see his face when she tells him. She tosses the magazine with its pictures of skinny celebrities in their fancy houses back on to the table.

'Mrs MacFarlane.'

She stands up and follows the young doctor through to the small box of a room. She sits down and looks around her while he rearranges some folders in front of him. There are no family photographs on the desk, no brightly coloured crayon pictures of stick men on the wall, nothing to make the room personal. She guesses he's not old enough to have a family yet and probably isn't married either. Christ, he looks like he's just out of school.

At last he's ready and he leans forward and fixes his best professional smile. 'How can I help you?'

'I'm here for the morning after pill.' The doctor raises an eyebrow so she continues, 'I had unprotected sex yesterday and I need to make sure I don't get pregnant.'

'Was this sex consensual?'

She nods, aware that he's staring at her burst lip.

'Do you mind if I ask what happened to your face,' he asks.

'Look, all I need is a prescription.'

He pushes himself back in his chair and exhales loudly. Time is ticking by.

'Before I give you a prescription, maybe we should take a minute to look at all of the options. There are two main types of what we call emergency contraceptive.'

She interrupts him before he can say anymore. 'Just give me either of them.' Christ, she sounds like a cold bitch but she's never going to meet this man again in her life so all pleasantries are forgotten for now. 'The quicker we can sort things out the better.'

He's a young doctor and she's sure he's going to be lost for words. She waits on him to organise a prescription and dismiss her, but he doesn't. He scrolls through her notes on the computer in front of him and she knows he's going to see it any second now. 'If you can just give me a prescription.' He's still reading. 'Look, I could easily go out and buy something over the counter.' He leans across his desk and looks her in the eye. She tries to look away but her gaze is caught. She waits for what he's about to say.

'I see from your notes that you lost a baby recently.'

'It was a long time ago.' She didn't come here to talk about that.

'Four years,' he says. 'Not really so long ago.'

'It is to me.'

'You were six months pregnant when you lost it.'

'Her.'

'Pardon?'

'It was a girl.'

'Oh.'

'Sarah.'

'A lovely name.'

'I thought so.' She looks out the window. The sun is shining for once.

'How did it happen?'

She looks at him and he's waiting for her answer. How did it happen? Outside, the branches of a sycamore tree are swaying in the summer breeze against a clear blue sky. 'It was an accident.'

'An accident?

'I fell.'

He doesn't say anything and she watches as a magpie lands on a branch causing it to bend under its weight. One for sorrow.

'You were admitted to hospital with bruising across your abdomen.'

'Like I said, it was an accident.'

They're dancing around each other, playing a game. But Tracey's played this game many times before and she knows she'll be the last one standing. 'I fell down a flight of stairs and hurt myself against the banister on the way down.' The magpie flies away. He's looking at the faded bruise below her eye, the only trace from their argument on the night she left. 'I don't want to talk about it.'

'You don't need to talk to me about anything you don't want to but before I give you this prescription I'm going to recommend that you have a chat with one of our nurses.'

'You're not listening. I don't care if it's Mother Theresa or the bloody Pope himself that you suggest I see, I don't want to talk about it.'

'I don't mean to upset you but it's routine practice that when a woman comes in for emergency contraceptive she is asked to speak to someone from our nursing team. They'll discuss appropriate contraceptives.' He leans closer and his voice becomes a whisper. 'And they're also trained in grief counselling. Someone that you can talk to about the baby you recently lost.'

'Lost?' The word fires out of her mouth. 'Lost? I've lost my purse before. I've lost my car keys. But I didn't *lose* my baby. She died.'

He doesn't look away like she expects him to. 'I'm sorry,' he says.

'Please,' she begs. 'You don't understand. I just want to get

236

this over and done with so I can carry on with my life. Things are about to get much better for me and my boy and I can't let anything get in the way of that happening.'

'What age is your son?'

'Robbie?' She sits back. It feels good saying his name. 'It's his birthday today, he's thirteen. A teenager. He's at the academy now and he's getting on brilliantly. His English teacher says he's one of the brightest kids she's ever taught. Wants him to go to university early and everything.'

'You and your husband must be very proud.'

She doesn't speak.

'Does your husband know you're here?'

'We're not together.'

'Oh.'

The conversation stops. All she needs to do is insist on her prescription and then she can get out of here. She knows her rights. It's the twenty-first century, for Christ's sake, and he can't deny her contraception. The room is stifling hot and she looks longingly through the closed window to the leaves blowing in the breeze. She imagines it's a cool breeze.

'Are you okay?' She hears his voice but it sounds far off, in the distance.

It's a swelteringly hot day and Robbie is outside in the garden. He's built himself a den out of a pile of empty boxes. He loves making dens and tents, and sometimes she finds him asleep at night in his pop up tent in the middle of his bedroom floor. She's standing at the sink watching him through the kitchen window, her hand gently stroking her pregnant belly. Robbie's going to be a big brother in September and she can't wait to see him with the baby. He'll be great and It'll be good for him to have someone to play with. She imagines him reading a story to his little brother or sister as they look up at him with big wide eyes.

He's filled the den with cushions from the sofa and a pile of comics and books. He always hides amongst his stories when

237

he's upset about something and today he's angry with his dad because he's gone to the football without him. The bastard left this morning without bothering to tell his son that he wasn't taking him. As usual he left that job to her.

'Your dad's already left,' she told him.

'But he promised.'

What can she say? The boy's right. His dad's been promising him for weeks that they'll go and see Hearts play Hibs at Tynecastle. He's been drilling the boy with tactics and strategies like he's the bloody manager.

'He promised,' Robbie shouted and ran into the back garden. He refused to come in for lunch and so she made him a jam sandwich and left it outside the entrance to his den.

Hearts lost that day.

So did she.

It was her own fault. She should have known better but she was so tired and she only planned to have a little nap. She'd been awake the night before with heartburn and the baby was starting to kick more and more. Robbie was sulking in his den and it would be hours before his dad came home. *If* he came home. Sometimes he stayed out drinking and didn't come home 'til the early hours. She'd make dinner in a wee while after she'd snatched forty winks. But she must have fallen into a deep sleep and dinner wasn't ready when he got home.

He dragged her up from the sofa by the hair. 'Get up, you lazy bitch!' She was groggy from sleeping and didn't know what was happening. Where was Robbie, was he still in the garden?

'You fucking lazy bitch!' he yelled. Please, please let Robbie still be outside. Please don't let him hear what's happening and come inside. 'Lazy bitch!' He grabbed her by the wrist and she could feel it twist in his grip. 'Get through to that fucking kitchen and make me something to eat.'

'I didn't know when you'd be home. I thought you might stay out celebrating.'

The blow came out of nowhere, his fist meeting her shoulder.

She wasn't expecting it and the force knocked her sideways against the kitchen table and the edge slammed into her ribs.

'Celebrating? You smug bitch. You love it when we lose, don't you?' The second punch was aimed low and caught her on the hip. This was in the days when he still tried to hide the bruises and never touched her face. Perhaps if he had, her baby girl might have survived but his next blow was to her stomach and that was the one that was fatal. The pain ripped through her as he hit her and she fell to the floor screaming. Her pregnant stomach felt like it had been sliced open with a knife and the screams brought Robbie running in from the garden. She can still see the look on his face. He was scared. Terrified. But there was another look there too. She couldn't quite put her finger on it but if she had to choose one word to describe it she'd say he was curious. At first she thought he was wondering what her pain felt like but a week later she changed her mind. A week later Robbie was suspended for punching another child in the playground. He couldn't give a reason. Was he wondering what it felt like to inflict the pain?

Forty-Seven

I know he's mad at me as soon as I walk through the front door and I'm guessing Miss Green found the graffiti and the school have been on the phone. She'd know it was me as soon as she saw the words but don't they need proof before they can accuse me? The shouting starts as soon as I close the door behind me.

'What the fuck were you playing at, you lying piece of shit. Did you think it was fucking funny? Eh? Lying to your old man like that.'

I'm confused; is this about the spray paint?

'Did you think I'd never find out?'

I don't know what he's going on about but if I play it calm maybe I'll get off the hook. I take a step backwards towards the front door and let him keep talking. I know better than to interrupt.

'Do you think money grows on fucking trees, eh? I had to go without to buy you that shirt and you've only fucking worn it once, haven't you? You stood there and watched me tell Big Steve how you'd made it into the school team, stood there and let me buy you a cola to celebrate and I bet you were laughing on the other side of your fucking face. You lying little cunt.'

Shit. How did he find out? I take another step towards the front door, reaching out blindly behind me for the handle but I can't find it. He walks towards me, blocking the living room door, my only other escape route. I'm trapped and I need to calm him down.

'I've been training every night. Honest. It was Gran, she got the wrong end of the story. I've been training every night and

240

I've been wearing my shirt. I've got a try-out with the school team next week.'

'Ya fucking liar.'

'I'm not lying,' I say. Please God, he's going to hurt me. I look around the hallway. The photo frames that stood on the hall table when Mum was here are gone now and it's littered with unopened bills, empty beer cans and a pot plant that's dying. And then I spot them. There's a pair of gardening scissors close enough for me to reach.

'You're a fucking liar.'

What has he always told me? The only way to deal with a bully is to hit them harder than they hit you. He's too busy shouting to notice me pick up the scissors and slip them behind my back.

'You're lying,' he yells in my face. 'There's no fucking try-out. You won't even be in school next week.'

I freeze. What does he mean?

'You're suspended.'

Miss Green's told them it was me and the bastards aren't even waiting to get any proof. I turn the scissors over in my hand.

'What the fuck did you think you were doing? You knocked a pensioner to the ground. A pensioner. A man who's given his life to this fucking country and he gets hurt by a delinquent like you. Ya fucking idiot!'

I push myself forwards towards him, aware that the hand holding the scissors is now raised by my side. 'He fell down,' I say. 'It was an accident.'

'You didn't fucking mean it? You shoved him to the ground. Jesus Christ. Have I not taught you better than that?'

I flip my wrist over and the blades face upwards. Standing up to him is my only escape. Hit them harder than they hit you. 'Taught me better, have you? What? Taught me how to hit a woman where no-one can see the bruises?'

'You shut the fuck up. That's between your mum and me and it's none of your fucking business.'

241

'She left because of you,' I scream.

'She was fucking asking for it. Always telling me what I could do, what I could drink and what time to be home for. Nobody tells me what to do. Especially not a woman.'

'Mum's gone and it's your fault.' I grip the scissors tightly, imagining the metal cutting into him, making him bleed. I freeze. I'm back in the kitchen and I'm four years old. Dad is stabbing her arm with a fork and she's bleeding. She keeps saying sorry over and over. He's angry with her. Isn't he? But if he's angry with her then why is he smiling? He's smiling as he breaks her skin and watches her bleed. I open my hand and the scissors fall to the floor.

'We're doing fine without her, aren't we? Just you and me, eh? Who needs her?'

'I do,' I whisper. 'Me. I wish she was here.'

He raises his hand in the air and there's nothing I can do to stop it. The force of the first punch knocks me to the ground and before I can get back up he kicks me in the side. Hard. I try to move away from him but he doesn't stop.

'Please don't hurt me.' But he keeps coming and I can see there's only one way to make him stop. I reach for the scissors but he sees me before I can get to them and this time his fist meets my face and the pain causes me to scream. The high pitched wailing that comes out of my mouth makes him flinch and I seize my chance. I stretch my fingers and pull the scissors towards me. I grip them tight in both hands and throw myself upwards before he can land another punch.

'Hit them harder than they hit you,' I shout as I plunge the scissors into his throat. The blades are in deep and I let go of the handle and fall backwards. Blood bubbles and splutters from his neck and he drops down on to the floor beside me. I close my eyes and pretend I'm sailing down the Mississippi beneath the stars and I make a promise to myself.

I promise that I'll never be like him.

Forty-Eight

Her evening shift at the pub starts in five minutes and she's walking as fast as she can because she hates being late. Her headphones are blasting out some old disco classics and she's strutting along the street as if she owns the world. The music is loud and she doesn't hear the sirens.

She pauses at the kerb and looks both ways, ready to cross, but then she stops. Blue flashing lights bounce off the walls of the council houses to her left and instead of crossing the road she turns and walks up the side street towards the ambulance. She knows she's definitely going to be late now but Jerry won't complain, not if she's got the gossip. There's a friendly match on tonight so the pub will be busy and everyone will want to know what happened. If she can supply them with a bit of juicy news they might give her a better tip. The neighbours are out in force and she wanders up the street as far as she can go until finally a policewoman stops her. There's nothing much to see yet so she joins the crowd and listens to the word on the street.

'Kept themselves to themselves.'

That's not going to help her get a decent tip.

'She left a few weeks ago.'

Everyone will want to know who...

'Poor lad's been left to bring himself up.'

That's better but she's going to need a few facts or maybe see a bit of action.

She shuffles to get to a better viewpoint and is just in time to see a stretcher being carried out of the house. She recognises the young boy immediately. It's the same lad that was in the pub

243

with his dad a few nights ago, and his name is on the tip of her tongue but she can't quite grasp it. He told her he was named after one of the top strikers but that doesn't help her much. She remembers how polite he was when she gave him a glass of cola and a packet of crisps and she pushes away the tingle of guilt that is threatening to surface. Maybe she should have followed him out of the pub that night, asked if he was okay.

But it was none of her business. Was it?

Forty-Nine

She's there when I open my eyes and I want to scream at her. I want to give her hell for abandoning me, for leaving me, but now she's in front of me.

She reaches into the plastic bag by her feet and takes out a book. She places it on the table beside my bed and I turn to look at the front cover. It shows a boy dipping his bare feet into a river. The boy is *Tom Sawyer* but this is a new copy. This isn't Miss Green's book.

'I'm sorry I took it,' she whispers.

'What?' Every word takes effort.

'I took the book from your bedroom when I came back to collect some of my things.' She chews at her fingernails and I see they've been bleeding.

'You took Miss Green's book?'

'I wanted something that was yours. I couldn't be with you so I thought that having something of yours would make me feel like you were close by.'

'Where is it?'

'I left it behind.'

'But it doesn't belong to me.'

'I'm sorry.'

'It belongs to a friend.'

'I'm sorry,' she says again and looks down at her hands. There's a white band where her wedding ring used to be.

'Did it work?' I ask her.

'What?'

'Did you feel closer to me?'

'No, you still felt a million miles away.'

'How far away were you?'

'Only a couple of miles. I used to watch you coming out of school in the afternoon.'

So I was right; I had seen her.

She passes me the book and it feels heavy in my hands. My ribs hurt but I don't put it down. The smell of the new book stirs a memory and I'm back in the kids' section of the library. We used to go to the library every week and I'd walk home with a pile of books so high that I could barely see over the top of them. Then we'd sit in the middle of the living room floor amongst the mountain of books and I could never choose which story I wanted her to read to me first and we'd always end up having to do eeny, meeny, miny, mo. Then we'd cuddle up and I'd feel the steady beating of her heart as she began the first story.

I turn the copy of *Tom Sawyer* over in my hands.

'It's yours,' she says. 'I bought it especially for you. I guess you could say it's your birthday present.'

I open it at the first page and my heart skips when I see her handwriting.

To Robbie,
Wishing you a happily ever after x

She takes the book from my hand and turns to the last page. She begins to read:

So endeth this chronicle. It being strictly a history of a boy, it must stop here; the story could not go much further without becoming the history of a man. When one writes a novel about grown up people, he knows exactly where to stop – that is, with a marriage; but when he writes of juveniles, he must stop where he best can.

Most of the characters that perform in this book will live, and are prosperous and happy.

Her tears fall onto the white hospital sheet but there's still something I need to ask.

'Why didn't you speak to me when you watched me coming out of school?'

She looks away.

'Why didn't you come home?'

'I thought you'd be better off without me.'

I don't understand.

She brushes my cheek with the back of her hand like she used to do when I was a wee boy to help me get to sleep. 'I thought if I left you, you'd be safe. He only ever got mad at me. Never you. He always said you were his lucky mascot.'

I close my eyes. Everywhere hurts. 'Mum,' I whisper, 'I didn't want to be his lucky mascot anymore.'

THE END

Reading Group Discussion Points

The story is told from both the point of view of Robbie and from the different women in his life. How do the different points of view complement each other? Do they work together successfully?

Can you comment on the way in which the story explores the relationship between fathers and sons?

Can you discuss the father's resentment towards books?

The author sets the book in Edinburgh. Did this increase your enjoyment of the book?

How well does the story explore the link between football, alcohol and domestic abuse?

What connections can you draw between Mrs Carmichael and Robbie's mother?

Did your opinion of Robbie's mother change over the course of the book?

Towards the end of the book an onlooker questions if she should have intervened at some point, 'But it was none of her business. Was it?' Why do you think the author put in this line?

What have you taken away from the story? What do you think it is trying to say?

Fantastic Books
Great Authors

Meet our authors and discover our exciting range:

- Gripping Thrillers
- Cosy Mysteries
- Romantic Chick-Lit
- Fascinating Historicals
- Exciting Fantasy
- Young Adult and Children's Adventures

Visit us at:
www.crookedcatbooks.com

Join us on facebook:
www.facebook.com/crookedcatpublishing

Lightning Source UK Ltd.
Milton Keynes UK
UKOW02f2155190814

237199UK00001B/3/P